"Oh, Molly. My hu... ...
What am I supposed to do now?"

I rose and looked at Preston. He was on his back.
His shirt was drenched in blood. How could this
be happening? Was Stephanie crazy? I wasn't a
therapist. I created greeting cards. All I wanted to
do now was get out of there. Maybe write her a
truly touching condolence card from the safety of
my own home.

But she was pregnant, her husband's dead body
was lying there a few feet away and she'd asked
me for help. I couldn't leave her like this.

★

Also available from Worldwide Mystery by
LESLIE O'KANE

DEATH AND FAXES

Just the Fax, Ma'am

Leslie O'Kane

WORLDWIDE®

TORONTO • NEW YORK • LONDON
AMSTERDAM • PARIS • SYDNEY • HAMBURG
STOCKHOLM • ATHENS • TOKYO • MILAN
MADRID • WARSAW • BUDAPEST • AUCKLAND

JUST THE FAX, MA'AM

A Worldwide Mystery/November 1997

First published by St. Martin's Press, Incorporated.

ISBN 0-373-26254-X

Printed in U.S.A.

To my fellow critique group members

*In Boulder: Marie Desjardin, Claire Martin,
Claudia Mills, Ann Nagda, Phyllis Perry,
Ina Robbins, and Elizabeth Wrenn*

*In Denver: Kay Bergstrom, Carol Caverly,
Diane Mott Davidson, Dolores Johnson,
Chris Jorgensen, Peggy Swager,
and the inimitable Lee Karr*

My thanks and appreciation to each of you, always.

ONE

Did I Catch You at a
Bad Time…Again?

THE INSTANT I opened my door, Preston Saunders blurted, "Molly, I've got to show you something, but first you have to promise not to kill me."

It was early morning on a quiet, brisk spring day—quiet because my children were at school, and brisk because here in upstate New York, the actual thawing and burgeoning of spring lags its calendar assignment by a good month or so. A pyramid of dirty snow, remnants of my son's first snow-fort, still graced a corner of the redbrick front porch on which Preston now stood.

I held up my palms. "I'm unarmed…but I haven't had my coffee yet, so all bets are off." I smiled, but his steel gray eyes still held no trace of humor. "Would you like to come in?"

He nodded, stepped inside, and shut the door behind him blindly, as if afraid to turn his back on me. "I can only stay a minute. I'm on my way to the office."

As usual, Preston Saunders was impeccably attired and drop-dead handsome. The tailored black suit on his tall, lithe body screamed *Gentleman's Quarterly*. I, too, was dressed for work—in my basement office: jeans, University of Colorado sweatshirt, pink moccasins.

"What is it you wanted to show me?" I asked, noting that his hands were empty.

"I'm not entirely sure how to broach the subject, Molly." His gaze did not meet my eyes, and he cleared his throat while he smoothed his flawless, prematurely gray hair.

"Why don't we sit in the living room?"

He shook his head, his eyes still focused on some spot past my shoulder. With this hesitant demeanor on top of his inauspicious opening line, horrendous explanations for his visit raced through my mind. The only one that made sense was that he was about to inform me he was leaving town, thereby leaving his very pregnant wife, Stephanie, and he wanted to recruit me as his replacement coach during labor.

"Guess I'll just...take it out," Preston murmured. He unbuttoned his jacket, then untucked his front shirttail.

"Stop!" I took a backward step toward the kitchen. "Preston, if I'm about to get flashed, at least let me get a cup of coffee first."

A look of confusion passed across his handsome features. Then he snorted. "It's not what you're thinking. It's just that I couldn't let your neighbors see me carrying this to your door." He reached under his shirt and pulled out a magazine, which he began to page through.

I caught sight of the cover: a woman, naked except for a holstered gun on each thigh. Appalled, I asked incredulously, "You came over to my house to show me a dirty magazine?"

He paused. "You have to keep this confidential, Molly. I have a post office box Stephie doesn't know about. If she finds out I subscribe, she'll have my head. Or worse."

My mind raced. That he wanted to show me a particular picture in the magazine was more than a little daunting. Stephanie had modeled for a while after high school. Maybe some of her modeling had been of the "disrobed" variety.

"Here it is." He folded the magazine open to the one page he wanted me to see.

Automatically I looked away, afraid I'd see Stephanie naked, or worse, their daughter, Tiffany, who was only fourteen. "I really don't want to do this. I have to get back to work." That was true. I run a faxable greeting card business and needed to finish my current assignment.

"You have no choice, I'm afraid. It's your picture."

"My *what?*" I grabbed the magazine so forcibly I'd have disconnected his arm at the shoulder if he'd tried to hang on. There on the page was the one raunchy cartoon I'd ever created. It showed a man clutching a towel to cover himself as he opened the door to a priest. In the corner are two buxom women in bed, wearing caps with sheep ears. The smiling priest asks the man, "Did I catch you at a bad time?" As always, the cartoon bore my last name, Masters, worked into some cross-hatching in the lower right corner.

"How did the magazine get my cartoon? Who did this to me?" While I spoke, I flipped to the front to learn its name. *"Between the Legs!"* My stomach lurched. "Good Lord. I'm a contributor to a magazine called *Between the Legs?* Won't *that* look great on my résumé." I could almost see my fictitious résumé, the lines flashing before my eyes like credits at the end of a movie. Molly Octavia Masters. Devoted wife. Mother of two. Owner of Friendly Fax. Smut cartoonist.

"I submitted it under the name *Mike* Masters," Preston interjected, "but before you get upset—"

"Too late!" I clenched my fist, my jaw, and every muscle in my body as I scanned the facing page that Preston had folded down. There was a photograph of Preston Saunders, identified as Mike Masters, the new cartoonist for their magazine. I glared at him. "You submitted *my* work to a trashy magazine and took the credit for it!"

"Let me explain," Preston said, holding up one palm while he reached into his jacket pocket with his other hand.

"You stole the cartoon from my file! And you submitted it without my consent! Preston, you've broken copyright laws. You've—"

As if it were a shield, he held out a check written to Molly Masters for a thousand dollars.

I gaped at it and continued, "...got a large sum of money

there for one mediocre cartoon. But that doesn't justify what you—''

''They want to hire you. A thousand dollars a month, for four to eight cartoons each edition. And since you're listed as *Mike* Masters, nobody has to know it's really you.''

I glared at him. ''What's in it for you?''

''This all started out as a joke.'' He tossed the check onto my coffee table as if it were merely a used napkin. ''I was at the country club with some friends of mine. I'd had too much to drink and said I was going to enter this cartoonists' contest, and, well, the guys bet me a thousand dollars apiece I couldn't win. The only way I could win, since the cartoon was signed Masters, was to convince them to print *my* photograph. I told the editor you were my wife, but you wanted to keep your identity hidden and that printing my photo was part of the ruse.''

''It's out of the question. These magazines exploit women. I don't condone them, let alone want to contribute to them.'' I intended to thrust the magazine back at him, but a paragraph of text below his photo caught my eye. I froze. To my horror, it was a brief biography. I began to read aloud. ''Mike Masters loves his hometown of Carlton, a small suburb outside of Albany, New York.''

In the meantime, Preston opened the door and backed onto the porch.

''How dare you? We're the only Masters in the Carlton directory. I have two young children to think about!'' Unable to control my fury, I followed him onto the porch, rolled up the magazine, and swatted him. ''Get out of here! You were right. I *am* going to kill you!''

''I'm leaving. But let me just point out that this house is actually your *parents'* home and therefore, the phone book lists it under the name *Peterson*.''

''True. But we got listed under this address and phone number in the new directory, too! We thought it would be more convenient!''

''Oh.'' Reddening, he turned and trotted down the brick stairs. He shook his head and said over his shoulder, ''I don't know how I'll explain this to the publisher. I already signed a year's contract on your behalf, as your agent." He rounded his Mercedes, which was parked in my driveway.

"But you're *not* my agent!" I toyed with shouting at him, "What's breach of contract when you've already broken copyright laws, privacy laws, and stolen my personal property?" But, to my annoyance and embarrassment, a pair of women in jogging suits on the sidewalk had paused and were watching Preston and me. Apparently they had already gotten enough of a collective earful. They resumed their jogging as soon as I looked at them.

"Good morning," I called, though I didn't recognize either of them. Neither turned toward me. They both lifted one hand in a perky, gotta-keep-goin' wave and crossed my driveway at a truly impressive clip. That no doubt slowed once they rounded the corner.

Though typical of Preston's egocentric oblivion to want his picture in a magazine that he secretly subscribed to, it *was* odd that the publisher had agreed to print "Mike Masters's" photograph. It wouldn't have taken much thought to figure out that if the cartoonist wanted to hide her identity, printing her "husband's" picture and naming their hometown wasn't the way to accomplish that. Then again, maybe the editor in question was a man who assumed that even if he and "Mike Masters" had figured that out, Mike's little wifey wouldn't have enough smarts to do the same. Editors who recognized women's intelligence and dignity were probably not inclined to work for a magazine entitled *Between the Legs* in the first place.

Much as I disliked the task, I sat down on my couch and flipped through the magazine, trying to learn its circulation and the editors' names. The circulation was not shown. The editor-in-chief was listed as "Butch Blake." Probably a pseudonym for someone whose real name was less masculine.

I paced between the back and front doors, mentally establishing a list of things to do. My husband, Jim, needed to be clued in on this as soon as possible, but this was

Monday, which meant he was in an all-day meeting. With all-day meetings once a week, it was no wonder Jim's year-long "temporary" assignment, which eight months ago had brought us back to my childhood home, had been extended to "indefinite."

Though I was ashamed of myself, a *thwock, thwock* sound kept reverberating in my brain. That was the sound of me hitting a tennis ball in a brand-new court in the yard of my beloved home back in Boulder. Financing a court through my business earnings was a personal goal I'd established to mollify myself when I got homesick. At what that fantasy court would cost, divided by my income to date, I would be lucky to thwup even one ball prior to toddling off to the retirement home.

After a half hour or so of pacing and pondering, I decided once and for all to call the publisher and demand a retraction, but still wasn't sure if I should rip up their check. The cartoon was already published. They may as well pay me for it, but would my cashing the check mean I had agreed to their contract? I needed a lawyer.

The doorbell rang. I marched over and flung open the door.

A young man with half his hair shaved and the other half dyed electric blue peered at me from beneath droopy eyelids. "Yeah, hi," he muttered. "Is your mom or dad home?"

Through a tight jaw, I answered, "I don't know. I'd have to call them in Florida to find out. Why?" Because I was thin and had long brown hair, even at thirty-five I still occasionally had to pull out my driver's license to assure cautious bartenders that I was a major, not a minor. But this was the first time someone nearly half my age had made that mistake.

"Hey. Don't get all ticked off."

"My house, my rules. I get to decide when to be annoyed. And if you're selling something, you're off to a cruddy start."

"I'm just a messenger, lady." He produced a clipboard

from a khaki-colored knapsack. "I'm s'posed to deliver a package in person to Mike Masters. Is he here?"

A package for Mike Masters? Already? What on earth could it be? Perhaps a copy of the contract Preston had signed. "That's me."

The messenger snorted and curled a lip at me. "Yeah. Right."

"It's short for Michelle."

He snorted a second time and didn't move. After staring at the logo on my sweatshirt, or perhaps my body, but I preferred to think it was the logo, he finally handed me the clipboard. "You gotta sign for it, uh, *Mike*." I did so, and he sneered at me and said, "Thanks, *Mike*. Here ya go." He pulled out a small, unmarked package wrapped in brown paper and handed it to me.

The box was light. It was only a couple of inches deep, six inches or so wide and long. Not the right dimensions for a written contract. Fan mail seemed unlikely. A bomb perhaps? I listened for ticking. "Who sent this?"

The young man was already clomping down the porch steps. "I don't give out the names of my customers, *Mike*. Maybe there's a return address someplace." He got on a dirt bike and took off.

Still somewhat fearful of setting off an explosion, I brought the package inside and carefully set it on top of the smutty magazine atop the coffee table. If it *was* an explosive, the least I could do was make darned sure the magazine went up with it. I got a pair of scissors from the kitchen and gently cut the string and brown paper. Beneath that was a white box. Glued to the lid of the box was a postcard-sized sheet of pink paper that read:

Mike Masters:
This is what we think of you and your cartoon.
Sisters Totally Opposed to Pornography

"No return address," I mumbled. Thanks to an unmistakable odor, I already had a pretty good idea of what was in the box, but curiosity bested me and I lifted the lid. Sure enough. Dog poop.

Though it was probably not the reaction STOP would've wanted, I chuckled. I imagined how the lucky member of their organization must have felt when he, or more likely *she* since these were sisters, found out she was in charge of this particular task. "You want me to box up some what?" Whose job title would that normally fall under? Vice president, I suppose. Maybe STOP had a mascot that was box-trained.

The phone rang. I answered and heard a woman sobbing into the receiver. My first thought was that a Sister felt so betrayed by my cartoon she was too emotionally overcome to shout obscenities at me.

My second thought was this was my least favorite human being, Stephanie Saunders, Preston's wife. The last time she'd called me in tears, it was because the cleaners had "forever destroyed" her favorite blouse. Therefore she "couldn't possibly" make it to preside over that night's PTA meeting, so as secretary-slash-treasurer, she needed me to take over for her.

"M-m-molly."

I recognized Stephanie's whimper. She was considerably more overwrought than she had been over the blouse. *Uh-oh. She's gone into labor and can't locate Preston. Either that, or this time the cleaners ruined an entire evening-wear ensemble.*

"What's the matter?"

"Preston. Oh, dear Lord. Preston."

"What about Preston?"

No answer, just more sobs.

"What's happened, Stephanie?" I asked again, starting to worry that, this time, she truly was in trouble.

She took a deep, noisy breath, then blurted, "Molly. Come quick. It's Preston. He's dead."

TWO

Help, Officer! There's Been a Pregnancy!

As I NEARED the Saunderses' palatial house, my every instinct screamed, "Go back! You're getting yourself into trouble!" I screeched my Toyota Corolla to a halt in Stephanie's circular driveway and yanked on the parking brake. There were no police cars out front. There were no vehicles of any kind.

I breathed a sigh of relief. Preston couldn't have died in their home, as I'd assumed when Stephanie called; otherwise, the police would have been here by now. I'd asked Stephanie no questions, just dropped the phone and sped to her house, battling tears at the thought that Preston, that *any* man, should die just before his child's birth.

Less than an hour ago, Preston had told me he was on his way to the office. He must have been in a car accident. Or died at work, maybe from a sudden heart attack. Granted, he was barely brushing up against forty, but stranger things have happened.

My emotions in turmoil, I pocketed my keys and headed up the stately flagstone steps toward the ornate, hand-carved front door. I took a deep, calming breath, trying to prepare myself mentally for dealing with a distraught Stephanie Saunders. This was a woman who had been blessed with the classic beauty of the prototypical prom queen, which she had, indeed, once been. If she'd been even half as lovely on the inside, we'd have been friends

for life. Instead, she'd been the bane of my existence from
junior high through high school—and ever since my return
to Carlton. I rang the doorbell but opened the door without
waiting, not wanting to force Stephanie to answer it in her
state of grief.

"Stephanie? It's me." A pungent odor filled the air. I
sniffed. Cleaning fluid.

"M-mm-moll, oh, Moll," came Stephanie's still-
overwrought voice from another room. "I'm in here. Be
careful where you step."

I glanced at the floor. The intricate pattern of hand-
painted Mexican tile in the foyer led to wall-to-wall white
carpeting. Were those soapsuds up ahead?

"The...the carpet's wet."

That explained the smell. Poor Stephanie. She must have
been shampooing the rug when she heard about Preston.
Years ago, my obstetrician had told me that a sudden urge
to clean was part of the "nesting instinct." Now, at that
thought, dread seeped into me. My doctor had also warned
that as a result of that nesting instinct, many women went
into labor *while* they were cleaning. Stephanie's official due
date was sometime this week.

Trying to muss as little of the carpeting as possible, I
tiptoed toward the sound of Stephanie's sobs. Just beyond
the formal dining room, the soapsuds grew denser and took
on an odd, pinkish hue. Though Stephanie's home was
enormous and I'd only been in it once before, I was pretty
sure this path led toward the kitchen.

To brace myself, I took a deep breath, then rounded the
corner...and barely stifled a scream. Blood was everywhere. Stephanie, on her hands and knees with a wash rag
and a bucket of soapy, reddish water, scrubbed at it.

"Stephanie! What in heaven's name are you doing?"

She looked up at me, tears streaming down her cheeks.
"I have to clean this. Now." She dried her tears on the
sleeves of her yellow terry-cloth robe. "Do you have any
idea how hard it is to get a stain out of white wool carpet

once it sets in?'' She went back to her scrubbing. Her belly was so swollen it nearly touched the floor.

Two thoughts flashed into my mind, virtually simultaneously. One: Stephanie was in shock and was cleaning because of the dementia. Two: Stephanie had murdered her husband and wanted to enlist me in the cover-up of her crime.

Number two was not out of the realm of possibility. Several months ago, just before Stephanie had learned she was pregnant, she'd also learned Preston had cheated on her—with my best friend. But the sight of Stephanie washing the floor in her current condition was so pathetic that I opted to believe number one.

I took another step. Preston's body was behind her, on the oak kitchen floor. I gasped and averted my eyes, trying to focus on Stephanie. Even nine months pregnant, her face blotchy, her bleached-blond hair damp and pulled into a sloppy ponytail, she was pretty. I knelt and gently touched her shoulder. "Steph? Listen to me. You're in shock. Stop cleaning. I'll call—''

She jerked away and karate-chopped my hand. "I most certainly am not in shock. Just help me get the rest of this…'' She let her voice drift away, then resumed her cleaning. "It's bad enough having my husband get killed. I don't want to lose my carpeting, too. This will cost a fortune if I have to have it replaced.''

Something was out of whack. Not even Stephanie was *that* heartless. Her downturned face looked grim and determined. If I didn't know better, I'd think she was deliberately trying to make it look as though she'd killed her husband. "Why are you doing this, Stephanie?''

No answer. She continued to rub hard enough to give her hands rug burns.

"Did you move him into the kitchen?''

"Oh, Molly. My husband. The father of my baby. What am I supposed to do now?''

I rose and looked at Preston. He was on his back. His

shirt was drenched in blood. How could this be happening? Was Stephanie crazy? I wasn't a therapist. I created greeting cards. All I wanted to do now was get out of there. Maybe write her a truly touching condolence card from the safety of my own home.

But she was pregnant, her husband's dead body was lying there a few feet away, and she'd asked me for help. I couldn't leave her like this.

I put my foot on her wash rag, only just now realizing I still had on my moccasins.

"Molly!" she cried, once again sounding not even remotely sorrowful. "You're grinding the stain in by doing that!"

With the calm, careful enunciation I sometimes used to talk to my children, I told her, "I know you don't think you're in shock, but you are. That's the only possible explanation for this behavior. Unless you killed him. That's the other explanation. Did you? Did you kill Preston?"

She relinquished her grasp on the wash rag and sat up. She opened her mouth to answer, then hesitated and studied my face. "No," she finally said, her voice quiet and sad. "I thought he'd gone to work, just after Tiffany left for school. I went upstairs to take a bath. I had the radio on. I thought I was alone. All I know is, suddenly I heard two gunshots. It scared me half to death. I put my robe on, came down, and...and...he was lying right where you're standing. I dragged him into the kitchen to get him off the rug, then I called you."

Uneasy at the concept of my feet now occupying the spot where Preston had perhaps taken his last breath, I stepped back toward the wall. "The police need to see...this is all evidence. Why did you call me? Why didn't you call the police?"

"Just as soon as I get a moment, I *will* call the police. Preston wouldn't want anyone to see him like this. He certainly wouldn't want the police, and who knows how many perfect strangers, traipsing through our house when it's in such a mess."

I stared at her. I repeated incredulously, "Preston wouldn't want... This is nuts! *And* illegal. Do you *want* to go to jail?"

Stephanie merely pursed her lips. I had to call the police. But the horror of the situation had fully sunk in, and I felt sick to my stomach. Throwing up on her precious carpet would put her even farther over the edge. I veered in a direction where I hoped I'd find a bathroom. "Just let me—"

She groaned and doubled over. "Damn it!" she panted. "*Now* we're in trouble. That was a labor pain."

Please, God. Not now. Not till I'm out of here. "Maybe it was just a Braxton-Hicks. In any case, we've got a long time till—"

She groaned again. "You've got to get me to the hospital. I was only in labor with Tiffany for forty minutes. It takes twenty-five just to get to the hospital where my obstetrician is located. My Mercedes has leather seats. We'll have to take your car in case my water breaks."

My nausea forgotten, I gritted my teeth and silently launched into a string of curse words at my stupidity. I should never have moved into my parents' northern home. When I returned to Carlton and learned Stephanie was still in town, I should have insisted we move to an unlisted address. I marched to the phone and dialed 911.

A woman dispatcher answered. "There's a dead man here," I told her. "He's been shot. His name's Preston Saunders. His wife's just gone into labor. Send an ambulance."

The dispatcher confirmed the address, then asked, "There's been a shooting?"

"Yes, and a pregnancy." I looked at Stephanie. She moaned again, in obvious pain.

While I gave the dispatcher my name, Stephanie yelled,

"Shit," repetitively and pounded the soggy floor with her fists. That reminded me. I glanced at my watch.

"Just get the police and ambulance here right away." I hung up and dialed my husband's office. I cut off the receptionist and told her, "This is Molly Masters. I've got to speak to Jim Masters immediately. It's an emergency."

Moments later Jim greeted me with "What's wrong?"

"Preston's been killed. I'm at Stephanie's house. She's in labor. I'm going to the hospital with her. Nathan's kindergarten bus arrives at noon. You have to get there first. There's a smutty magazine, a large check, and a box of dog shit on the coffee table. Put those where the kids won't see them, but don't throw anything out. It's all evidence."

"What? Start over. I could've sworn you said—"

Stephanie groaned again.

"I've got to go. I'll explain later. Bye." I hung up and rushed to Stephanie's side. "Let me help you to a chair. Can you stand up if I steady you?"

She groaned, her face red and her forehead beaded with perspiration. "I'm sure as hell not going to give birth on my carpet."

Since she now outweighed me by a good fifty pounds, getting her and the baby to her feet was no easy matter. She demanded I help her toward the "sitting room" and started shuffling toward the foyer. Good. Every step I took toward an exit made me feel a bit better.

Mid-waddle, she glanced back at the kitchen and said, "Damn you, Preston. How dare you do this to me? I'll never forgive you."

Two steps away from the entrance to the sitting room, she had another strong contraction and grabbed me for support. Her prenatal vitamins had done their job. She and her nails were so strong she dug into the flesh on my forearm and drew blood.

By now sirens wailed outside, growing louder as they neared. As soon as the contraction passed, I pulled down the sleeves of my sweatshirt to protect my skin. "Let's just go out to the porch and wait for the ambulance there, shall we?"

She nodded, tight-lipped. We made our way outside. The air was chilly, and I shivered uncontrollably. An ambulance pulled into the circular drive, followed by two police cars.

"I forgot to get my keys," Stephanie said, lurching toward the door. "I have to lock up."

I grabbed her arms. "You don't *need* to lock your house. The police are here. They'll have to get inside."

Stephanie started weeping as two paramedics, both young and male, rushed toward us. Just at the appropriate moment, she pushed me away and half fell, half twirled, in some sort of romance-heroine's swoon. The men caught her, one on each side.

"Thank God you're here," she wailed. "I need drugs." She gestured at me with a toss of her head. "Molly. Go back in and get my bag. It's all packed for the hospital. It's right inside the front coat closet."

While the paramedics helped Stephanie into the ambulance, I rushed back into the house, threw open the first door that appeared to be closetlike, shoved aside a batch of long coats, and scanned the floor. Amid boots and shoes was a leather carry-on suitcase. I slung its strap over my shoulder, then froze as a box that had been near the suitcase tumbled toward my feet.

It was a small, white box. Though upside down, its dimensions were identical to the one I'd just received. I knelt and shook the box. Empty. I chewed on my lower lip as I turned the box over. Fastened to the lid was a typed note on pink paper that read:

Mike Masters:
We are watching you. We will not rest until we have rid the world of scum like you.
Sisters Totally Opposed to Pornography

THREE

This Might Be Tougher than It Looks

"DROP THAT! Now!" a man shouted from Stephanie's open doorway behind me.

I dropped the box, then cautiously turned toward the voice. A young, uniformed police officer glared at me, his hand a millimeter above his holstered gun.

"It's just an empty box," I said, my voice a cracked whisper.

An instant later, Sergeant Tommy Newton stepped alongside the armed officer. Tommy looked at me, then at the officer, and shook his head. "It's okay, Yates. She's not dangerous, just nosy."

Under these circumstances, my relief at seeing Tommy, who'd been in my classes from kindergarten through senior high, was so strong I could have hugged him. Nonetheless, I rose and said, "That's not fair, Tommy. This is the last place in the world I wanted to be, but Stephanie called me and—"

"So you took it on yourself to plant your fingerprints all over the scene." Tommy stepped inside, his green eyes scanning the room.

"That wasn't my fault." I glared at him. He was in full uniform except for his cap, which, as usual, had left a band-shaped dent in his thick red hair. "I came over here because—"

He brushed past me. "Take her statement, Yates." The

other officer pulled out a notepad as Tommy mumbled, "So I take it the body's back here, somewhere."

"Preston's in the kitchen," I called after him. "Unfortunately, by the time I got here, Stephanie was—"

"Aw, jeez!" Tommy cried. "Did you move the body, Molly?"

"No, I—" I started to follow him into the kitchen.

He met me halfway down the front hall and interrupted, "Somebody sure did. You 'spect me to believe Stephanie was more concerned about cleaning up than calling for help?"

"Yes, I expect you to believe that," I snapped back at him. "You know me, and you've known Stephanie for more than twenty years. Which of us do you think would be worried about a carpet stain...me or Stephanie?"

He raised an eyebrow at me, then gestured at his fellow officer. "Better get her statement outside. Let's secure the scene. Tape's in my car." He put a hand on my shoulder. "Molly, you gotta go wait—"

A third uniformed officer rushed into the house. "Excuse me, sir," he said to Sergeant Newton. Then he said to me, "Are you Molly Masters?"

"Yes."

"That woman in the ambulance. Seems her labor's too far along for drugs. She's grabbed one of the paramedics by the...the...she says she's not leaving till you come with her."

"Go ahead," Tommy instructed me.

Still carrying the suitcase, I dashed out to the ambulance and climbed through the back doors. Inside the air bore a slight ammonia odor. Stephanie had already released her grip on the paramedic and was now lying on a cot and screaming her head off. She managed to stop long enough to glare at me and yell, "Where have you been?"

Having a spot of tea with the Queen, I thought to myself but, by reminding myself that she was in a lot of pain, managed to resist saying aloud.

It was easy to tell which of the two men Stephanie had assaulted. One of them merely sneered at her, then got out and shut the doors. The other was as far away from Stephanie as possible in the tight quarters, rocking himself slightly. "Are you all right?" I asked him as I sat down beside him.

He grimaced and muttered. "I hate this job."

The other paramedic got behind the wheel, flipped on the siren, and pulled out onto the road. My eyes adjusted to the muted lighting from the small one-way glass window behind me. With efficiency that would have made my mother proud, every available nook and cranny was neatly packed with blankets, medical equipment, and supplies. I was about to compliment the paramedic on the clever use of space when a curse word spewed from Stephanie's lips with the intensity of a volcanic eruption. Then she cried, "For God's sake! Somebody help me!"

Stephanie's victim scoffed and shook his head. It was up to me to comfort Stephanie. Trying to ignore my queasy stomach, I knelt beside Stephanie and let her grab my hand with her talons.

After the contraction passed and Stephanie was merely whining and panting, I told her, "You cannot treat people like this and expect them to help you."

She rolled her eyes.

"You can do this, Steph. You've given birth before. You know it's both painful and joyful, but the pain part goes away."

"It does, huh? Wait till *your* kids reach adolescence."

"My point is, you made it through Tiffany's labor. You can do it again."

She grabbed me by the front of my sweatshirt and shouted into my face, "You idiot! You don't understand. I promised myself I would have morphine this time! I want to be unconscious!"

As I reclaimed my seat, my eyes met the paramedic's. He murmured, "Tell her I'll make her unconscious, just as

soon as I find a baseball bat.'' By then Stephanie was yell-
ing and all but frothing at the mouth from another contraction, so she couldn't have overheard.

"Oh, God," Stephanie cried. "The baby's coming!"

"Drive faster!" I hollered at the man up front.

The paramedic with me sprang into action. "Baby's
coming, Dave. Pull over and get back here."

We came to a screeching stop and, moments later, the
paramedic who'd been driving joined us. He instructed me
to help support Stephanie's upper body as she pushed.

For several minutes, the three of us shouted out words
of encouragement over the earsplitting noise of Stephanie
panting and crying and screaming and uttering more pro-
fanities than were in a year's worth of action-adventure
movies combined. All I could think was, if this child un-
derstands English, he or she is going to have an unparal-
leled vocabulary of four-letter words.

And then, in the midst of this mayhem, like the sun
breaking through the worst of storms, a baby boy was born.
A perfect, beautiful baby boy. Though I had witnessed my
daughter's and my son's births, my vantage point had been
considerably different. Without experiencing firsthand the
labor pains that had then kept me grounded in reality, wit-
nessing this newborn's birth felt like nothing short of a
miracle. My eyes teared up and my smile was so wide my
face hurt.

The paramedics let me help swaddle the baby in one of
their many red blankets. I cuddled him and tried in vain to
avoid seeing Stephanie deliver the placenta—a sight that
brought to mind one of my daughter's favorite sayings:
"Eww! Sick!" Then I placed the baby in Stephanie's arms.
Her tears of pain and physical effort changed to tears of
joy as she took him from me, and I found myself weeping
with joy, too, and hugging her.

In the male equivalent of hugs, the men gave one another
high-fives and slapped each other's backs. Stephanie tearfully apologized to us. The same paramedic who, not fifteen

minutes ago, had told me he hated his job now told her
how much he admired her and that this was a day he would
never forget as long as he lived.

His words, though, brought the reality of the full situation back home to me. The rest of the way to the hospital,
I forced a smile each time Stephanie met my eyes. I agreed
every time Stephanie asked me, "Isn't my baby beautiful?"
But my thoughts were in turmoil.

Suddenly I'd been sucked into a matter of both death
and life. Some three hours earlier, I'd been minding my
own business, literally, trying to complete a drawing for a
product demonstration for a company that sold fax machines. Ironically, that cartoon showed a woman in an even
more precarious predicament than mine: A solitary man
shields her from a huge battalion of armed men on the
nearby shore. All the while, their boat is sinking and is
surrounded by both alligators and sharks; overhead is a
helicopter where a dozen men with rifles aim at them. The
man is scratching his chin thoughtfully and says to the
woman, "Hmmm. This might be a little tougher than it
looks."

My head was filled with unanswered questions. Who
killed Preston? Who put that box in his closet? Was the
bullet that killed him meant for me, the creator of the cartoon?

We pulled into the emergency entrance to the hospital,
an ugly, brown, boxy building in downtown Schenectady.
I got out of the way and watched the men unload Stephanie
with baby. I called to her that I'd catch up with her soon,
then stayed outside for a few minutes to clear my head.
The chilly air felt good on my face but reeked with car
fumes from the busy street nearby.

Eventually I went inside the stark emergency room,
where a thick antiseptic smell masked even less desirable
odors. Along with four or five would-be patients and one
of the uniformed officers I'd seen at Stephanie's, my friend
the police sergeant was already seated in the waiting room.

The damp leather of my moccasins scuffed against the linoleum as I walked over to him.

"Tommy. I'm surprised you're here already."

"Can't do anything at the Saunders residence till I get a search warrant. It's a little matter called 'expectation of privacy.'"

I stared at him blankly, not having a response to his statement, and not knowing when to begin to try to explain everything that had happened.

"So, Ms. Masters," Tommy began, flipping open a notepad he'd taken from his pocket. Apparently, since he'd addressed me so formally, Tommy wanted to waste no time getting my statement.

A nurse came up to me and asked if I was Molly Masters. To my nod, she explained that Stephanie Saunders was in an observation room nearby and had asked to speak to me immediately. The nurse then gave me instructions on how to get there.

Tommy led the way. He pushed the door open and muttered to me, "Just what you always wanted, right? A police escort."

We entered a small, brightly lit room with white walls and maroon linoleum flooring. Everything was on wheels: the monitors, the cart of medical supplies, the baby's clear plastic bassinet, Stephanie's cot. Tommy greeted Stephanie solemnly and ignored the infant sleeping in the bassinet beside her, though, once I laid eyes on him, it was impossible to look anyplace else. The baby was sleeping on his side, his perfect, pink lips slightly parted. A tuft of blond peach fuzz peeked out from below a stocking cap—off-white with a blue-is-for-boys band.

"Molly?" Stephanie said quietly.

I reluctantly turned away from the adorable infant and met Stephanie's gaze. She looked exhausted, yet, amazingly, still attractive.

Apparently accepting the fact that Tommy was going to

eavesdrop, she said, "I've decided to name my son after you."

I waited, but when she didn't go on, I asked, "You're going to name him Molly?"

"I'm naming him the closest male alternative to Molly I can think of. I'm naming him Michael."

I winced. "Michael? As in long for Mike?"

"That's right. Michael Saunders."

My stomach knotted. I desperately didn't want this angelic baby named Mike, forever to remind me of "Mike" Masters. "Gee, Stephanie. Thanks. But...Michael is so hard to spell. Nobody ever knows which comes first, the *a* or the *e*. Couldn't you just make Michael his middle name? Call him Preston Michael Sanders?" I paused. "Never mind. That would make his initials PMS and you wouldn't want to do that. How about Preston Junior?"

She pursed her lips and shook her head. "I've made up my mind." She smiled lovingly at her child. "This is Michael. My little Mike." She looked at Tommy for a long moment, then cleared her throat. "Could I have a minute alone with Molly, please?"

Tommy shook his head. "I have to talk to each of you separately first. I need to get both of your statements."

"Please, Tommy," Stephanie said. "This is urgent, and it has to do with the care of my baby. Nothing whatsoever to do with my husband's murder."

Tommy's gaze went from Stephanie to me and then back. "I'm putting myself on the line here cuz of our friendship. So I'm warning you. Don't say one word about what happened in your house till I've had a chance to talk to you privately."

"I won't." Stephanie held up three fingers and flashed her Miss America smile. "Scout's honor."

Still maintaining her perfect smile, she watched Tommy leave. The instant the door swung shut behind him, her expression changed to a sneer. "Like I was ever a Scout."

She studied my face. "Molly, I have a confession to make."

My stomach muscles tensed. *Oh, no. You have an infant who needs you! Don't be the killer!*

"The reason I was cleaning up the blood?" Stephanie said quietly. "When I came downstairs and saw Preston, he wasn't dead. He said one last word to me. And then...he was gone. That's why I tried to clean. To make it look like *I'd* killed him. Now, I'm next to this tiny person that's a part of me, and I realize, I can't go to jail.

"I didn't kill him. I swear to you as a mother. I swear on the life of my baby. I didn't kill Preston."

"But you know who did?"

She nodded, tears coming to her eyes. "I'm afraid I might. Preston's last word to me was 'Tiffany.'"

Oh, dear Lord. Tiffany? She thinks her own daughter killed her husband! "But she was his daughter. Maybe he was just thinking of her. How could you possibly think that—"

"On Saturday, Preston caught Tiffany and her boyfriend...in the act. Preston said he was going to file statutory rape charges and...I've never seen Tiffany so out of control. She threatened to kill him."

From her frequent baby-sitting stints at my house, I was well aware that Tiffany had been at odds with her father for some time now over her continuing to defy his orders and date Cherokee Taylor. All along, I could see both Tiffany's and Preston's perspectives. But this time I could empathize strictly with Preston. Tiffany was only fourteen! Heaven forbid, six years from now, I were to discover *my* daughter...I shuddered.

Stephanie gently took my hand. "Molly, if she killed her father, I want you to help her. If she didn't, I want you to find out who did so he can be brought to justice. I'm never going to tell anyone what Preston said, and I called you because I know that regardless of the fact you and I have had our differences, you're the one person in this world I know I can trust to always do the right thing.''

"But, I—"

I stopped and turned as the door squeaked open. A nurse leaned into the room and smiled at Stephanie. "The doctor needs to examine you now, ma'am."

My head was spinning from this emotional roller coaster I'd suddenly been flung onto.

"Promise me, Molly. Please."

I looked at Stephanie. For all our shared experiences during our lifetimes, this was one of the very few times I knew unequivocally that she was being utterly sincere.

I nodded and left the room. I felt stunned. My baby-sitter a murderer? No. It just couldn't be. She was flaky, self-centered, high-strung—a typical teenager. Not a killer. Now she was supposed to cope with her father's murder *and* her own mother suspecting her?

I had to help Tiffany.

Tommy Newton was waiting for me in the hospital corridor just outside Stephanie's room. "What'd she say?" he promptly asked.

I forced myself to meet his eyes. "She just wanted to thank me for helping her with the birth."

"Did she tell you who did it?"

"No, I swear. She just thanked me."

"Uh-huh."

Tommy and I knew each other well. Though he'd since broadened considerably, back in high school he had been the runt of the graduating class in which I'd been class clown. Last fall, he had erroneously arrested Lauren, my best friend. Tommy knew from that painful incident how single-minded I could be when the situation demanded it. I learned that Tommy deliberately gave the appearance of having a whole lot less on the ball than he actually had. My husband, Jim, was even a little jealous of our relationship, though he needn't have been. Aside from the fact that

I loved my husband and would never be unfaithful to him, Tommy and I rarely saw eye to eye on anything.

I studied his lightly freckled face. Despite his blank expression, something about his physical bearing indicated he knew all too well that I was lying. He had used *me* as bait to eavesdrop on Stephanie! I clenched my fists.

"You listened in on our private conversation, didn't you?"

FOUR

Across the Sands of Time

Y'ALL PROMISED not to talk about the murder," Tommy replied. "What exactly was said during your 'private conversation'?"

"Give me a break, Tommy. '*Y'all* promised?' We both know you've lived in upstate New York your entire life. That good-ol'-boy routine of yours is just a technique you use to interrogate suspects. And I'm *not* a suspect."

"You're not, eh? Glad to hear it." He put a hand on my elbow and tried to lead me down the hall. "S'pose we take a seat in the lobby. You can tell me exactly what happened from the get-go."

"First I want to check something." I headed in the opposite direction from where Tommy wanted me to go. He followed. Just a short distance away was a nurses' station. As I suspected, from an unseen speaker somewhere in the station, I could hear Stephanie's voice cry, "But I don't *want* my uterus massaged! It hurts! It's *my* uterus, isn't it? Massage your own blasted—"

"I knew it!" I whirled and leveled a finger at Tommy. "That was a rotten thing to do! Neither Stephanie nor I knew you were listening, so it's not admissible!"

"Prob'ly not," Tommy answered calmly, his face blank, his eyes trained right on mine. "That is, *if* I were listening in on you, which I'm not saying I was. But, just in case, how 'bout you tell me exactly what was said? That way we won't have to worry 'bout me drawing the wrong conclusions."

I stormed past him, hoping I could find my way out of the hospital despite my horrendous sense of direction.

"Where you goin'?" he called after me.

"Home!"

"You still haven't given me your statement."

"I know. But I don't feel like talking to you right now, Sergeant. And I need to get home to my children."

Feeling a small moment of personal triumph, I pushed through a set of double doors and found myself exactly where I wanted to be: the emergency waiting room. I marched past the officer still in the same seat he'd occupied when I'd first spotted Tommy.

I pushed through the glass exit doors, then realized how minuscule this "personal triumph" truly was. My car. It was still parked in Stephanie's driveway. I had no purse, no money for bus fare, not even two dimes for a phone call home or to a taxi company. Besides, there were no phones out here. No choice but to turn and go back inside.

Why couldn't life be like the movies? Why couldn't I make a good exit, just this one time? I'd had every right to storm out of there. Tommy Newton had done something reprehensible, both to me and to a woman who'd just lost her husband *and* given birth—a woman he'd known his entire adult life.

Knowing the longer I stood on the sidewalk, the greater would be my embarrassment, I straightened, turned on a heel, and reentered. As I'd feared, Tommy now stood next to the other officer. Both sets of eyes were on me. The seated officer was grinning, but Tommy maintained his typical placid expression.

"On second thought," I said evenly to Tommy, "if your partner here could give me a ride afterward, I'd be happy to tell *him* exactly what happened this morning."

BY THE TIME I got my car and drove home, followed by Officer Tommy, it was midafternoon. I felt exhausted and emotionally drained. Given half a chance, I would climb into bed, curl into the fetal position, and do my best to pretend this day never happened.

My pretty, petite daughter, Karen, home from second grade, met me at the door to the garage. I gave her a hug and kissed her soft cheek.

"Guess what, Mom? I can spell Mississippi *and* Massachusetts *backwards!*"

"That's great, sweetie, just so long as you can spell them forwards." Karen skipped along behind me as I trudged through the house toward the front door to await Tommy's arrival. The oval-shaped cherrywood coffee table was a tad dusty but otherwise clear. Jim had, as asked, removed the box, magazine, and check. "Where are Nathan and your daddy?"

"I think he's in his room. He says he doesn't want to be in this family anymore."

"Nathan?" If she meant Jim, my husband was more perturbed about my weird emergency phone call than I'd hoped.

Karen nodded and said, "Mm-hmm," her fine, light brown hair bobbing, then she launched into an animated description of the latest "Daddy's Mad at Nathan Because..." She said something about Nathan hammering nails into tires, but by then Tommy had arrived and Karen's voice drifted off as she fell into her usual awed silence at the sight of him in full uniform. Maybe I should get a police uniform myself to wear around the house.

Jim emerged from the basement, no doubt having been working in my office. He was thin and six feet tall, and had brown hair now flecked with white, a mustache, and soft brown eyes that could melt an ice maiden's heart, as well as mine—even after twelve years of marriage. He was wearing brown wing-tips and the gray slacks from his suit, but he'd changed into a green plaid flannel shirt, a triangle of white undershirt showing at his neckline. A handsome man, but a lousy dresser.

"I *thought* I heard you come in." His eyes darted from mine to Tommy's. "Hello, Tom."

True to form, Jim shook Tommy's hand and chatted about his current troubles with Nathan, who had indeed flattened one of the radials on the Jeep by hammering a roofing nail into it. Granted, that was bad behavior on our six-year-old's part, but it paled in comparison to Preston's murder, and the fact that somewhere in this house was possible evidence. Jim's social graces were so firmly entrenched that, even if Tommy were currently in the process of reading me my rights and handcuffing me, their friendly exchange would've gone much the same way.

Ever since his wife had died two years ago, Tommy was single-handedly raising two boys, and he assured my husband that his sons had gone through a destructive stage that lasted "thirteen years and counting." This led to Jim asking what his sons were "up to these days."

Thankfully, Tommy opted not to offer a lengthy response and merely answered, "Just fine. Growing like weeds. I hear you've got some things for me to take back to the station." He was being vague out of sensitivity to the fact that Karen still stood just a few feet away, watching us wide-eyed.

"Yes, they're in the laundry room," Jim answered. "I put everything in plastic bags."

Just then, Nathan slunk down the stairs toward us. He was the portrait of self-pity: red eyes and pink cheeks, chin down, lower lip protruding, his curly hair every which way. He flopped onto the bottom step in a puddle of despair. Then he caught his first sight of Tommy.

"Hello, big guy," Tommy said.

Nathan's expression changed to one of sheer terror. He scrambled up the stairs and raced into his bedroom.

Both Jim and Tommy looked at me, perplexed. "He thinks you're here to arrest him for putting a hole in the tire," I explained to Tommy. "Jim, I'll go get the stuff from the laundry. Could you please go assure our son you didn't call the cops on him?"

As he went upstairs, my vision drifted to Karen. She was listening to all of this, utterly fascinated.

"Don't you have some homework to do in your room?"

"Already finished. Um, Mom? What did Daddy put in our laundry room?"

I gave her a quick kiss on her forehead and said gently, "Go upstairs and see if you can figure out how to spell Connecticut backwards. I'll quiz you on it in five minutes."

Karen had been on to all of my diversionary tactics for a good four years now. She rolled her eyes, in practice for her upcoming adolescence, but then acted her age by following my instructions.

Tommy and I went to the laundry room, not the neatest room in the house, but then I'd been remiss in my cleaning duties of late so all rooms were competing for that honor. In fact, my mother would faint to see her house and its antique furnishings in this unkempt state. The laundry room had built-in shelves opposite the washer-dryer. The STOP box and contents were on the top shelf, along with the magazine and check, all sealed into individual Ziploc freezer bags. As I handed them to Tommy, it occurred to me I hadn't written down the address and phone number for *Between the Legs* and needed to resolve the problem of the contract Preston had supposedly signed for me.

"Do you need all of these things?" I asked.

"Yeah. For now, at least. Can't even let you keep the fertilizer. We'll have to get that analyzed."

Analyzing dog waste? Now *there's* a great job. "Judging from size, my guess is the perp's a German shepherd, though I'm no expert. But what I'm wondering is, do you need the magazine and the check? They probably won't tell you anything about Preston's killer."

"We'll need to have 'em fingerprinted, just in case." He eyed me. "Don't worry. You'll get to cash it, eventually."

I accompanied him to the front door. Seeing the box from

STOP again reminded me of something that had puzzled me about the second box. "Did that box I found in Stephanie's closet have...stains in it?"

"Can't examine it till we get the search warrant, which'll be any minute now." He paused in the doorway and narrowed his eyes. "Got a friendly warning for you, Molly. Don't go pokin' your nose into this."

"That's an interesting figure of speech, considering you're carrying dog doo-doo."

He turned and called over his shoulder. "Don't leave town. I'll be in touch."

Now wearing sweats and sneakers, Jim headed back down the stairs, holding Nathan's hand. "Nathan and I are going to fix the tire. I'm skipping the rest of my meeting so I can get some real work done at home on our computer."

This was pure Jim-speak. He didn't want to admit it, but he was too worried about me to go back to the office. I smiled lovingly at him. Jim gave Nathan a reassuring pat on the shoulder. "Go on ahead. I'll be right there."

Nathan rushed off, nearly jumping for joy at the chance to atone for his wanton hammering. Jim promptly gave me a big hug. He seemed to be trembling slightly. Then, as Jim held me even tighter, I realized my body was actually the one trembling. "Don't worry," he whispered. "Everything's going to be fine."

"I hope so."

"Did Stephanie do it?" Jim asked, releasing me from his warm embrace.

"Do what?"

"Kill Preston." He furrowed his brows as he stared into my eyes. "Did she?"

"No, but she's afraid Tiffany did it."

"Tiffany? Our baby-sitter?" Jim's face paled. We shared the dreadful, unspoken fear that someone we'd trusted to watch our children could be a murder suspect. "Did Stephanie witness the—"

The heavy door to the garage creaked open, and, after a clatter and a bang, Nathan rushed in, carrying a crescent wrench. "Is this what we need, Daddy?"

"That's too small. But you're on the right track." He followed Nathan toward the garage, then, as he opened the door for Nathan, turned and said, "Let the police handle this."

"Bye, Mommy!"

"Do a good job," I called after them.

My thoughts warred. Jim was right. I should play it safe—trust Tommy and his fellow officers to solve the murder. But how could I desert poor Tiffany? Just having to *be* a teenager was punishment enough in this world. Having her father die a violent death, let alone be suspected by one's own mother of the murder, was just too horrendous.

Jim's partial question nagged at me. Could Stephanie have actually witnessed Tiffany shooting Preston? Is that why Stephanie tried to incriminate herself?

Later, after the tire was repaired, we encouraged the kids to watch cartoons and locked ourselves in our bedroom as I recounted the events of that morning. It was a frustrating experience, because whenever I tell him something upsetting, Jim interrupts frequently to ask questions. In this case, his questions were not only off the main point, but unanswerable. "How did Preston get the cartoon? How could he sign a contract for you? Why did the magazine want to hire you on the basis of one cartoon?"

When I came to the part about Stephanie's "confession" at the hospital, I was unable to convince him that I knew Stephanie was telling me the truth.

He stared into my eyes. "Uh-oh. There's…that look on your face."

"What look?"

"Remember that time we were on a softball team and the other team was short a player, so our captain told them you'd play for them? You had that same look on your face when you stepped up to the plate and hit that home run."

The memory made me grin. That was perhaps the only time in the history of Boulder co-rec softball when the pitcher cheered for having a grand-slam hit against him. Jim had been pitching.

"Promise me you'll stay away from the Saunderses," he went on.

"I can't. I promised Stephanie I'd help Tiffany."

He furrowed his brow. "Stephanie's manipulating you."

"I don't let her manipulate me. She just—"

"She manipulates everyone. She senses everyone's weak spots to use against them. Asking you to help her *daughter* is the best way to con you into helping *her*. Maybe Preston cheated on Stephanie one time too many, so she killed him. Now she wants to send you on some wild goose chase, hoping you'll turn up something to deflect everyone's attention off of where it belongs. On *her*."

Jim's words made me bristle, though I suspected I wasn't really angry at him for making the suggestion, but at Stephanie, who was indeed so manipulative that Jim's theory could be correct. "But our whole family knows Tiffany," I said. "The kids are crazy about her. I couldn't live with myself if I turned my back on her and Stephanie now. She's a *recently widowed new mother!*"

"If you go chasing after some murderer," Jim shot back, "you might just turn *me* into a recent widower."

"I'm not going to put myself in danger. But I am going to talk to Tiffany and her friends and try to find out if she's involved. Because either way, she needs help. She's a teenager and she's just lost her father. The time I stop caring about the people in my life is the time I *hope* I stop living!" This last remark was an overstatement, but as a former debate-team captain, verbal sparring brings out the occasional drama queen in me.

Jim grimaced and dragged both hands through his hair, a gesture he only used when he felt defeated. "Can't you *care* from a safe distance? For the sake of our family?"

"I can't. I'm sorry." I felt like a wishbone, with the

Saunders family tugging on one side, my family tugging on the other. And some wacko group called STOP wielding a meat cleaver.

Jim shook his head and unlocked the door. He was not the sort who'd battle for the last word.

"Jim, I've got to go next door and tell Lauren about Preston. Can you keep an eye on the kids?"

"I'll be at the computer, but I'll be here." He didn't look at me, just headed down the stairs. It was painful to see him this worried about me. My spirits were sinking to basement level as well.

The air was downright frigid, but I dashed across the lawn without a coat, my thoughts on Lauren. She had played a part in virtually every significant memory from my childhood. During our late teens, our friendship survived despite a couple of traumas that had threatened to rip us, as well as our friendship, apart. Now when we were together, I experienced an almost magical blending of past and present—the little girl in pigtails I once skipped rope with, and the elegant woman who talked and laughed with me while our daughters skipped rope.

Then, last summer, Lauren and Preston had had an affair. Her husband had died shortly after learning of his wife's infidelity, leaving Lauren in emotional shambles for some time.

In the last two or three months, she had started to put her life back together. She had taken on a part-time job in the principal's office at the high school building of the Carlton Central campus. She'd recently admitted to me that she'd finally forgiven herself for the "terrible mistake" she'd made with Preston. She once again seemed to be the Lauren Wilkins I knew and loved.

What the news that Preston had been murdered would do to her I could only guess. But I wanted to tell her myself, not have her hear it over the eleven o'clock news or, worse, from our small-town grapevine, which occasionally reached out and choked us.

Inside, the house was warm and smelled like cinnamon. It was clear the moment our eyes met that Lauren was already aware something was wrong. Her daughter, Rachel, raced to join us. Our daughters were in the same second-grade class and were best buddies.

"Where's Karen?" Rachel asked.

"She and Nathan are home with their daddy."

"Can I go play with them?" Her eyes focused on mine, then her mom's.

We agreed to let her go, though I called Jim first to let him know there would be a third child under his supervision. He tended to get so absorbed in his work he wouldn't notice the house was burning down till his clothes caught fire.

I sat on a barstool at her kitchen counter and we made small talk as Lauren microwaved us some tea. She was a fairly large woman—"big-boned," being the euphemism of choice—and had a round face with shoulder-length brown hair. A stranger might not even find her especially attractive. But she had an undeniable presence about her, along with a stunning smile. I thought of her as nothing less than beautiful.

She slid a cup toward me and took the stool next to mine. As if her sitting signified it was time to get down to business, she said, "I saw a police car in your driveway a few minutes ago. What's wrong?"

"It's Preston. He was...someone shot him."

She paled. "Oh my God. Is he dead?"

I felt suddenly inarticulate, while watching Lauren's face for signs of the emotional upheaval I imagined she must be experiencing. I blundered through an account of Preston's visit, Stephanie's call for help, and the bizarre scene at Stephanie's house. Lauren listened silently until I told her about the birth in the ambulance.

"Good Lord," she murmured. "Steph's baby was born on the same day her husband died. How is she handling this?"

I held up my palms. "In pure Stephanie style, frankly. I've never been able to fathom her behavior, even under the best of circumstances.

"So," I continued with my chronology, "when we got to the hospital, she asked to speak to me alone and told me that…" I stopped, remembering that Stephanie had said she was never going to tell anyone what Preston's dying word had been. I had already told Jim, but he would never repeat it. That was not necessarily true with Lauren.

"What?" Lauren prompted.

"That she didn't do it."

She waited. "And?"

"That's it."

She sat back, studied my face, then shook her head. "Molly. I know you better than I do myself. I can always tell when you're lying."

I averted my eyes. I hadn't actually promised Stephanie I'd keep her secret, only that I'd help Tiffany. And because Lauren worked in the high school office, she could be a tremendous asset when arranging to talk with Tiffany's friends. "I'm sworn to secrecy on this, so don't tell anyone, but she's afraid Tiffany may have been responsible. The thing is, I'm almost positive Tommy listened in and knows about Tiffany."

Lauren sat in silence, absorbing my news. "This is all so horrible. Preston, murdered. It's as if every man I've ever slept with gets…thank God I was working at school all morning. Otherwise it'd just be my luck Tommy Newton would think I did it, once again."

I studied her, making no comment. At length, she met my eyes, then rose and crossed over to the window that faced my home. "What's wrong with me?" she asked, more of herself than of me. "I should feel…torn up about this. After all, he was my lover, once. I'm *sad* that he's dead, but that's all. The truth is, he was such a sleaze I can't believe I ever actually slept with him." She leaned on the countertop for a moment, then straightened and added wistfully, "I just...wish I knew what to do for Stephanie. Should I visit her? Bring her a baby gift? We've made a point of avoiding each other, and I haven't even *seen* her in six months."

I resisted the temptation to point out once again that I was the last person she should ask what to do where Stephanie was concerned. "Maybe you should call her at the hospital and say you'd like to visit and see what she says. But Stephanie is tough as nails. It's so weird. She cares more about the mess on her carpet than she does about her husband's death. At this point, I just feel bad for Tiffany, losing her father."

"True. The thing is, though, Stephanie's already succeeded at creating Tiffany in her own image. Don't you think?"

Because Lauren was actually quoting me from a conversation we'd had months ago about Tiffany, I couldn't disagree. "Well, yes, but Tiffany's only fourteen. Theoretically, there's still time for her to change. And lately, I have found myself liking Tiffany more, mostly because my kids think she's so wonderful."

Lauren studied my face. "Do you really think Tiffany could have killed her own father?"

I thought about that for a moment. "No. But I do believe one of her friends might have. You can't even read the newspapers now without coming across some article about some child shooting someone with a gun."

But that begged a very important question: If *I* couldn't believe Tiffany had murdered Preston, how could Stephanie? Was Tiffany's possible involvement just an irrational fear on Stephanie's part, indicating she truly *was* traumatized by the murder? Or was it because she knew her own daughter so much better than I did? To answer those questions, I was going to have to get to know Tiffany better.

TO MY SURPRISE, the three children and Jim were engrossed in a game of Old Maid when I got home from Lauren's.

Times like this made me want to design a "World's Best Dad" coffee mug for Jim. It also struck me that this was a golden opportunity for me to purchase a copy of *Between the Legs* privately. I told Jim I was going to put some gas in the car and headed across town to a self-serve station that sold cheese snacks and cheesy magazines.

As I filled the tank, I realized I should've simply asked Jim to get me a copy. He would have been considerably less conspicuous asking for a "girly" magazine. Then again, I was here now. May as well go through with it.

I washed every window in my car twice while waiting for other customers to leave. The clerk was a gruff-looking man in his sixties. Behind him was a small wire rack of various men's magazines, each sealed in plastic. I told him what my total for unleaded was, then tried to sound casual as I added, "Oh, and could I get a copy of *Between the Legs*, too, please?"

He smirked, but silently fetched a copy. He rang up my bill with gnarled fingers so discolored with cigarette stains they looked like old cigars.

Unless the threats from STOP were a bizarre coincidence, the killer had to have seen a copy of the edition that printed my cartoon. If we happened to have selected the same store and the same clerk, I might be able to get a description.

As he slipped my magazine into a brown bag, I asked, "Have you sold many copies of this lately?"

He shrugged. "Two or three."

"You wouldn't happen to remember what the people who bought 'em looked like, would you?"

He grinned, revealing rotted teeth. "Why? Trying to start a fan club?"

My cheeks warmed. "I'm just...I want to make sure my...husband hasn't bought any copies. This is a birthday present for him and I want to be sure he hasn't already got it."

He let out a wheezy laugh. "You're giving him a porno

mag? Whooee! You must have some interestin' birthday parties. Are you gonna hire a stripper to pop out of his cake?"

Not about to dignify that with an answer, I ignored my ever-warming cheeks and pressed on. "My husband is average height, typical looking. Does that sound like any of your customers who've bought this magazine?"

"Don't recall. Tell you one thing, though. You're the second woman I've sold it to."

Aha! A STOP member! What woman, besides me, would pay good money for this trash? "Really? What did the other woman look like?"

He peered at me. "Why?"

"Well, because..." How could I lie my way out of this one? My mind was blank. "I'm just curious. Can you describe her to me?"

He chuckled again, blatantly staring at my chest. "Attractive. In her thirties or so. Blond, I think, but I can't swear to it. That was 'bout a week or so ago when our April editions first arrive. I only remember that much 'cause she was the first woman I ever sold the mag to. You're the second." He glanced back at the rack of magazines. "It must have cross-appeal. Maybe I should order more copies."

I murmured thanks and turned away.

"Sure thing. Hope your hubby has a real *special* birthday."

Trying to ignore my inner voice that was screaming "Stephanie" in response to the female magazine-buyer's description, I drove home. The clerk would've mentioned if the woman customer had been eight months pregnant. There was no reason for me to jump to the conclusion that Stephanie had bought this magazine and plotted her husband's demise.

Actually, as my astute husband had already pointed out, "no reason" was an exaggeration. Knowing that spouses were always the first suspects, Stephanie could have learned about the cartoon and plotted the whole STOP thing as a blind. That would explain the empty box in the closet. She couldn't stand the thought of having actual dog doo-doo in her own house, so she put just the box in the closet. She kills Preston, calls me to set me up, and sends me for her suitcase, knowing I'd see the box and get my fingerprints on it.

"Stop it," I told myself aloud. In times such as this it's imperative to trust one's instincts. In my heart of hearts, I believed Stephanie was innocent and was telling the truth about her fear for Tiffany.

And after all, "attractive, in her thirties" fit any number of women in this town, any of whom could be members of STOP. I reflected on the two women joggers this morning who'd overheard my exchange with Preston. Either one of them loosely fit the clerk's description. Perhaps they were from STOP and had been jogging around my block to spy on "Mike" Masters.

THE NEXT MORNING, Jim left for work, the kids were off on the bus, and I tried to return my office to the same state of organized chaos I liked it in. Jim had straightened, which annoyed me to no end. He had to be prodded to do the dishes or to clean any room except for the one room in the house I considered "Mine All Mine."

I finished my drawing for the office-supply store that was my main customer, then doodled on my drawing pad for a while. When I had no current orders, I often freelanced for card companies. This being the end of March, the card companies would currently be seeking Christmas cards.

I used to work for a greeting card company in Boulder, which produced poetic cards on pastoral scenes. When my husband's job had forced us to relocate, opening my own business allowed me to focus on my strength, cartooning. Serious Christmas cards, however, always outsold the humorous ones. So I drew a desert scene where, on the horizon, a camel laden with Christmas presents is led by a man in Arabian robes. The panel would take up the entire front of the card, and would open to read:

May the Joy and Peace of the Holiday Season
Stay with You
Across the Sands of Time

The challenge facing me was to paint the picture well enough to inspire feelings of peacefulness. I envisioned the rich hues of a desert at dusk, but as a self-taught artist— my bachelor's degree was in journalism—what I envisioned and what I produced were often quite different.

My work was interrupted when the fax machine began to whir. As always, I hoped it would be a job order, but it was merely a résumé from some woman who'd seen my name in a greeting card trade magazine. This was a common occurrence; the amount of actual work my business ads generated was always neck-and-neck with the number of job applications they inspired. The popular opinion seems to be that any idiot can write greeting cards, which may be true, however this is one idiot who can't afford to hire a staff.

The applicant's work history was in "the food-service management industry"; read: a waitress. She was sure I'd want to hire her. A sample stanza was included, with a hand-printed copyright notice to prevent me from plagiarizing: My love will always be true/Without you I could never do/Say you'll be mine/Please be my valentine.

"Wow!" I cried, indulging myself with some sarcasm. "I never thought of rhyming *mine* and *valentine*. The woman's a genius!"

The machine began to whir again. Apparently, this applicant was more persistent than most and was sending me yet more atrocious poetry. I snatched the sheet off the tray and read a letter.

Molly Masters:
We know what you're doing. You are a
traitor to women everywhere! You didn't
even have the guts to admit you were a
woman. Instead you used a man's photograph in that disgusting piece of filth.
Now you're trying to frame our group for
murder! S.T.O.P. is innocent. We are
nonviolent. Your actions force us to
make an exception! *You* will be our first
victim!
Sisters **T**otally **O**pposed to **P**ornography

FIVE

Raw Hamburger

LESS THAN thirty minutes after I'd notified the police about my threatening fax, Sergeant Tommy Newton rang my doorbell. I let him inside and said, "Thanks for responding so quickly."

He nodded and removed his cap. I couldn't help but stare. Either his head was growing, his cap was shrinking, or he needed a haircut. The dent in his red hair was now so pronounced his head looked like a pinched orange balloon.

There was a twinkle in his eye as he glanced at the coffee table and spotted the fax. I knew his sense of humor. I snatched up the piece of paper and warned, "If you say, 'Just the fax, ma'am' to me even once, I'll scream."

"Uh-huh," he murmured. That was his catch-all response, but this time it sounded a little disheartened, as if I'd ruined his fun. I handed him the fax and took a seat on the couch.

He sat on the stuffed high-back chair and took so long to read it he must have been committing it to memory.

"What-all do you make of this?" he said at last, peering at me.

"That was my question for you."

One corner of his mouth raised a little, but he remained silent, studying my face.

"I can't figure out much about the fax, except that I don't feel particularly threatened by it. They're certainly not going to kill me now, knowing the police are hot on their trail. Right?''

Tommy merely shrugged.

Though less than encouraged by this response, I continued, "The tag line shows it was sent from one of those self-serve copy shops in Albany. I called the store right away, but none of the clerks had any clue about who might have sent it. Since my first name is used this time, the sender could have looked that up in the phone book or maybe knows me personally, and either truly didn't know my first name yesterday or wants to give the police the impression he or she didn't.''

Tommy sighed, rubbed his forehead, and murmured, "Uh-huh."

"Also, the sender wants the police to think he or she is from STOP and that they had nothing to do with the murder. That's either because they're innocent or guilty.''

"Innocent or guilty, huh?'' Tommy raised an eyebrow. "That's pretty impressive theorizing.''

"Well? You asked, and I told you I didn't know much. But I do have some theories about Preston's murder. Want to hear them?''

"No, but odds are you're going to tell me anyway, so go ahead.''

"The way I see it, there are three possibilities. One: STOP actually did murder Preston Saunders thinking he was Mike Masters, in which case there's at least one certifiably insane feminist in Carlton who scours all the men's magazines and flipped out when she discovered smut had come to our little town. Two: The STOP messages were a bizarre coincidence and someone killed Preston for entirely different reasons. Three: Someone in town spotted my cartoon in the magazine or heard about Preston's plot to win the contest using my cartoon, then concocted this whole STOP thing to cover up his or her personal motives.''

I paused, expecting him to be impressed. He blinked.

"Uh-huh," he said at length. "And which theory do you think is correct?"

"I go back and forth on that. Having such a crazy feminist in town seems unlikely. After all, people do and say things every day that are more offensive to women than that cartoon of mine. On the other hand, Preston coincidently getting killed on the same morning we both got threats from STOP is a little hard to swallow. Yet, would anyone really go through such an elaborate hoax to hide a murder? I mean, wouldn't it be easier to...make it look like a shooting during a burglary or something?"

"Yep. You done a good job of poking holes in your own theories." He rose and fitted his cap back onto its headslot. "Keep up the good work."

"What about the box at the Saunderses' house? Was it stained?"

"Yeah. Used to have the same general contents as your box." He headed toward the door, taking the fax with him.

"So tell me, what do *you* think about the fax?"

"That's the trouble. Right now, we don't have a whole lot of facts, just theories that don't hold much water."

"I mean the faxed message that STOP sent me. What do you think it means?"

"Think it just goes to show you attract trouble quicker than raw hamburger attracts flies."

"Thanks a lot. That's a charming image, comparing me to uncooked meat."

He opened the door. "Coulda compared you to something a lot worse. And like you told me earlier, 'You asked.'"

LAUREN, her daughter Rachel in tow, dropped by later that afternoon. Karen and Nathan raced me to the door, but they'd been engrossed in their daily one-hour allotment of cartoons—which occasionally lasts two hours when I'm pushing a deadline—and so were a step behind me.

Though she wore a particularly flattering outfit—a royal

blue cardigan over a beige turtleneck, with perfectly matched, loose-fitting dress slacks—Lauren seemed out of sorts. She absentmindedly combed her fingers through her brown hair and chewed on her lower lip.

"Have you gone to see Stephanie today?" she asked me over the noise of our children's chattering.

"No, though I'd planned to earlier. I never got the chance." The fax from STOP had disrupted my day, but I wanted to find out why Lauren seemed upset before I mentioned my own problems.

As soon as the children were out of earshot, she slumped onto the stuffed high-back chair in the living room and said, "Well, I took your advice."

"Uh-oh. I gave you advice? I hate it when I do that."

"I called Stephanie at the hospital. I'll just give you the highlights. She called me a husband-stealing bitch."

"Maybe she…" I began, compelled for some neurotic reason to defend Stephanie.

But Lauren held up a hand and said, "No, wait. That wasn't an exact quote. What she said to me was, 'You bitch. Wasn't stealing my husband enough for you? You had to murder him, too?'"

Though my mind raced at how or why Stephanie had now leaped to the conclusion that Lauren, not Tiffany, had murdered Preston, all that came out was a meek "Oh, dear."

With her lovely hands, Lauren gestured helpless resignation. "I, of course, told her that I didn't kill him. I also pointed out that I didn't exactly 'steal' her husband. We just had a brief affair that ended a long time ago."

"What did she say to that?"

"She hung up on me." With a glance in the direction of the family room where our children and TV cartoons blared, Lauren leaned toward me. She met my eyes and said quietly, "I can't go through this again, Molly."

She was referring to the time Tommy erroneously arrested her last fall. I winced at the thought of her being thrown in jail a second time for a murder she didn't commit.

Her eyes filled with tears. "I've paid for my sin of infidelity many times over. I've tried so hard to build a good life for Rachel and myself after my husband's death. You have to help me, Molly. I haven't even seen Preston in months. Tell Stephanie that. Convince her. And tell Tommy, too. I know he's going to suspect me. I just know it."

"But you told me you were at work yesterday morning. You've got an ironclad alibi, so you don't have to..."

She was shaking her head and had shielded her face with her hands, struggling to collect herself. She dropped her hands and chuckled sadly. "I'd forgotten about a half-hour errand I'd run. The auditorium was being used, so the band held their practice in the cafeteria, right across from the office. It was so noisy I wanted to get away for a while, so I offered to run some forms out to the district office. I drove out there and took my time to make sure I'd miss all of the rehearsal."

Preston had been at my house a few minutes after nine, and Stephanie had called me just before ten. As long as the band practice didn't happen to fall between nine and ten, Lauren was in the clear. "What time was this?"

"Around nine thirty."

I punched my thigh in frustration. Lauren merely watched me, then said, "I'll keep an eye on the kids, if you want to go visit Stephanie now."

Lauren was one of the few people, not counting my family members, whom I would do anything for, including paying Stephanie an otherwise unnecessary visit. I sighed and stood.

A half hour or so later, I entered Stephanie's hospital room. She was propped up in bed, watching an afternoon talk show while filing her nails. Perhaps digging them into my flesh yesterday had damaged them.

The air smelled sweet. Every available flat space was

taken with flower arrangements. I felt a little guilty about coming empty-handed, but Stephanie had already spotted me so it was too late to double-back to the hospital gift shop.

We exchanged a few niceties as I sat down on an orange vinyl chair. Where would one go to purchase such a chair? I wondered. There must be a furniture store someplace that specializes in especially ugly chairs for hospital rooms.

Stephanie told me that Tiffany would be here shortly and Michael was napping in the nursery. She asked where my children were, but showed no reaction when I then mentioned Lauren's name in reference to watching them. So I took the initiative and said, "Lauren told me she spoke to you on the phone."

Stephanie sneered. "I take it that's my cue to say how bad I feel about the things I said to her."

"Do you?"

"Feel bad? Ha! If she killed Preston, I'll make her feel a hell of a lot worse than she does now."

"But you just said 'if.' Lauren said you accused her. Do you really think she's guilty?" Stephanie merely pursed her lips, so I continued. "Do you think that after some six or seven months of no contact whatsoever, Lauren would suddenly burst into your house and shoot your husband?"

She flicked a hand in my direction. "Since you put it *that* way, no, probably not. But the woman was one of my dearest friends, before she slept with my husband. Miss Manners would agree that under the circumstances, I'm not socially required to welcome her with open arms."

"Of course not. But accusing her of murder is at the extreme other end of socially acceptable responses."

She narrowed her eyes. "Tit for tat, as they say." She glanced at the clock by her bed. "Oh, dear," she murmured, straightening her covers with rapid, jerking motions that were doing more harm than good. "Tiffany's going to be here any minute."

Why was Stephanie acting nervous at the idea of seeing her own daughter? "How is Tiffany?"

"Distraught."

"Have you talked to her about...what Preston said before he died?"

"No, but maybe I will after the funeral tomorrow."

"The funeral's *tomorrow*? Shouldn't you delay that? You're still in the—"

"I'm checking out of the hospital tomorrow morning. I need to have the funeral immediately so I can move ahead with my life." As if the soundness of her decision to bury her husband hurriedly were readily apparent, she went on. "Since you brought up the subject of Tiffany..." Stephanie paused and searched my face. "Could you stay and talk to her? She seems to really like you." Her tone of voice implied she found the concept of liking me unfathomable, but I let it slide.

"Wouldn't I be intruding? Don't you want some private time?"

"We haven't been...since this past weekend, when Preston caught Cherokee and Tiffany"—she made a sweeping gesture with both hands—"in the throes of passion, shall we say, she's been living at her aunt and uncle's house. To say the least, things have been tense between us."

"You saw her yesterday, though, right?" Stephanie looked away without answering. In horror, I continued, "She's seen her baby brother and you talked with her about how she feels about her father's death. You *have* done that, right?"

"Molly," she said evenly. "Until you are a parent of a teenager yourself, until you come to realize your fourteen-year-old daughter is promiscuous with someone your husband detests, until that day arrives, you have no right to judge me."

"I'm not judging you, Stephanie. I'm just trying to understand. Your daughter needs you. If you shut her out now, you'll never get her back. Yesterday you begged me to help her. The best way I can do that is to tell you to be her mother now, above all else.''

To my surprise, Stephanie burst into tears. ''You're right. I love Tiffany so much. I don't know what I'd do without her.'' She grabbed a handful of tissues and swiped at her face. ''But, Molly,'' she said in a hoarse whisper, ''she may have killed Preston.''

''She may not have. Why do you suspect her?'' I dropped my voice and asked, ''Did Preston abuse her?''

''Absolutely not! How could you even think of such a thing?''

''Because that strikes me as the most logical reason why any mother might suspect a daughter of killing her own father.''

She frowned. ''Yes, I suppose it would have been a very good motive, but it happens to be untrue. He never hurt her in any way, except through general neglect and disinterest. Preston was a womanizer, a philanderer, a cheat, an all-around morally bankrupt individual, but he was not, repeat not, a pedophile.'' She scoffed and met my eyes. ''Some commentary on my husband, isn't it? The best thing I can say about the man is he wasn't incestuous.''

Appalled and astounded at this blatant contempt for her late husband, I murmured, ''I had no idea the two of you were—''

Stephanie suddenly grabbed my hand and dug her nails into my skin as she looked at the door. I managed to avoid crying out in pain and turned. Tiffany entered and said, ''Hi, Mom,'' in a voice barely above a whisper.

Though it had been less than three weeks since the last time I'd seen Tiffany, she looked radically different. She had gone from being a fourteen-year-old to an elegant-looking young woman. Either she was stuffing her bra or she'd grown from an A cup to a C since I'd last noticed. But more strikingly, gone was the makeup, the baggy pants, the bare-midriff T-shirt and bulky vest, the popular hair-style of both short and long hair lengths all willy-nilly. Now she wore tan slacks and a beige knit sweater, and her short hairstyle accentuated her high cheekbones and doelike eyes.

Tiffany turned her gaze toward me and murmured, "Hello, Mrs. Masters."

She knew I preferred to be called Molly, since I only associated "Mrs. Masters" with my mother-in-law, but it was entirely appropriate under these sad circumstances. I rose and said, "Hi, Tiffany. I am so sorry about your father."

She nodded.

"If you ever feel the need to talk to someone, I'll always be available."

"Thanks," she said.

Stephanie finally spoke. "Did you see your baby brother yet?" she asked gently.

Tiffany smiled, her eyes tearing up. "I saw him through the nursery window. They had the name tags in view, but I'd know him anywhere. He's just beautiful, Mommy."

I had a lump in my throat that was rapidly growing, but I managed to mutter, "I should be going now." Just then, Stephanie held out her arms and Tiffany rushed into a hug.

As I pushed out the door, I heard Stephanie tell her, "Come home, baby. I need you."

THE NEXT AFTERNOON the large funeral home was more than half full, though there wasn't a wet eye in the place. Not even Stephanie's or Tiffany's.

Lauren had found a baby-sitter, but we'd decided to bring Nathan and Karen because of their ties to Tiffany. Karen wore her navy blue crushed-velvet dress, which I'd bought for her eighth birthday and wished came in my size, too. Her hair was neatly combed and she looked every inch the angel she is—when she's not egging her brother into a fight. Nathan's hair had grown too long for his liking— unfortunately he detests his curls—but he'd carefully parted it and slicked it down. He'd paid close attention to what his daddy was wearing and matched outfits perfectly: the white long-sleeve dress shirt, the black pants, and the tie, although Nathan's was pink and a clip-on. For the first half hour of the service, he even managed to match Jim's somber expression. To kick off the second half hour, however, he repeatedly tried to stretch our definition of "sitting quietly" to include lying on his back, head dangling and feet straight up in the air.

Afterward, Stephanie thanked and hugged each person as they came through the line, but she seemed merely to be playing the role. She even hugged Lauren, which either qualified her for an Academy Award or meant she was on Prozac. Tiffany, frankly, seemed bored.

Outside the funeral home, on a sidewalk still damp with melting snow, we waited for Stephanie to lead us to her neighbor's house for a memorial service. Karen slipped her warm, delicate hand into mine and stood beside me quietly. The snippets of conversation I caught from surrounding mourners were all of a superficial "How-'bout-them-Mets?" or "Love-your-outfit!" nature. Not a word about Preston. I scanned the faces, most of whom I'd never seen before, and wondered: Had one of these ordinary-looking people fired two bullets into Preston Saunders's chest?

In a loud voice, Nathan announced. "This is taking too long. If anyone dies in our family, we should bury them close to our house so we can get home *quickly*."

Just then Stephanie and Tiffany emerged, arm in arm, and strolled stoically toward the parking lot. We shushed Nathan and followed. He soon realized we weren't driving home and complained vehemently, but changed his mind when we arrived at the reception and he discovered that pretzels and potato chips were being served.

The reception was held at the house next door to the Saunderses' home. The home was upscale, though, like the couple who owned it, old. Hardwood floors were adorned with Oriental carpets; the walls and ceilings were plaster. As I sat between my husband and Lauren on an antique couch, I examined my own duplicity. I hadn't liked Preston, never could stand Stephanie, had only slowly warmed to Tiffany in the past few months. Yet with all of my soul, I wanted to find Preston's killer. Why?

Stephanie had said I was someone who would "always do the right thing." Certainly I aspired to that, as, I liked to think, do most people. But if I hadn't become involved thanks to Preston's submitting that damned cartoon, I would never have promised to help find the killer. Plus there was an undeniable doggedness in the way I was drawn to any kind of mystery.

When I was in college, Watergate was still fresh in everyone's minds, especially among would-be journalists. Though by now I'd long since dropped journalism as a career goal, I'm not sure I ever dropped the dream of myself as the heroic ace reporter who single-handedly exposed some unconscionable crime against humanity. Which was not to say that killing Preston Saunders qualified as an unconscionable crime against humanity. But then, I wrote humorous greeting cards, not startling newspaper exposés.

Lauren tensed and shot me a pleading look as Tommy approached. She was still expecting him to arrest her at any given moment. Tommy merely nodded to her and said, "Sad business. Preston should be sharing his new baby's first day at home today. The days my sons were born were the happiest of my life."

"Mine, too," Lauren said. "I'll never forget how overjoyed I felt when Rachel was born."

"Mom?" Karen asked in a voice slightly muffled by potato-chip remnants. She and her brother were kneeling at the coffee table by a plate of hors d'oeuvres. "Can I go get us some orange soda?"

"No," Jim interjected. "You can't drink soda in here." He pointed toward the kitchen. "You'll have to—" He stopped abruptly, and I followed his gaze. Tiffany had entered the room with her boyfriend, Cherokee Taylor, followed by two girls about Tiffany's age.

"We have plenty of soda at home," Jim said. "Let's

go." He got up, hustling the children to their feet as well. He gave me a quick glance. "Sorry, sweetie. I need to get back to work."

And, I thought, you want us to leave now to stop me from investigating the murder. Jim knew my first task was to talk to Tiffany and her friends. I eyed Cherokee as I rose. I had only seen him once before, through my car window. He was a tall, solidly built young man. The mohawk hairstyle he'd worn months ago had grown out. He now had lots of brown curls.

Tiffany brushed Cherokee's hand from her shoulder and shot him a withering look, then turned on a heel and trotted upstairs. Cherokee winced. The two girls shrugged and started wolfing down food.

"Guess we're leaving now, Tommy," Lauren said, rising. She had ridden in our car.

As we drove home, I realized that Jim had done me a big favor by preventing me from talking to the teenagers. Cherokee couldn't possibly remember me from our lone, brief, distant encounter. And, except for Tiffany, I'd had virtually no contact with high school students in this town.

As soon as Jim dropped us off and left for work, Lauren said, "So, I'll bet I know why we made that hasty exit. You're sleuthing again and Jim's not taking too kindly to it. Am I right?"

"I've been thinking. The teenagers will never open up to me or to the police. There's only one thing to do. Go back to school."

"You're going to pretend to be a teacher or an aide or something?"

I struck a goofy pose, twirled the ends of my hair around a finger, and grinned at her. "I'm, like, gonna, ya know, pose as Tiffany's cousin."

SIX

Bahugen Buzzkills

JIM WAS WORKING late to make up for Monday's unplanned absence. Having decided to keep my husband unaware, I now had the opportunity to plan my foray into high school. Granted, keeping Jim in the dark was a less than noble decision on my part, but the fact that both of us knew when to keep quiet was a major reason our marriage had lasted for twelve years now.

After putting Karen and Nathan to bed, I called the Saunderses' house. A woman with a deep voice answered. A few moments later, Tiffany got on the line. I asked her if she was taking tomorrow and Friday off from school.

"Mom thinks I should, but I'm, like, getting behind in my classes. I may as well go back tomorrow." Her voice sounded trouble-free, almost happy. How could she be so glib with her father murdered just two days ago? Did Tiffany, like her mother, have no sense of human compassion whatsoever? If that proved to be the case, I wasn't going to let her watch my children ever again.

"There's *nada* for me to do 'round here," Tiffany went on. "Mom hired a live-in nurse to help out for the next couple weeks and that lady won't let me near Michael. Like, what? I'm gonna drop my baby brother or something? Does this nurse-lady think she's the next Betsy Ross?"

Florence Nightingale, I corrected silently, pondering the image of the Saunderses' nurse sewing mini American flags for diapers and baby blankets. That explained the woman with the husky voice. But how would *I* explain my plan to pose as a teenager in Tiffany's school? This was not the normal request one makes of one's bereaved baby-sitter.

"Did your mom talk to you about the last thing your father said before he died?" I asked.

Silence. Then: "Yeah. But I didn't do it, Molly. I told Mom that, too, but she seems to think Cherokee did it, and that Daddy meant to warn me about him."

The same suspicion had crossed my mind, more than once. "Does she have any reason to think so?"

"No way. It's just…dumb stuff. Daddy was shot at nine forty. And Cherokee and his friend Dave and this other guy, José, got nailed for skipping third period. But Cherokee told me they just hung out at the mall."

"So, third period is around nine forty?"

"It's from nine thirty to ten twenty. But, like I said, they were at the mall."

The mall was within two miles of the school, and less than a mile from Tiffany's house. "Did Cherokee drive? He has a car, doesn't he?"

"Yeah. But so what? A lot of seniors do." She paused. "Why are you asking me so many questions? You're worse than my mom. I already told you, Cherokee didn't do it!"

I felt a tinge of guilt for questioning her at this time, but it was impossible to be respectful of Preston's family's mourning period when, by all appearances, they weren't experiencing any remorse, let alone grief. Nevertheless, I softened my tone. "Of course he didn't, Tiffany. But what about the two other guys, Dave and José? Is it possible one of them has a gun?"

"Like, how'm I supposed to know? They're Roke's friends, not mine. They keep telling him I'm too young for him. I can't hardly go ask 'em about guns and stuff."

"Your mother told me about the charges your dad was going to file against Cherokee. Are Dave and José such good friends of his they might've decided to confront your father on his behalf?''

"I dunno. Maybe."

I waited her out through a long silence.

"What should I do, Molly? I know Cherokee's innocent, and I'm innocent, but how would I know about Dave and José? If they did it, the police might think Cherokee was behind it, but he wasn't.''

"As a matter of fact, I have a suggestion. I was thinking about having your older cousin come to visit for a few days and go to school with you.''

"What cousin? I don't have any older cousins.''

"You do now. But she could use a little help with her wardrobe and speech patterns.''

"Huh?''

I WAS SEATED at the vanity table in our bedroom, blow-drying my hair, when my husband got home. He paled as he looked at me. "What did you do to your hair?''

"I just henna'd it. Don't worry. It'll wash out.''

He grabbed the box. "This says it's supposed to add natural-looking highlights! Why is your hair purple?''

"I left it on my hair a little too long.''

He scanned the directions desperately, as if seeking an antidote for poison. "So you're actually going to go out in public like that? How long till it washes out?''

His horror was beginning to annoy me. I didn't look *that* bad. "Don't worry. I bought a Bozo the Clown costume earlier, so my hair will blend right in.''

He set the box down and glared at my reflection.

I inwardly chastised myself. If I'd come home and discovered he'd dyed *his* hair purple, I wouldn't have been especially complimentary, either. "Sorry. Thanks for noticing. Most wives would be thrilled to have their husbands notice they've changed their hair.''

"Most husbands don't come home to purple heads.'' He

patted my shoulder. "I wouldn't go near any gardens if I were you. Bees might mistake you for a giant petunia."

THE NEXT MORNING I awoke at an ungodly hour. Tiffany's bus would arrive at seven fifteen, and I wanted to be at her house for a dress rehearsal an hour early. My heart sank when I saw myself in the mirror. My eyelids belonged on a basset hound and there were suitcases under my eyes. I'd be lucky to be mistaken for a *live* person, let alone a young one.

I told Jim while he was still too asleep to listen that I had an early breakfast meeting. I drove to Stephanie's house prior to my children waking. As planned the night before, Tiffany was waiting by the door so I wouldn't have to knock and wake the household.

She was back to her normal "grunge" attire: baggy shorts, undersized T-shirt covered by an oversized plaid flannel that resembled my husband's favorite shirt. It was a weird comment on the state of the world when Jim's clothing was now considered fashionable.

She eyed my jeans and white long-sleeved dance leotard. "You're not thinking of wearing that to school, are you? You look forty!"

"Horrors. Of course not." In truth, I *had* hoped merely to toss on a shirt of Tiffany's as a top layer. "The leotard stays, regardless. It holds me in so I don't jiggle in any unteenlike places."

"Gross. Well, come on upstairs. We'll raid my closet. I just hope you don't make me look like a cretin maggot in front of my friends."

"We wouldn't want that." I followed her to her room, telling myself to be sure to use the term *cretin maggot* at least once today.

"What am I supposed to call you, anyways?" she asked, rifling through a pile of shirts on the floor of her closet. She grabbed one that looked ready to be turned into a cleaning rag and presented it to me.

"How about Molly? Your friends don't know a lot about your extended family, do they?" She looked confused, so I continued, "Would they know about your cousins?"

"Nah. We don't talk about junk like that. The only reason any of us goes to school is to get *away* from our families."

"All right, then." I put on the shirt, taking care not to poke my hands through any tears in the fabric. "My last name can be Saunders. I'll be your cousin who lives in Colorado. I'm a sophomore at the University of Colorado in Boulder. My family is staying at your house, and we tried to fly in yesterday for the funeral but our flight got delayed. We're staying through the weekend to help your mom with her new baby."

Tiffany rolled up my sleeves and fussed over my shirt as if she were a tailor who specialized in rips and wrinkles. Then she demanded that I take off my pants. I didn't even get one leg out before she cried, "Stop. Never mind. I was gonna have you put on some shorts of mine, but those are not the legs of a twenty-year-old. Sorry."

"So am I, but I'm rather attached to them. Haven't you got some baggy pants I could borrow?"

She shook her head. "They'd be too short on you. Besides, they're ripped up and we need to hide your knees. What's the nine-one-one on why you're going to school with me?"

"The nine-one-one?" I repeated as I indignantly pulled my jeans back on to spare the world from the sight of my ancient legs.

"You're not ready for this at all!" She stomped her foot. "This is hopeless! The nine-one-one means…information. It's the same as 'shake me up.'"

"So, when I want to ask someone what's happening, I say, 'Shake me up,' or 'What's the nine-one-one?'"

She nodded, but looked on the verge of tears.

"Don't worry. I'm a fast learner, Tiff, and I have a knack

for languages. But why isn't it 'What's the *four*-one-one?' since that's the number for information?''

"Cuz 'What's the *four*-one-one?' sounds stupid.''

"Oh.''

Next Tiffany led me to her private bathroom, which was even messier than her closet, and sat me down at her built-in vanity table. She'd once told me she "wanted to be a cosmologist,'' though she'd meant makeup, not star-gazing. She clicked her tongue and shook her head at the enormity of her task. Then she boldly applied makeup to my face and wove some red and blue strings into a small, long braid that dangled down my left shoulder.

Finally she said, "Just stay out of direct light and we'll be okay. Also, you may want to move around a lot so nobody can get a real close look at you.''

I stared at my reflection in dismay. The transformation was remarkable. I really did look like a teenager...or at least like a thirty-five-year-old with a severe case of arrested development.

"What are you going to tell my friends when they ask why you're hangin' at my school?''

"I'll tell them I want to teach school when I graduate. This seemed like a good opportunity to check out what I'd be doing in a couple of years.''

"You're a sophomore in college, and you already forgot what high school's like? Talk about a *demoto*.'' In answer to my perplexed gaze, she explained, "That means an unmotivated student.'' She gestured at my watch. "Take that gold thing off. Nobody'd be caught dead wearing that.''

While I applied makeup to hide the tan line around my ring finger, she located a plastic watch that looked as if it came out of a bubble-gum machine. *Much* more fashionable than the Swiss quartz watch my husband had given me for our tenth anniversary.

By now I'd concocted a new story and shared it with Tiffany. "I wanted to get away from my folks. Going to school with you was the lesser of two evils.''

"That flies. 'Course, if you say, 'get away from my folks,' and 'lesser of two evils,' everyone's gonna think you're a real lamen."

"I take it I don't *want* to be a lamen?"

She rolled her eyes, then headed out of the room. I followed. We were partway to the stairs when a door opened and an exhausted-looking Stephanie emerged, wearing a lacy pink nightgown. She smiled at Tiffany, took a quick glance at me, and started to greet us. Then she did a double take and gaped at me. Her hand flew to her mouth. "Good heavens, Molly! Why in the world..." She whirled on a heel and said, "Never mind. I had twenty-two minutes of sleep last night. I don't want to know." She closed the door behind her.

Tiffany and I headed downstairs. "Can I borrow a coat or a jacket?"

She shook her head. "I don't wear a jacket unless it's like, twenty below."

"But I'm cold-blooded," I protested.

"Trust me," she said, studying me with a scornful expression. "You're *not* cold-blooded. That means you're...really awesome." I followed her outside where the air was, unfortunately, chilly but not quite twenty below. "The best we can hope for in your case is not a total lamo. Lamo means a weirdo."

That much I could've guessed. We headed toward the bus stop. Up ahead, a group of kids waited on the sidewalk. My stomach fluttered nervously. "What's the word to use for parents?" I whispered.

She clicked her tongue. "Couldn't you just cop a case of laryngitis?"

"No. I have to blend in and ask questions."

"Parents are called peeps, or Mom duke and Pop duke."

Yuck. I had too much pride to use words like *peep* and *Mom duke.*

She pivoted and blocked my path before we reached the group. "Whatever you do, don't say anything to anyone, 'less they speak to you first. Also we need a signal. If I go like this,'' she said, and flicked the corner of her eye with her middle finger, ''that means 'chill.'''

''As in, 'Chill out, act a little more with-it,' right?''

''As in, 'Shut up; you're embarrassing me.'''

Though the four teenagers already at the stop shot little glances our way, no one spoke. This annoyed me. From their body language, they clearly knew about Tiffany's father but didn't offer a word of acknowledgment. The bus arrived. Tiffany and I were the last to get on.

The driver took off while we were still making our way down the aisle, and I nearly fell. A girl I recognized from the wake gestured for Tiffany to share her seat. The girl was thin, with dirty-blond hair and braces. She looked too young to be in high school, but then, so did everyone on the bus except me and possibly the driver. Perhaps my whole concept of how mature high school students look had been warped by the thirty-year-old actors who played high school students on TV. I battled an urge to scream, ''Stop the bus! I'm too old for this!''

''Hey, G,'' the girl said to Tiffany as she sat down, ''bahugen buzzkill 'bout your ol' man.''

''Word up,'' said another girl behind her.

Bahugen buzzkill? This is what young friends now say to one another upon the death of a parent? The thought of my writing such a thing in a grievance card caused an involuntary shudder, and once again I nearly lost my balance.

''Yeah, thanks,'' Tiffany replied. ''I'm still pretty mopped.'' Tiffany slid over and gestured for me to sit on the six inches of green vinyl seat that remained.

The two-mile trip to school seemed to take forever with my one-cheek perch. Tiffany never introduced me to anyone, and though I tried hard to listen, the conversations around me were mostly unintelligible.

As soon as I stepped through the doorway of the school, what little confidence I still had instantly deserted me. I had felt like an outsider throughout my entire four years of high school. What had possessed me to think that I could "blend in" seventeen years later?

Though I'd gone to school at Carlton, I'd never been inside the high school building. It had been built ten years ago behind the building that once housed all grade levels but was now the elementary school. The air smelled foul, a combination of floor wax, sweat, and cafeteria food. Swept along by the crowd, I eyed my surroundings. The linoleum floor was a dark gray, dulled by countless scuffing heels. Metal lockers lined the walls, the tan paint chipped and marred with graffiti. The noise of students chattering and lockers opening and banging shut was deafening.

I mutely followed Tiffany and her friend Madison, whom Tiffany had finally deigned to introduce me to once we arrived on school grounds. The total of the conversation between Madison and me had been: Hi. Yeah, hi. If the whole day went like this, I might succeed in posing as Tiffany's almost-but-not-quite-a-lamo cousin, but would learn nothing about the possible roles Tiffany's friends had in her father's death.

I found an empty desk in Tiffany's homeroom. The teacher, a short black man with wire-frames, kept looking at a notebook on his desk and at me. Finally he asked me, "I've never seen you before, have I?"

"She's my cousin," Tiffany immediately piped up. "She's here visiting today and tomorrow."

The teacher smiled as if relieved to learn he hadn't been hallucinating. "Take her down to the office and sign her in."

The office? Was Lauren at work yet? Tiffany rose and headed out the door assuming I would follow, which I did, for lack of a better plan, though I worried about Lauren's reaction when she saw me. She knew I'd be here today because we'd arranged for her to watch Nathan after kindergarten till I got home.

Lauren was seated directly in front of the notebook we needed to sign. She took one look at me and started to laugh, which she quickly turned into a fake coughing attack. Tiffany, who knew that Lauren and I were friends, said in a loud, rehearsed voice, "Yeah, uh, Mrs. Wilkins, this is my cousin, Molly Saunders, from Colorado. We need to sign her in as a visitor."

Lauren quickly stifled her giggles, met my eyes briefly, and shoved the notebook toward us. "So you're Molly Saunders? Just sign here, and make a name tag for yourself." She turned her attention to the ringing phone, winked at me, and said, "Enjoy your visit, dear."

Feeling awkward and embarrassed, I stuck my name tag on my shirt as we headed back toward homeroom. Tiffany froze and gaped at me. "Hey, Moll. Don't you think that name tag would make you look a little less lamo if you, like, put it on your forehead?"

"Where *should* I put it?"

She ripped it off my shirt and crumpled it, then jammed it into her pocket. We went to homeroom and waited out morning announcements.

At the bell, Tiffany told me, "I've got English class first period. Ms. Nesbitt is a...well, I guess you'll see for yourself soon enough. Class is always interesting, though."

We entered another classroom and Tiffany pointed out a desk for me to use directly behind hers. The woman in the front of the classroom wore old-fashioned, laced black boots and a faded paisley peasant dress that looked as if it had come from a secondhand store. Clearly visible along the low scooped neckline of the dress was a tattoo of a bird in flight. Her plain brown hair was piled atop her head in a frizzy rat's nest. While waiting for her students to take their seats, she marched back and forth in front of the blackboard as if charging her batteries. Her desk was such a mess it even made my office look well organized.

The moment the bell rang she clapped her hands crisply three times, then said, "*The Women's Room. The Color Purple.* What do those books have in common. Madison?"

"Um, they both start with the word *the?*" Madison replied self-consciously.

A couple of students snickered.

"Stupid answer," Ms. Nesbitt shot back. She scanned the room. "Someone with brains." She stopped at me and pointed. "You there, with no business being in my classroom. What do those two books have in common?"

Though startled, I stammered, "Both books portray men as...egotistical brutes."

"Good answer. You can stay, even if you're here by mistake."

"She's my cousin," Tiffany offered. "She's just—"

"Oh, Tiffany," the teacher said gently. "I'm glad you're back at school. I meant to go to your father's funeral yesterday to pay my respects, but I had a meeting that I couldn't rearrange. Please pass along my condolences to your mother."

I stared at the teacher in surprise. Why would she mention Tiffany's loss in front of the entire class? Could she have known Preston or Stephanie personally? Judging by the Saunderses' obsessiveness about physical appearance, they would probably have treated Ms. Nesbitt as a pariah.

Returning to her drill-sergeant's voice, she said, "So, Cousin of Tiffany. Do you agree with the authors' conclusions about men?"

"No. Overall, I think both books are excellent, but the portrayals of men aren't well balanced and the male characters are too stereotypical."

Tiffany turned her head and shot me a warning look.

"Ah," the teacher said, raising her eyebrows. "Stereotypical. Wouldn't you say it was high time *men* in literature were portrayed in stereotypical ways? Aren't you sick of male authors being termed 'brilliant' despite their paper-doll female characters? Don't you think, Tiffany's Cousin, it's *time* the combat boot was on the other foot?"

"Yes, actually I *do* think so, as long as the theme of the difficulties women face in a male-dominated society isn't so overstated that the reader suspects the author's agenda is to reinforce her own hatred of men.''

Tiffany started coughing wildly and waving her hand. When Ms. Nesbitt called on her, Tiffany wheezed that she had to get a drink of water. She threw her chair back so violently it slammed my desk into my stomach, then she left the room.

"Let's get some male perspectives on this, shall we?" The teacher paced in front of the blackboard. "Roberto. Do you think the men in these two books are accurate representatives of your sex?"

Roberto, a pimply-faced boy across the room from me, straightened. "I, uh, guess so."

"You guess so? So then, you *realize* that men are basically aggressive egomaniacs."

He shrank down in his chair, his cheeks reddening. "Some of us are. But only because we have to be to get ahead."

Ms. Nesbitt stopped pacing, smiled, crossed her arms, and rocked on her heels. "Aha. The fault lies in our society. So who makes the rules of society?" She waited a moment for Roberto to answer, then looked out at the faces. "Madison, are you ready to join us now in a serious discussion?"

While Tiffany quietly reentered the room, Madison nodded and answered that parents pass on social rules to their children. That led to one of the livelier debates I'd heard in some time, as Ms. Nesbitt engaged the class in a discussion of how and when society changes and what the individual's role is, especially with respect to the "war between the sexes." Realizing I was incapable of taking part in a debate while pretending to be an inarticulate youth, I managed to remain silent and spare Tiffany from another coughing fit.

Ms. Nesbitt had a tendency to cut off the boys and dismiss their comments. It occurred to me that she could harbor enough feminist anger to be a member of a militant women's group such as STOP. Yet surely, as a literature lover, she would be an adamant free-speech proponent. This begged the question: Would she belong to an antipornography group? When the bell rang, I raised my hand. She nodded at me.

I ignored the noisy intake of breath from Tiffany and asked, "What effect, if any, do you think pornography has on our society, Ms. Nesbitt?"

She narrowed her eyes. "Pornography is perhaps the major reinforcement to men who think of women as sex objects. As long as we continue to promote pornography in this country, women will never achieve equality. Class dismissed."

I rose and headed toward the door, but paused by Ms. Nesbitt's desk. I needed to find out if she could have left the building Monday morning when Preston was shot. "Ms. Nesbitt? Could I sit in on another of your classes during third period?"

"No. That's my free period." She turned and erased her scribblings on the blackboard.

We filed out into the hallway, my thoughts going a mile a minute as I considered the possibility that Ms. Nesbitt was Preston's killer. Tiffany yanked me by the shirt into a deserted doorway. Wagging a finger in my face, she said under her breath, "If that was the best you can do at pretending to be a teen, I'm sideways! You got that?"

"Well, actually, no," I whispered back. "What does *sideways* mean?"

"It means, 'I'm outta here,' you lamen!"

SEVEN

Toss Chow, Shoot the Gift, and Totally Sideways

I SAT THROUGH a second-period biology class in which I learned precisely two things: The man teaching it had very attractive blue eyes, and, some twenty years later, I still didn't know or care what an enzyme was.

I had high hopes for third period, though. This was the time slot in which Cherokee, Dave, and José had escaped the building on Monday. Giving the excuse that I was having a hard enough time learning teen-speak, I deserted Tiffany to her Spanish class and went looking for Cherokee. I found him in "study hall," an enormous room that sat some two hundred students, possibly twelve of whom were actually studying. The monitor, who was wearing earplugs and had his nose buried in a paperback, didn't even notice me.

I strolled up to Cherokee's desk and explained I'd recognized him from Tiffany's description and was her Colorado cousin, which he seemed to believe. The only description she'd ever really given of him to me was "(Sigh) He's just *too* studly." Actually, he was a bit blobby around the waist and pimply around the chin, but otherwise reasonably good looking: tall with lots of curly brown hair—a cute-faced Lyle Lovett.

He gestured at me to pull up a chair. The two boys on either side were watching me with interest, and to my delight, Cherokee introduced me to Dave and José, the two boys, I assumed, he'd cut class with when Preston was killed.

Except for his muscular upper body, Dave was a nondescript sort; his sandy-colored hair was cut short but for one tress that hung down his neck like a rat's tail. José was wiry and dark skinned, wearing those ridiculous billowing shorts in which the crotch was halfway down his skinny thighs. If his parents were to have insisted he dress like this, he could have charged them with abuse. His straight, black hair was closely cropped along his neck; the top was long and hung into his face. He was practically panting as he ran his eyes over me. Hooking up with someone half one's age is supposedly a popular middle-aged women's fantasy, but it was decidedly unappealing from where I was sitting—namely among three teenaged boys. Frankly, they weren't that great looking. With such silly hairstyles and clothing, what was left for future teenagers, such as Karen and Nathan, to do to their appearances when *they* wanted to shock their elders—seed their scalps with lawn turf?

"How's Tiffany doing?" Cherokee asked me. "I haven't talked to her since the funeral. Did she say anything about me?"

"Be a mensch," Dave said, swatting Cherokee in the arm. "You gotta get over her, man." He leaned around Cherokee and said to me, "You're her cousin and all. So you probably want to be loyal. But like, Roke here is *four* years older than her."

I made an appreciative whistle at the spectacular concept of four entire years.

"How old are *you?*" José asked, leaning closer to me.

"Twenty," I said, half expecting him to guffaw. Instead his eyes lit up. That is, the *portion* of his eyes that was still visible behind all that hair lit up.

"Yeah? I'm gonna be twenty in a couple months."

"Yeah, right," Dave interjected. "Make that in *fifteen* months."

Undaunted, José continued. "How long you gonna be here?"

"I'm leaving tomorrow."

"Better move fast, José," Dave said with a laugh. Then he settled back into his seat and said to Cherokee, "Did ya hear? Falmont got taken to the curb."

"By that skinz he was with last month?" Cherokee asked.

"Now he's sprung on Lisa. Galloway caught 'em mackin' it in his hoopty last night."

"No way."

"Yes way."

I felt like screaming, "Which way?" I'd have a better chance of understanding Tiffany's Spanish lesson. I needed to change subjects before they dragged me into this unintelligible one. "Any of you know where I can get hold of a gun?" I blurted out.

All three heads turned toward me. I grinned sheepishly. "I need it for, like, self-defense."

"Sorry, dudette," Dave said with a chuckle. "This ain't the gun club."

Cherokee, too, laughed. "Yeah. None of us bear arms or arm bears."

"But I'll show you my bare arm, if you're interested." Dave pulled up his sleeve and flexed for me. He was apparently all too aware that his muscular arms were his best feature.

"How about you, José? Do you know where I could get a gun?"

"Maybe, but—" He stopped and stared at a spot past my shoulder. I turned and watched Tiffany rapidly head toward us, looking as if she intended to strangle me on the spot.

"Hey, Tiff," José called to her. "It's been a grip. Sorry 'bout your Pop duke."

Her eyes met Cherokee's. The electricity between them was palpable. It was appalling to me that these two children had already "gone all the way." And what, pray tell, was *that* called nowadays? Bahugen badoinking, maybe. Cherokee grabbed her hand, but she quickly pulled away and focused on me. "Molly. You have to come with me now. Aunt Mary's waiting for you in the office."

I went along with her ruse and left. En route to her Spanish class, we agreed that I would not speak to Cherokee without her being present. In exchange, she would arrange for me to talk to Madison, Cherokee, Dave, and José during lunchtime, in an hour.

AT THE START of lunch recess, Madison, José, and Cherokee were leaning against a wall outside the cafeteria as Tiffany and I approached. Cherokee's eyes lit up as he watched Tiffany, and he greeted her with a hug. Once again she pulled away quickly, and the disappointment was written all over his face. In the meantime, José was undressing me with his eyes. If he only knew.

Dave sauntered toward us and gave José a friendly jab on the shoulder. "Got any dead presidents? It's dunkers at the caf. I want to bus one, get some grubbin' and, like, grind, but I'm clean out of bank."

"Think it ain't." José pulled out his wallet and opened it. "I got two Jacksons. Tell ya what. Let's all bus."

"Beauteous maximus, dude," Dave replied with a big grin.

Then the group agreed that whatever had just occurred was, indeed, "beauteous maximus," and they headed toward the exit.

"What do you say, Moll?" José asked. "Want to?"

Want to *what?* "Uh, sure. Why not?"

Us dudettes—Madison, Tiffany, and me—were led by the dudes—Cherokee, Dave, and José—to a rusty Ford Galaxy. José unlocked it. As luck would have it, I got positioned in the middle front between José and Dave. José used the excuse of the tight quarters to put his arm around me while he drove. This made me more than a little ner-

vous. Young male drivers have a hard enough time steering
with two hands, let alone one. Not to mention the possibility of his resting his arm on some stray lump of cellulite
that might reveal my true age.

José smiled at me. So much hair was in his face only his
left eye was showing. I had to bite my tongue to keep
myself from saying: For heaven's sake, comb your hair out
of your eyes so you can see well enough to drive!

"How 'bout gettin' on some phat flavor, Molly?" he
asked as we left the parking lot.

Fat flavor? Was he asking me if I wanted to stop for ice
cream? "Thanks, but I'm on a diet."

Dave laughed heartily, but José merely looked confused.
"I meant music." He gestured at a plastic box by my feet.
"Pop in a CD."

"Sorry. Where I'm from we call CDs...spoolers."

"So," Madison called from the backseat. "Where's your
dibs, Molly?"

"Colorado," Tiffany answered on my behalf.

Okay. So "dibs" had something to do with where I was
from. But did it mean my friends? Family? School?

"Yeah, um. Boulder. That's where I go to college, at
CU." I fumbled through the music collection, none of
which I recognized, and popped in a CD at random, hoping
it wouldn't be choir music. To my relief, it sounded horrible.

In the meantime, Tiffany engaged Madison in some
noisy, mindless chatter aimed at blocking me from potential
conversations. We pulled into the parking lot of Mc-
Donald's. When we reached the counter, I learned that José
intended to treat all of us to lunch. He was somewhat offended when I insisted on splitting the cost with him.

We found a table for six, and I promptly asked everyone
how they liked school, intending to work the conversation
around to what happened when they cut study hall last
Monday. I was answered with shrugs and grunts, along with
Tiffany flicking at the corner of her eye.

"We'd better toss chow," Tiffany then said anxiously.

"We've got time to shoot the gift," José replied.

"Thank goodness," I muttered.

Tiffany shot me a withering look and again rubbed at the corner of her eye.

José put a hand on my shoulder. "So, I hear Boulder's the bomb, dudette."

"Absolutely," I agreed.

"Sweet hookup for you, huh? Can you show me the sights if I get up there sometime?"

He was either asking to visit or making a sexual advance. I opted for a noncommittal shrug and, "No problem."

"Awesome." José grinned at me. "So shake me up on Boulder."

At last! A phrase I knew. "You want the nine-one-one, huh?"

"Yeah. Put it on the set. Do you, like, ski?"

All eyes were on me. *Ski.* Was he asking if I liked to go downhill with long, skinny boards strapped on my feet? Or was skiing now a euphemism for something illicit?

Oh, what the heck. Time to wing it. If I couldn't understand them, my safest bet was to make darn sure they couldn't understand me, either. "I gotta give you the Abe's, dude. Compared to Boulder, Carlton is bogus behoochies. You've got nothing but poodunks here. Out there, it's pure razinoids. And, of course, the skiing is major catoracts. You jet down those verts through powder that's like, pure snazz. We're talking alts to the minks! Not to mention the rays. When you're doing the 'tude anyway, you've got—"

"Molly!" Tiffany cried. "I've got something in my eye!"

"Must be a lash. Like I was, in Boulder, you're out there thirty minutes, max, and we're talking a major case of skin zaps."

She rose and said into my face, "You need to come help me. Now."

"I was just gettin' wound, Tiff. Can't you check your ref in the WR?"

She clenched her teeth and glared at me. Her friends all looked baffled. I followed Tiffany into the bathroom. The instant the door swung shut behind us, she whirled toward me.

"All right, Molly. I don't know what you think you're doing, but stop it right now! Otherwise, I'll put the word out and you'll never find another high school baby-sitter in this town again! You got that?"

"Got it." Anyone who thinks teenagers have no power in our society has never needed a baby-sitter. Tiffany brushed her hair and reapplied her lipstick. We went back to the table.

The moment we sat down, I said to the group, "Tiffany tells me you're not familiar with Colo-lingo. I have to admit, I haven't a clue about what you guys are saying, either. So, maybe we could all, like, pretend we're talking to...our peep dukes. That way we can...shake the gift."

Cherokee laughed. "Whoa. You really are in a different zone. But I can relate. I was a pseudo when I first moved here, too."

I managed then to steer the conversation toward my getting a gun, explaining apologetically to Tiffany that ever since "my uncle" had been shot I'd decided I wanted to buy one for self-protection. My efforts proved fruitless, though I hoped José might approach me privately later.

We went back to school and sat through a couple of uneventful classes. During the five-minute break before final period, it struck me that I still needed to check into everyone's alibis for third period last Monday.

Tiffany informed me that Cherokee had an electronics class now and she had algebra. I told her I needed to renegotiate our agreement about my not talking to Cherokee in her absence. She agreed to let me talk to him alone, on the condition that I "stay home tomorrow."

As I'd hoped, both Dave and José were in Cherokee's

electronics class. Seated in groups of three or four at large wooden tables, the students were working on projects that involved assembling little electronic doohickies. Dave, José, and Cherokee shared a table in the back corner. José spotted me, smiled, and waved. Dave turned to look at me, then leaned across the table and said something to Cherokee, who chuckled.

The teacher was a friendly-looking woman, who appeared to be about my age in real life. I quietly identified myself to her and explained that, as Tiffany Saunders's relative, I had some urgent personal business to discuss with a couple of her male friends. She gave me permission to talk with the three boys, so long as our conversation didn't disrupt anyone at adjacent tables.

"What are you doing here?" Cherokee asked me as I claimed the empty stool across from him and José.

"Oh, Tiff's got algebra, which is too boring. So I thought I'd come hang out with you guys."

José gestured at the doorway behind me with his chin. "Uh-oh. It's the five-oh again."

I turned, expecting to see a five-foot-tall person or someone in their fifties, but it was Sergeant Tommy Newton, heading straight at me. His jaw dropped as our eyes met. He stopped midstep.

"Molly. What the hell are you doing? Aren't you a little old for high school? Wasn't being a teenager *once* enough for you?"

I got up and strode toward him, saying loudly, "Yeah, it was, Sergeant Newton. Let me explain." Then I went past him and into the hallway.

Tommy followed. "This better not be what—"

I leaned against a locker and said quietly, "School's over in half an hour. Just give me the rest of today without blowing my cover. Please? The kids are starting to trust me. If Tiffany's friends have anything to hide, I'll be able to learn the truth from them a lot easier than you can scare it out of them."

"No way, Molly."

"Yes way," I responded with a smile.

Tommy merely glared at me. "How many times do I got to tell you to stop interfering with police investigations?"

"If you'd already learned everything you needed from these kids, you wouldn't be here, right? So what's the harm in letting me try? I'll tell you every word they say to me. Please?"

He shook his head, making no effort to hide his anger. "No chance."

"All right. Just give me...five minutes to go explain myself to them."

"Sure. Just do it *while* I'm with you."

Tommy and I reentered the electronics lab, where every face turned to watch us. Cherokee said, "What gives?" as I sat down again. Tommy crossed his arms and took a post between Cherokee and José where he could watch my every motion.

"Sorry, guys," I began. "The truth is I'm not...your age." I still hoped to do some damage control, especially for José's sake, who might never live down his having flirted with someone his mother's age. "I'm twenty-four. I just figured you'd all be afraid to be yourselves if you knew how old I was."

Tommy raised an eyebrow. I gave him a small shrug in apology.

José said gently, "You should've just put it on the set. I know a few cold-blooded people in their twenties. Twenty-four's not *that* old."

I scanned the room. Everyone appeared to be listening to us. Dave crossed his muscular arms and peered at me for a long moment. Finally, he said, "Name three rap groups."

"That's easy," I lied. My mind was blank. "Um, Vanilla Fudge, Snoopy Diggity Dog, and...that guy with the inverted-pyramid hair who does the fast-food commercials."

"Yeah, right," Dave snarled. "You're not twenty-four. You're probably at least thirty."

"Okay, okay. You got me. I'm thirty-five. I have two children who go to elementary school."

José recoiled in shock. Cherokee cried, "You've been on the shine all this time! Who do you think you are?"

"My name is Molly Masters. I'm a friend of...Tiffany's mother. I'm trying to learn who killed her father. I realized you knew more about what was going on in Tiffany's life than anyone. I just needed to find out, so I could help Tiffany. I didn't mean to cheat or embarrass anyone. I'm sorry."

"You got a lot of nerve, lady," Dave said.

"None of us had anything to do with Tiffany's dad's death," José said angrily. He turned toward Tommy and said, "Like we told you yesterday, Officer. We were at the mall third period. All three of us were together, the whole time. Then we came straight back to school."

Tommy shook his head. "Your alibi hasn't panned out. None of the waitresses at the mall restaurant you claimed to be at recall seeing you."

"I told you guys not to cover for me." Cherokee pulled out a jewelry box from his shirt pocket. He opened the box and set it on the table. Inside was a gold ring that bore a small diamond chip. "I was picking this out at the jewelry store. Dave and José came to help me. Ask the owner. He waited on us. I've got the receipt and it's time-stamped. See? Ten-oh-six a.m."

"Why didn't you just tell me this yesterday?" Tommy asked.

Cherokee sighed and closed the box. He glanced at his classmates, then said under his breath, "Cuz the ring proves...the charges Mr. Saunders made against me were true. I did...Tiffany and I were...anyway. I asked her to marry me. She said no."

With a pleading expression, he looked up at Tommy. "I made my bros here promise not to tell anyone what we were doing at the mall, and they kept that promise. If your girlfriend took you to the curb after you bought her a diamond, would you want everyone to know?"

"Word up," Dave added, chuckling. "And now Tiff's so weirded, she's told Cherokee to, like, check it."

Cherokee shot Dave a dirty look but said nothing.

Thoroughly embarrassed, I quietly stood and headed for the door. "I think I'll go...wait for you outside, Officer Newton."

I sat on the sidewalk next to Tommy's cruiser. The plastic watch Tiffany had loaned me that morning had already stopped, but judging by how cold my rear end was by the time Tommy emerged, it had to be almost time for the final bell.

I stood up and asked, "Can you give me a ride to Tiffany's to get my car?"

He wouldn't meet my eyes. Through a tight jaw, he answered, "Take the school bus." He drove off.

A minute or two later, the bell rang and a tidal wave of students poured out the main exit toward me. I scanned the faces, and eventually picked out Tiffany and made my way upstream to her. She looked unhappy. Perhaps she'd had a pop quiz in algebra.

"Hi, Tiff. I've got something to tell you, before we get on the bus."

"Oh? Could that something be that Sergeant Newton came into the electronics class and recognized you?"

"You talked to Cherokee already?"

She shook her head. "No, I heard it from someone I barely know passing in the hall. You'd be surprised how fast the word that 'some old bag's pretending to be Tiffany Saunders's cousin' can spread around. I think even the janitor knows about it by now. And he's deaf."

"Oh." My cheeks burned. I was not only an "old bag," but a deflated one. "Well, it was fun while it lasted. Right?"

We rode home, enduring everyone's stares. I would venture to say it was the quietest ride since the school bus was first invented.

Tiffany said nothing as we walked from the bus stop toward her home. I felt horrible. My intention had been to help her by learning who had killed her father, but all I'd done was make things worse. To top it off, I finally remembered this was Thursday; I helped out in Nathan's kindergarten class every Thursday morning, but I'd completely forgotten. In my misery, I sang to myself, "I'm a Bad Mom" to the tune of "It's a Small World" as we shuffled along.

Halfway up her driveway, I heard a loud bang and sensed, more than felt, something whiz past my shoulder. I automatically tackled Tiffany. The realization reached my brain just as we thudded onto the hard ground: Someone was shooting at us. She let out an "Oof," then an "Ow!"

Another bang. I forced Tiffany's head down, covering her body with mine as best I could. She was crying hard. I could feel her racking sobs. The shots were coming from behind the large juniper bush at the corner of the Saunderses' garage. "Help!" I screamed. "Help!"

The bush rustled. Someone ran away, across the Saunderses' lawn. The only glimpse I got was the hooded back of a gray, bulky sweat suit.

EIGHT

Screams from a Marriage

TIFFANY JUST KEPT sobbing when I scrambled off of her and asked if she was all right. Before I could assess our injuries, a door banged, and Stephanie, wearing a pink floor-length bathrobe over a nightgown, ran toward us.

"Gunshots! I heard gun—" Her face turned white as she spotted Tiffany lying next to me. "Oh my God!" Stephanie rushed beside Tiffany and fell to her knees. "Baby, are you hurt?"

"No-o-o," Tiffany puffed. She pointed at the bushes the gun-person had run from. "Somebody...shot at us."

Stephanie helped Tiffany to her feet, and I got up as well. Tiffany's knees and one elbow were bleeding. Nothing was hurting me, but I was so numb I may not have felt even a serious injury. Stephanie whirled toward me. "Look what you did to my daughter!"

"Don't yell at her," Tiffany scolded between sobs as she swiped at her cheeks with her sleeves. "She saved my life."

Stephanie pursed her lips. She wrapped her arm around Tiffany's shoulders and helped her inside. I followed. Tiffany was still whimpering as Stephanie led us to a denlike room just off the foyer. She sat Tiffany down on the couch, then reached into a drawer and took out a blue-and-white wool afghan, which she wrapped around Tiffany's shoulders.

"Estelle!" Stephanie cried. "Get in here. My daughter's hurt."

By now I was shaking uncontrollably. My teeth chattered. I sank onto the nearest chair, a hard-back just inside the doorway. I was lucky to be alive. My life could have been over, just like that. And for what? Why had somebody shot at me? Because of one stupid cartoon I never wanted to publish in the first place? I felt faint. I leaned over and put my head between my knees.

"Sorry," called a woman's husky voice from the hall. She rushed into the room. "I was bathing the baby and couldn't—" She gasped, then said, "Tiffany, are you all right?"

"Of course she isn't," Stephanie snapped. "Someone shot at her! Look at her knees!"

"I'll get some bandages," the nurse said. She stopped in front of me. I could see her brown laced shoes and sturdy-looking ankles. "Are you all right?"

"She's fine!" Stephanie said. "I'm paying you to take care of my family!"

The nurse left the room.

"You're not going to throw up, are you?" Stephanie asked me, demonstrating her love of carpeting that was so freaking adorable. I sat up a little and shook my head, wishing I had the strength to inflict severe bodily harm to her.

Stephanie marched over to an antique-style white-and-gold phone in the corner and dialed 911. She waited, then said, "This is Stephanie Saunders. Some maniac fired two shots at my daughter. I need Sergeant Tom Newton out here immediately." She paused and listened. "No. Sending just any patrol car won't do. I want Sergeant Tom Newton." She listened for a moment, then yelled, "Listen, you obfuscating ignoramus! My daughter just got shot at! I want Newton here, this instant!" She slammed the phone down. She glared at me. "I don't know why you persist in calling that man Tommy."

"Because he *asked* me to."

She sat down next to Tiffany and put her arms around her daughter. "That's why this...this killer is still loose on the streets. Because we're stuck with a police sergeant who sees himself as a little boy."

I glared at her, wanting to defend Tommy, but stopped myself. Her husband had been murdered and now she thought someone had attempted to kill her daughter. Anyone in her shoes would be lashing out at the world. "He was shooting at me, not Tiffany," I said.

"So it was a man? Did you recognize him?" Stephanie asked hopefully.

"All I saw was a gray sweat suit from the back. I'm not even sure it was a man."

"Then how can you know he...*it* was shooting at *you?* Your own family wouldn't recognize you from a distance, wearing that trick-or-treat costume."

"We weren't far away. The shooter was behind the bush by your garage. And we were walking right toward him. Or her."

Estelle, a chunky, dark-haired woman, returned with a full medical supply kit and ministered to Tiffany's wounds. This was the first time I'd seen their nurse and wanted to introduce myself, but Stephanie kept me occupied as she argued about why the shooter had waited for me here, instead of at my own house.

My car, I replied wearily, had been parked in her driveway, and sooner or later I was going to come back for it. At my house, I'd have driven into my garage and shut the door automatically while still in my car. I'd been an easier target here. And what, Stephanie then wanted to know, made me such an expert on the deranged workings of the criminal mind? I had no response to that—the truth was I had become devious, if not quite deranged, while trying to stay one step ahead of my children—but not wanting to examine too closely what that said about me or my children, I kept quiet.

We heard sirens—welcome relief from the current conversation. Soon the doorbell rang, and the nurse taped the last bandage in place on Tiffany's knee and rose. "Estelle, can you get that?" Stephanie asked after Estelle was already halfway to the door.

A tense-looking Tommy Newton soon filled the doorway, and, after Stephanie stopped babbling about what a lousy job he was doing protecting her family, he turned toward me.

"Come with me, Ms. Masters." Stephanie, still seated beside Tiffany, started to rise as well, but Tommy gestured for her to stay put. "Just Molly. Be back in a moment to get your statements."

I eagerly followed Tommy out the front door, hoping to leave this house forever.

"Show me exactly where everyone was at the time of the shooting."

I did so. A spot of blood revealed the exact patch of pavement onto which I'd tackled Tiffany. I watched as Tommy followed a line of sight from the bushes down the driveway, and eventually fished a knife out of his pocket and removed something from the broad trunk of an elm tree at the base of the driveway. In the meantime, I sat on the bottom step of the porch, reassessing my life.

At length, Tommy headed up the driveway and sat beside me. "Found a slug. Could be from a twenty-two, just like in Preston's shooting. I'll send it to the lab and find out for sure." He gave a heavy sigh. "Guess this is my fault."

I looked at him in surprise. "How can you blame yourself?" Though it may have been caused by the pattern of shadows and light from the late afternoon sun on his face, he looked enticingly handsome sitting there. The lighting lent his hair flattering auburn tones, as well.

"Never should've made you go home on the school bus. I should've known something like this might happen." He met my eyes. "Molly, please. Do yourself a favor. Take a vacation for a couple weeks. Leave town."

I shook my head. "I wish I could. But I can't run away from Carlton again. I've tried that before. It doesn't work."

He was quiet for a moment. "That last time you were gone for seventeen years, not a few weeks. Nobody was shooting at you then. Different circumstances."

"True." I rose. "But it feels the same."

He looked up at me. "Lauren's forgiven you. What's it gonna take till you forgive yourself?"

I fought back tears and struggled to take an even breath. "I don't know, Tommy. I just know I can't run away a second time."

"I LIKE MY BORING life. So sue me." Jim ran both hands through his thick brown hair and paced in front of our antique four-poster bed. It was late at night. Karen and Nathan were fast asleep, as I wished I were, instead of sitting cross-legged atop Mother's hand-sewn quilt, arguing with my husband.

In the fifteen years since we'd first met, I'd never seen him this upset. He was insisting that the kids and I leave immediately for Florida and stay with my parents until the police arrested Preston's murderer.

Jim continued, "I like to know that my wife and children are still going to be alive when I get home at the end of the day."

"So would I. Every person on the face of this earth would like to know that we and all our loved ones won't be the victims of violence. But life doesn't give us any guarantees."

"I'm not asking for guarantees. I'm asking you to protect yourself! I'm asking…I'm *telling* you to get out of here while you're still alive. I didn't marry a policewoman; I married someone who writes greeting cards. This wasn't part of the deal!"

A chill ran down my spine. Until now, the times Jim had been angry with me were always over petty concerns: my not tightening jar lids, or not cleaning his hairbrush after borrowing it. "Sure it was. Our vows stated, 'For better or for worse.' Having me get shot at qualifies as worse."

Jim cursed under his breath. He strangled a post at the foot of the bed with both hands. "I'm your husband. I want to be able to protect you."

"You can't protect me from all evil. However much you might like to, you can't." I struggled to keep my voice steady. "Please, Jim. I can't just leave Carlton every time something goes wrong." Jim knew about the guilt that had driven me from town years ago, but he thought that issue was resolved. I had thought so, too, till this happened. "I need your support. I didn't deliberately set out to put my life in jeopardy. That happened because of something Preston did, which I had no control over."

"Maybe so. But now you're—"

"I can do what you want," I interrupted, scooting closer to place my hands gently on his. "I can run away. I can hope that the police find Preston's killer in a reasonable period of time so the kids won't miss out on too much school. That they'll survive being uprooted and separated from their daddy one more time. That they won't secretly believe we're getting divorced. That five of us can live in my parents' tiny, one-bedroom condo without going nuts."

Jim released the bedpost from its death grip and resumed his pacing, slower now. His anger seemed to be dissipating. "Maybe you should go by yourself. I'll take some time off and stay home with the kids."

"Absolutely not. The police still have no idea who's behind the shootings. I refuse to be separated from my children until Tommy solves this thing, if he ever does. Besides, what makes you think the killer won't follow me to my parents' place in Florida? Or simply lie low until I return, then…shoot me through the window, or something?"

Jim sighed. "You've already made up your mind to stay, haven't you?"

"Yes. I want to help catch the person who's doing this to me. And I want your emotional support."

He shook his head. "I can't support your doing something dangerous. You're determined to nose around and turn yourself into a duck at a shooting gallery."

"No, I'm not. I'm just—"

"We'll give the police another week to catch this maniac. In the meantime, you steer clear of the murder investigation. If you get shot at or physically threatened one more time, you're leaving on the next plane."

"Absolutely," I said, and gave him a hug. "My poor, long-suffering hubby."

"My wiff," he murmured and kissed the top of my head. "I don't know what I'd do without you."

THE NEXT morning, after we'd shared a quiet breakfast, Jim and the children left. I was tired from a mostly sleepless night, but time was of the essence. A week from now I'd have to become a Floridian unless this thing was solved. I called the high school.

When Lauren got on the line, I asked if she had a minute to talk privately. She said yes, that she was alone in the principal's office. I asked what she could tell me about Ms. Nesbitt, Tiffany's English teacher.

"Oh, let's see," Lauren replied. "Her first name is Deborah, but everyone calls her Deb. She's popular with students and staff, but not parents."

"Not parents?"

"She's in her first year of teaching, and she was a bit of a flop at the open house. Most teachers dress up for the occasion, but not her. Afterwards, Preston Saunders was trying to get her dismissed."

"Because of her *clothes?*"

"That and her tattoo. He claimed she wasn't a good role model."

Hmm. Preston had carried quite a bit of weight in the community. He was the sole owner of a small but immensely profitable import-export business. His threatening to get her fired wasn't a motive for a sane person to commit murder, but I didn't know Ms. Nesbitt well enough to assess her sanity. And she had a free period right when Preston was murdered. "Could she have left the school during final period yesterday?"

"No, she's got a class then."

That let her out as a suspect in yesterday's shooting. If she was a member of STOP, though, she could easily have had an accomplice or two.

"Do you know what kind of car she drives?"

"A VW bug. Baby blue. Badly dented." Lauren then looked up Deb's phone number and address and gave them to me.

"Great. And who's her emergency contact person?"

"Marjorie Shoman, listed as 'roommate.'"

"Thanks for the information."

"Don't tell anyone where you learned it. Working in the principal's office may not be glamorous, but I enjoy it. I don't want to get fired. Okay?"

"Sure. One last question. Do you know her personally?"

"No. She looks like quite a character, though. I wish I could drop in on her class, but I'm not willing to go to the lengths you did. By the way, did you get any pictures of yourself in that getup?"

"No, thankfully. I shampooed my hair twenty times after I got home to get the purple out. Took me an hour and a half in the shower. Now my *skin's* purple and water-logged. I look like a giant prune."

She chuckled, and we said our good-byes.

My ears were ringing so loudly I couldn't hear myself think. Someone had put my life in a blender and pressed the Puree button. The only benefit I could glean from all of this was it should be good fodder for freelance cards. I grabbed my drawing pad. I doodled for a while and eventually drew people playing charades. Standing in front of the others is a couple, their mouths open as if screaming while they pretend to strangle one another. A woman in the audience waves her hand and says, "Ooo! I've got it! It's that movie starring Liv Ullmann...*Screams from a Marriage!*"

The drawing had absolutely no marketing potential—what's known in the business as "sendability." Discouraged, I put my pad away. I was too exhausted to be funny.

I decided to go help out in Nathan's class to make up for yesterday's absence. Nathan smiled and gave me a wave as I entered the classroom, which was brightly decorated with piñatas hanging from the ceiling and children's colorful paintings on the walls.

The children were doing centers—three or four related projects set up at table clusters from which the students choose on their own. Nathan's table had worksheets with *I see a green leaf* written across the top of a page containing the outline of a big leaf. He'd colored his leaf green, but unlike his classmates was now drawing what I recognized as his self-portrait, a smiling figure with a Humpty-Dumpty body dangling from the leaf stem as if it were a helium-filled balloon.

His kindergarten teacher, an elderly woman who, like the teakettle in the children's song, was short and stout, pulled me aside and explained to me that they were "currently doing a color unit." Then she narrowed her eyes and said in a near whisper, "In my thirty years of teaching kindergarten, your son is the first little boy I can remember whose favorite color is white."

"Yes, well, I use that to my advantage when it's time to get him to brush his teeth." I was kidding, but she still peered at me as if expecting me to register alarm. Months of weekly encounters with this teacher had taught me it would be senseless to point out to her that yes, my little boy's favorite color was white, but he was also a little boy who would take a dull task like coloring the one leaf on the page green and turn it into a creative, imaginative project. "Does that worry you?" I asked.

"Not at all," she answered in a chirpy voice that might work on five-year-olds but was annoying to me. "It's just...unusual."

"Good. I wouldn't want to raise 'usual' children. What can I help you with today?"

FOR SOME REASON, Karen and Nathan weren't into the spirit of our tailing Ms. Nesbitt after school. Their periodic moans of "This is so bor-r-ring!" kept wafting from the backseat of our Toyota, where we were parked a few rows away from Ms. Nesbitt's VW in the high school lot. I told them we were lucky to get the chance to experience this "family time." They wouldn't even keep their heads down when people looked our way. Maybe I hadn't let them watch enough cop shows on TV.

"*Why* are we doing this, Mom?" Karen asked for the third time.

"I told you. I want to watch where the person in the blue VW goes so I can see if she knows anything about who might have been mean to me yesterday."

"Did someone shoot real bullets at you?" Karen asked.

Both of the children's bedrooms—my sister's and my old rooms—were right across the hall from the master bedroom. Karen must have overheard some of our private conversation last night. So much for protecting them from unsettling news. "They were probably just blanks, like they use in movies."

"Are we doing something bad now?" Nathan asked.

"Bad? No." Stupid, maybe, but not bad. "We're just going to follow the car for a few minutes."

"Is a bad person going to be driving it?"

"The woman who owns that car isn't a bad person. I'm just hoping she can *lead* me to the bad person. But we're not going to get close enough to her car to be seen; we'll just drive away and tell Sergeant Newton where she went."

Just then, Ms. Nesbitt came out of the building. She wore a brown leather jacket and a skirt so worn out it was practically see-through, her hair once again in a messy pile on top of her head. I ducked below the dashboard until I heard her car start.

"Here we go," I announced. "Fasten your seat belts."

I waited until she'd pulled out of the lot before starting my engine. She turned right at the exit, pulling out in front of a large silver van. The van would prevent her from seeing me in her rearview mirror, but might block *my* view when she made a turn.

Deb headed south on the Northway—an oxymoron caused by the name of this particular highway. Maybe they should have named it the Snorthway. It could intersect with the Weastway. *Enough,* I chastised myself; my mind rambled idiotically far too easily when I was sleep-deprived. Deb was going a full fifteen miles over the speed limit, but I kept pace, planning what I could say if I got pulled over for a speeding violation. "It's not my fault, Officer. I just happen to be tailing a lead-foot."

She took the exit for Colonie, a town that borders Albany. Less than half a mile later, she pulled into the parking lot of an espresso bar. Why would she come way out here when there were plenty of other espresso bars much closer to school and her home? I wanted to keep an eye on her long enough to make sure she actually went inside, then I would drive home. Tomorrow, while my children were safe at school, I could come back here and nose around.

There were no other business lots immediately adjacent to this one, so I went ahead and turned into it too and parked by the exit. I had stayed a good distance behind her on the highway, and even if she'd noticed my car she would probably assume both of us happened to be simultaneously craving caffeine.

Actually, I didn't care for cappuccino, or any other espresso product. It tastes to me like coffee that's been left on the burner till most of the water boiled away. Why are people willing to pay four times as much for *that* as they would for a cup of coffee? Isn't that the same as a breakfast café charging extra if they burn your toast?

Ms. Nesbitt went into the restaurant. I decided to wait just another minute to make sure she was staying.

"Mom," Karen wailed. "I have to go to the bathroom."

"Okay, we'll be home in a couple—"

"I have to go right *now!*"

I glanced back at her. Her legs were crossed and she was rocking in her seat. "All right. We'll use the bathroom in here and then go straight home."

We got out of the car, but I felt discouraged and worried. I'd had no intention of getting my children in the same building with Deb Nesbitt, just in case she was indeed meeting the "bad person." This hitch in my plans was unexpected. To my knowledge, James Bond never had to blow his cover because of a potty break. With luck, though, Deb Nesbitt wouldn't pay any attention to a mother and two children dashing into the rest room. She probably wouldn't even recognize me in my postpubescent state.

We crossed the lot and I held open the door. Warm air with a delectable coffee and cinnamon fragrance greeted me. Karen tried to enter, but Nathan grabbed her arm and wedged his shoulder ahead of her.

"It's my turn to go in first!" Nathan shouted. "*You* got into the *car* first!"

"But I have to pee!" Karen screamed at the top of her lungs.

Embarrassed, I scanned the room, which resembled an old-fashioned ice cream parlor with its chrome tables and green vinyl chairs. All eyes were on us, including Ms. Nesbitt's, who was standing by a table right in front of us. Just then Nathan gave Karen a spin move that would've made a wide receiver proud and bolted into the room. He crashed full force into Ms. Nesbitt.

"Whoa," she said, grabbing Nathan to steady him. "Watch where you're going."

Nathan recoiled in horror at having bumped into a

stranger. In the meantime, Karen darted past us and into the rest room.

"I'm sorry," I said to Deb, deliberately speaking a tone or two higher than normal to disguise my voice. "I've been somewhat remiss in teaching my children the proper decorum when entering a restaurant. We don't get out much."

She snapped her fingers and studied me, an amused expression on her face. "Hey. I know you. You're the woman who pretended to be Tiffany's cousin. What are you doing here?"

"Using the bathroom, actually. Excuse me for..."

A petite young woman called from behind the counter, "Sorry, ma'am. Bathroom's for customers only."

"We are customers." I put my hand on the back of the nearest chair to demonstrate that I was staying. Caffeine this late in the day gave me the shakes, but I could always get Ms. Nesbitt something. "Can I buy you a drink? This is my son, Nathan, who still owes you an apology for bumping into you."

He murmured "sorry" so quietly Ms. Nesbitt had to read his lips.

"It's okay. But be nicer to your sister from now on." She sat at the small, round, chrome-topped table and gestured for us to join her.

We introduced ourselves, and she told me to call her Deb. "You won't need to pay for my order, Molly. My drinks are on the house." With a jerk of her head, she indicated the short woman behind the counter and explained, "That's my roommate, Marjorie. She owns this place. I'm a not-so-silent partner." She then signaled the waitress, a plump woman with bull-froggish frown lines around her mouth. Deb told her, "I'll have the usual."

The waitress grimaced, but nodded, then turned her unfriendly gaze to me.

"Mommy," Nathan said, "I'm hungry."

"Do you have any coffee ice cream?" I asked.

She growled. "Naw," and handed me a menu. It had

several flavors of latte, along with numerous words that ended with the suffix -ino. Apparently hard-core coffee drinkers of the world were trying to keep pace with teenagers at inventing words. I read the list of baked goods to Nathan, but he shook his head to each one, his scowl deepening. The daily special was some blend of espresso with a double dollop of whipped cream. "I'll have the special, with whipped cream on the side. And two spoons. And you may as well hold the espresso."

"Ya just wanna bowl of whipped cream?" the waitress replied, sounding as incredulous as if I'd ordered hot ice water.

"Yes, but it doesn't have to be a bowl. Any container you have handy would be fine. And you can charge me the full price for the drink."

While I spoke, Karen returned from the rest room and immediately elbowed Nathan. He responded with a right cross to Karen's shoulder. I pried them apart quickly and demanded they sit on either side of me. In their current state of antagonism, expecting them to share an order was out of the question. I called out to the waitress, "Make that two daily specials and bring two separate containers of whipped cream, please."

Deb Nesbitt laughed heartily. "Didn't I see this in a Jack Nicholson movie once?"

"Yes, but I promise not to flip the table afterwards. So. Have you lived in Carlton for long?"

"No, I moved here from New York City. I wanted to get away from the madding crowd, so I applied only to small schools upstate."

"Carlton High School is lucky to have you. I enjoyed your class yesterday."

"Why were you pretending to be a student?"

I glanced at Karen and Nathan, who were now sitting peacefully, listening to our every word. If I lied my way out of this, I'd be setting a horrible example. If I told the truth, I'd be giving more information about the trouble their

mother was in than any six- and eight-year-old should have
to know. "It was research. I'm a freelance writer, of sorts."
Just then, the waitress returned to our table, a welcome
distraction from this particular conversation. "Oh, good.
Here come our drinks."

"Drinks?" the waitress said from the side of her frown.
She set Deb's coffee by-product on the table, then slammed
down two narrow glasses filled with whipped cream.
"What? Now you want straws?"

I ignored her and asked Deb pointedly, "Have you been
a part *owner* here for long?" Our cranky waitress merely
slapped the bill on the table and shuffled off. Apparently
she didn't care much about keeping this job.

"Only six months." She studied me for a moment. "So,
you're doing some research for a story on teens, huh?
That's an odd coincidence. I assumed you were there because of Preston Saunders's murder."

I winced. Sure enough, Karen and Nathan perked up at
the word *murder*.

"Actually, that's true, but I can't explain at this time.
Did you know Preston well?"

"Only met the man once." She grimaced and muttered,
"That was a memorable encounter. He came for open
house last September. Sat through my fifteen-minute pre-
sentation without opening his mouth. He came up to me
afterwards and said, 'People like you shouldn't be allowed
to come in contact with young people.' Then he turned his
back on me and left." She paused and grinned. "Apparently he objected to my appearance."

I gave a quick glance to my children, who were giggling
at one another's whipped cream mustaches, paying no attention to our conversation. "That must have infuriated
you."

She shrugged. "I'm used to it. But I'd rather dress as I
see fit than try to impress people like the Saunderses."

"Under the circumstances, I'm surprised you wanted to
go to his funeral."

A momentary look of confusion passed across her features. Then she said, "I would have gone for Tiffany's sake. Mr. Saunders wouldn't have had the opportunity to object."

Nathan now wore a devilish grin and was holding his spoon as if he planned to catapult whipped cream at Karen. I leaned close to his ear and said in my most menacing voice, "Don't even think about it." He quickly redirected his spoon into his mouth to polish off the last of his whipped cream. He and his sister still sported white mustaches. "Would one of you please get us some napkins? There's a dispenser on the counter."

Karen and Nathan jumped up.

"No racing! First child to reach the napkins *loses.*" While the children did their impression of a moonwalk through molasses, I said quietly, "So, Deb. I agreed with what you said at the end of class about pornography. I sure wish it would be banned. Do you know of any active antipornography groups I could join? One that has a chapter in Carlton?"

She tensed and downed the rest of her cappuccino in one swig. "Sorry, I don't."

"You don't belong to any women's groups who share your sentiments?"

"I do belong to one women's group, but I don't know if they agree with my politics." She rose.

"Is that something I could audit sometime? I'm fairly new in town, and I'd like to meet more people."

She chuckled and shook her head, gathering her belongings. "It's a closed group, and I very much doubt you'd qualify for membership."

I wouldn't qualify? Why? She seemed to be getting ready to leave, so I had to ask a more pressing question. "Have you heard of an organization called Sisters Totally Opposed to Pornography?"

"No." Though she met my eyes, I didn't know if she was telling the truth or not. "I've got to run. Nice meeting you, Molly." She held out her hand, which I shook. She dropped a dollar tip onto the table.

She smiled and waved at her roommate, Marjorie, behind the counter, who winked and returned the smile. Just as Deb pushed out the door, Marjorie called, "Don't forget. The group meets at our house tonight. Seven o'clock."

"Ready to go, guys?" I called out to the children, who were still only halfway to the napkin dispenser. I rose, grabbed the tab, and gasped when I read it. Fourteen dollars and change. I could have bought prime rib for that amount. Let that be a lesson to me; next time I went on a stakeout with the children, I was bringing a tub of Cool Whip.

"I'm still hungry," Nathan said and ran up to me, followed by Karen. He'd already used his sleeve as a napkin. At least that was a good sign he was outgrowing his neat-nik stage. "Can I have some more?"

"Not without sacrificing our financial security."

The waitress barked from across the room. "Wait. I'll take that up for you."

"No, thanks. Don't tucker yourself out on my account." I carried my bill to the counter, where Marjorie Shoman stood near the cash register. Her long brown hair was pulled into a ponytail. She had an impish face and a button nose. At a glance, she could have passed for a teenager without any effort.

She gave me a thoroughly engaging smile and said, "I see you know my friend Deb. How was everything?"

Everything? "I didn't actually have anything to drink. But my chair was perfectly comfortable and the table didn't wobble." I grabbed my wallet. "Do you take Visa?"

"Oh, it's no charge. You didn't get a bill, did you?"

"Sorry," the waitress said, racing up beside me. She snatched the bill from me and shredded it. "I must have misunderstood your instructions, Marjorie."

Marjorie glared but said nothing.

"Thank you," I told her. "This was really generous of you." I was tempted to tell her that now I could afford to feed my family tonight, but instead silently handed napkins to my children. Maybe Nathan could use his to clean his sleeve.

"Any friend of Deb's is a friend of mine. Stop in again anytime."

I was lost in thought as I drove home. Neither Deb Nesbitt nor Marjorie Shoman struck me as the murdering sort. But the waitress...that woman I could imagine shooting someone in cold blood for not leaving a tip. She would probably relish the task of scooping dog doo-doo into a box. Maybe she was a renegade member of the women's club scheduled to meet at Deb's house tonight. Perhaps their relationship as fellow STOP members explained why she felt she could get away with her brazen behavior to her employers.

I already knew Deb Nesbitt's address. Now I just had to tell Jim to be sure to be home before seven so I could get there in time.

It was five after seven. Jim was late. This was a man who had never been late for a sporting event or a business meeting, but couldn't manage to get home on time to save his wife. Though I'd tried to plan ahead for this and had called Lauren to watch the children, she wasn't home.

Finally, at quarter after, I heard the garage door open. I called good-bye to Karen and Nathan upstairs. I was doomed. I had planned to park my car and watch the arrivals, especially keeping my eye out for Attila the Waitress. By this time everyone would've already arrived. Now what? Creep along her house and peer through the windows?

For lack of a better idea, I rifled through the coat closet for something black to camouflage me. All I could find was Jim's navy blue down coat. I always hated that coat. It puffed out between its horizontal stripes of stitching and made anyone wearing it resemble the Michelin Tire Man.

And the thing was so old that little feathers periodically fell from it like a molting chicken.

"Sorry I'm late," Jim called as he entered. "I got pulled into an impromptu—why are you wearing my coat?"

"It was the darkest thing I could find. I'm in a dark mood. See you later."

I chastised myself as I sped to Deb's home. The nylon coat swished every time I moved. Someone was sure to notice a noisy, molting trespasser encased in a hot-air balloon, even if it *was* a dark color.

I arrived, parked nearby, and quietly got out of my car. I'd tell any witnesses I was looking for my lost dog. That story, of course, wouldn't wash if Deb Nesbitt spotted me. May as well tell her I was looking for my six-foot-tall invisible rabbit.

If only I owned a dog, I could have stashed him under this silly coat and released him near a window. I decided to name the fictitious dog Soapy, after a springer spaniel that lived in my old neighborhood.

I trekked through the crested snow alongside Ms. Nesbitt's house, a modest ranch-style home. There was a well-lit window up ahead, and the curtains were slightly parted. From inside I could hear the muffled tones of classical music. That would no doubt prevent me from eavesdropping on their conversation. At least I could try to see if the waitress was there.

I tiptoed toward the window, wondering if I should start calling "Here, Soapy" now, or wait till somebody inside screamed upon spotting me.

NINE

Women Do Get Weary

THE CLASSICAL music was so loud that the stereo speakers must've been right next to the window where I was crouched, behind some large, prickly bushes. While this hid me from the street, huddling behind bushes made my story about searching for a dog a bit implausible—unless my dog happened to be of the small, burrowing variety.

I rose slowly, not wanting to make any sudden movements that might catch someone's eye. If anyone happened to be looking at this window, I was in trouble no matter how slowly I moved. Someone would call the police and report a "peeping Tomette." My husband would turn me in to my parents and never speak to me again.

My heart was pounding as I peered inside. A group of about eight women was gathered around a baby grand piano, which Deb played beautifully. Her roommate played a flute, and everyone else played stringed instruments. Their attention was so focused on their music, no one noticed me.

I ducked back down. Deb was a member of a chamber orchestra! No wonder she didn't know if her "women's group" shared her political views. But why had she said she "doubted" I'd qualify for membership? Did I *look* tone deaf? Actually, I could plink my way through simple tunes on the piano, so long as the first note was "C" and I only had to play the white keys.

Still hunched over, I dashed to my car, throwing in a whispered "Here, Soapy" for good measure, and drove home.

Deb Nesbitt was a dead end. She was at the school at the time of the second shooting. She had ample reason to dislike Preston Saunders, but so did most discerning people. Under the circumstances, I couldn't rationalize tailing Deb to see if she was lying about not belonging to STOP.

Besides, there was a better way to learn about that particular group. Jim would approve of my plan, since it ostensibly had to do with resolving my contract dispute with *Between the Legs.*

WE ATTENDED church regularly—provided, that is, Jim was in town since he was the staunch Catholic and I a staunchless Protestant. I groaned when I spotted the bald-headed, elderly priest making his way to the pulpit. His sermons tended to wander, as did my attention. This time, though, his homily about the love-thy-enemy commandment had me enthralled, especially when he spoke about how "the most dangerous enemy is often ourselves."

In one of the readings, Jacob was quoted as warning that "anger locks a man in his own house." Fear, I thought, was quite a prison warden as well. Ironically, the song during Mass was the beautiful and stirring hymn "Be Not Afraid." Too choked up to sing along, I could only mouth the words.

Later that morning, during my return trip from dropping the children off at a birthday party, I was alarmed to see Tommy's police cruiser in Lauren's driveway. Lauren had nothing to do with Preston's murder. If Tommy was there to arrest her I'd punch his lights out. Then she and I could share a cell. The heck with "love thy enemy"; forced to choose, I was going with "love thy neighbor."

Though I mentioned my concern to Jim, all he had to say on the subject was, "She'll probably call later and let you know all about it." I didn't want to have Jim catch me being nosy, and I certainly couldn't call Lauren to ask what was going on with Tommy still there. Because the window over the kitchen sink happened to give the best view of Lauren's house, I hand-washed every dish in the house. Twice. A set of glasses was now on its third washing. I had all but scrubbed off the painted design. Finally Tommy emerged from the house, followed by Lauren.

"Oh, no, Jim," I cried. "Tommy's taking her some-place! I knew it! I knew he'd arrest her!"

Jim, who was watching a basketball game on TV, called out, "He's probably just—"

"Never mind. She's waving good-bye to him. He's driving off alone."

"Sure you don't want to chase after his car?" Jim grumbled.

That remark gave me pause. Had the children told him about Ms. Nesbitt's VW? If he found out I was still "on the case," I'd better stock up on sunblock.

I waited and waited, but Lauren didn't call. Finally I could stand it no longer. I had to sneak next door to talk to Lauren. I ran upstairs, put on my jogging suit, and came back downstairs.

"I'm going for a run."

It was my bad luck that a furniture commercial happened to be on, so he gave me his full attention. "Why? You haven't jogged in years."

"I know, but...I've been meaning to take it up again for a while now." After all, the last ten minutes counted as "a while now."

I left promptly and jogged to Lauren's house. I used the sidewalk instead of cutting across the lawn, took a lot of extra steps, and raised my knees really high so as not to have lied to Jim. She answered the doorbell and greeted me breezily, ushering me inside.

"I saw Tommy over here and was worried. Was he asking you about the murder?"

"Actually, it never came up." She casually shook her

hair back from her shoulders. She wore a schoolgirlish grin as she leaned back against the wall of her foyer. "We were just chatting. We sort of…agreed we'd like to see each other."

My heart skipped a beat en route to my throat. "You mean 'see' as in *date?*"

"Yes. Why are you so surprised?"

"No reason, really. It's just that…he did throw you in jail several months ago. Those kinds of misjudgments generally put a damper on romance."

"You're not jealous of me and him, are you?"

"Jealous? Me?" Now I was not only astounded, but also affronted. "I'm happily married. I love Jim. Why would I be jealous of you and Tommy?"

"Because it's nice sometimes not to feel *too* married. To hang on to an innocent flirtation."

My first thought was that Lauren should know there's really no such thing as "innocent" flirtation. Her relationship with Preston Saunders should have proved as much to her. "I'm too blunt to be any good at flirting, even if I wanted to. I hope he makes you happy. You deserve to be. Think I'll go get some exercise, seeing as I'm dressed for it." Then I said good-bye and rushed off.

I deliberately headed in the same direction as the two women joggers who'd witnessed my argument with Preston. There was a remote possibility of my coming across the women, and if I did, I fully intended to grill them about STOP. Half a block away, I passed a man walking his golden retriever. I looked him over for small white boxes, but his hands were empty.

Tommy and Lauren. Dating. How weird. My thoughts were in such turmoil that the next thing I knew I was clear across the neighborhood where the birthday party was being held, almost two miles from my house. My sides were killing me. My organs must have been bumping into one another. The party was scheduled to end in thirty minutes. I tried to decide which would be less painful: Hanging around with ten children under the age of nine for thirty minutes till Jim picked up the three of us or jogging home. I turned around.

Using a series of four-letter words as a mantra, I eventually neared my house. Tommy was at Lauren's again. This time he had driven his personal car. Two redheaded boys, hair the exact shade of Tommy's, were sitting in the backseat. Tommy was escorting Lauren and Rachel down the front steps, and they all looked up just as I limped past.

"Keep up the good form, there, Molly," Tommy called, laughing.

I was too breathless to make a snappy retort, even if I'd had one.

EVERY MUSCLE in my body was sore Monday morning, but I got the family out of the house on time, then called *Between the Legs,* identifying myself as the Ms. Masters who'd won their cartoon contest, and asked to speak to Butch Blake. A woman with a pleasant speaking voice identified herself as Susan Wolfe, Mr. Blake's assistant, and asked if she could "be of any assistance."

"Your company printed my cartoon without my permission, and we need to get the matter resolved as quickly as possible."

"Without your permission? The cartoon was submitted by your husband and agent, Preston Saunders. If—"

"He's not my husband. And he was never my agent."

There was a pause. "I'm sorry. He gave us every impression that he was your agent. In fact, he showed us a signed copy of his contract for representation."

"He must have forged my signature." I paused, confused. "How did you know his real name? I thought he'd represented himself to you as Mike Masters."

Another pause. "He told us Mike Masters was the pseudonym he used for his agenting ventures. Apparently all of us need to sit down and, as you say, get this resolved as quickly as possible. I have Mr. Saunders's phone number. I'll give him a call and—''

"Preston Saunders was killed last week," I interrupted, somewhat surprised the police hadn't contacted them yet.

"Oh my God," she murmured.

"Could I possibly see Mr. Blake this afternoon?"

"Just a minute." She put me on hold. Her voice had sounded as if she were quite shaken by my news. Perhaps she had gotten friendly with Preston during their negotiations over my contract. Then again, it was more likely she was understandably concerned about having entered into an illegal business agreement. Her voice was tense when she clicked back onto the line a couple of minutes later and said, "Ms. Masters? I think it would be best if we have our respective legal representatives meet instead. Do you have a lawyer?"

"Yes, but..." That would ruin my opportunity to learn more about STOP. "It seems clear to me that Mr. Saunders misrepresented himself. I don't consider your magazine culpable whatsoever for printing my cartoon. I'd just like to talk to Mr. Blake face to face and work out a logical, expedient solution, and then maybe pick his brain about some...organizational problems I've been having."

We scheduled an appointment for 2 p.m., and I made round-trip train reservations. That meant six-plus hours on the rails, but I would make it home by dinnertime. Once again, Lauren agreed to watch the children after school. By now our baby-sitting co-op was so out of balance her daughter Rachel might as well take up residence in my house for the entire month of May.

I spent the next hour or so on the phone to other "men's" magazines. I asked if they had heard of STOP, having identified myself as an investigative reporter for *20/20*. My house address here happened to be 2020 Little John Lane.

Two of the five magazines I called admitted they had received "hate mail" from STOP last week. In both cases, the mail consisted of empty but brown-stained boxes, with a card attached to the lid that stated in a sentence or two that they were to cease publication, "or else." Though no return address was listed, the boxes to both magazines had been postmarked from Albany. Neither publisher had heard of the group before last week, or heard from it since. Also, in both cases, the men I spoke to gave me this information freely, then asked what STOP had done to interest *20/20* in a story, a question I had to "decline to answer for professional reasons."

During my last conversation, however, the magazine's representative said, "It's about that murder upstate, isn't it?"

"Murder?"

"Yeah. A police sergeant spoke to me a few days ago, asking the same questions you are. He wouldn't tell me anything, 'cept that this all had to do with a murder investigation. Is this STOP group full of wacko, murderous feminists?"

Uh-oh. If I kept on the line, sooner or later I'd make a mistake that would reveal I wasn't really on the staff of *20/20*.

I held the phone away from my face and called, "Just a moment, Barbara, I'll be right there," then said into the phone, "Thank you, sir," and hung up.

So. Tommy had been in touch with men's magazines to try to learn about STOP. That meant he had probably spoken to personnel at *Between the Legs* as well, and just hadn't happened to speak to Susan Wolfe. Whatever he had learned about their contact with STOP I could learn too in my meeting with Butch Blake.

I put on the pair of silk panty hose I reserved for business meetings, black high-heels—which were technically "flats," but they were high compared to the moccasins or sneakers I usually wore—and my favorite dress: Windex blue with a matching jacket. Just as I was about to leave, the doorbell rang. I swung open the door and nearly gasped when I saw Sergeant Newton, arms akimbo.

"Tommy. What a surprise. I'd love to invite you in, but you happened to catch me on my way out."

"You're 'way out,' all right. Going to New York City to see Butch Blake."

"How did you know that?"

"Called down there myself 'bout an hour ago. A Ms. Susan Wolfe told me you were coming down this afternoon. So am I."

"Why? Haven't you already spoken to Butch Blake?"

"No, the editor was out of town last week."

"So you don't know if they've gotten any nasty mail from STOP, huh?"

"They have. Last week they received an empty box from 'em."

"Postmarked from Albany?"

"Uh-huh. How'd you know that?"

"Lucky guess." I leaned out onto the porch and saw Tommy's police cruiser. "So, I guess I can cancel my train reservations."

"Naw. I'm not takin' the squad car all that way, but I'll give you a ride to the station. I'm riding the train with you."

"Good. That'll give us a chance to shake the gift."

"You mean *shoot* the gift."

"Whatever," I murmured.

Why would anyone want to *shoot* a gift? A person might *shake* one to figure out what was in it, but *shoot* it? Was it asking too much for young people's expressions to make a little sense?

That thought brought another question to mind: Why all these empty, stained boxes? Had STOP's dog died? Even so, surely dog excrement was one of the more readily available, affordable commodities. Perhaps there was some significance to the fact that I'd gotten the real thing. Copy-dog mailings, perhaps?

Or maybe the culprit was afraid that sending such a thing through the mail was a punishable crime...abuse of the U.S. Mail. But that seemed so strange: "Okay, I'll kill some guy, but I'm not gonna mail dog doo-doo. Too danged risky. I might have to pay a fine if I get caught!"

ON THE TRAIN, Tommy offered me the window seat, and we were soon on our way to New York City. I decided to wait a few minutes before asking him how the investigation was going. After turning toward him with the intention of making small talk, it hit me that he was now my best friend's boyfriend. That was followed by a truly horrendous moment during which I unintentionally flashed on the thought of him and Lauren in one another's arms.

Tommy must have seen me blush, for he raised an eyebrow and said, "A penny for your thoughts."

Caught off guard, I guffawed so loudly the old woman across the aisle leaned forward to peer at me. I cleared my throat and said quietly, "So, Tommy. How's the investigation going? Any suspects?"

"I got a possible or two."

I waited, but judging by the set of his jaw, there was no sense asking him who these "possibles" were. Instead, I asked, "Have you located the messenger? The one who brought me the box from STOP?"

He shook his head. "We've contacted every delivery service within a fifty-mile radius. None of 'em recorded a delivery to your house, and we can't locate anyone fitting the description."

The young man's most notable feature had been his hair, shaved to his scalp down the exact middle of his head, the other half dyed blue. "Maybe he was wearing a disguise and kept the whole transaction off the books." Tommy said nothing, so I continued, "Someone could have bribed him to keep the whole thing secret, and if so, he probably would've assumed he was making a drug drop-off."

Tommy nodded. "Yeah, that's our theory, too. In which

case, us finding him is gonna be next to impossible, unless
he comes forward, which he's not gonna do, since he thinks
he was an accessory to a drug crime.'' He paused, then
said, ''There is one thing you could do that might help us
locate him.''

''You want me to draw a picture of him?''

''Yep. I'll get that out to the local papers and we'll see
if it shakes him out.''

I snatched a small drawing pad I always kept in my purse
and set to work. I had to compensate for the movement of
the train, which not only gave my rendition unwanted blem-
ishes and jagged lines, but made me carsick. It didn't take
me long to realize that the messenger's bizarre hairstyle
had distracted me from fully noticing his facial features.

The results were disappointing. It could have been almost
any Caucasian male having a distinctly bad hair day, but
Tommy thanked me as he carefully put my drawing in his
inside jacket pocket. Then we chatted pleasantly about our
children, and for once I thoroughly enjoyed being with him.

At a stop, I chuckled at the sight of a large woman wearing what had to be the ugliest dress I'd ever seen. It was
composed almost entirely of peacock feathers.

''Some dress, hey Moll?'' Tommy said as he spotted the
woman. ''I can see you in something like that.''

''It's a bit too plain for my taste.'' That gave me an idea
for a cartoon, so I doodled a drawing of a woman in an
outlandish outfit almost as bizarre looking as the real thing.
While her husband looks with popping eyes at the price
tag, she says, ''Well, as you know, Fred, we women do get
weary, wearing the same simple dress.''

Tommy peered over my shoulder at my sketch and said,
''I don't get it.''

''It's poking fun at the line from the song.''

He furrowed his brow as if confused, so I sang a stanza
of ''Try a Little Tenderness.''

He shrugged. ''Your cartoon's pretty sexist. Keep it up

'n' you're gonna get STOP to change their name to STOMP: Sisters Totally Opposed to Molly's Puns.''

That remark stung. I replied in clipped tones, "Maybe so. But, after all I *am* a woman, so all I'm doing is laughing at myself."

"Uh-huh. So if a woman makes a joke about women, she's laughing at herself, but if a man makes a joke about women, he's sexist."

"Touché. I stand not only corrected, but humiliated."

"Just makin' conversation to pass the time. No need to get upset."

I shoved the notepad back into my purse and feigned sleep. Tommy sat in silence for several minutes, then started to whistle "Try a Little Tenderness."

WE ARRIVED at Penn Station, and I had to admit I was now very glad Tommy was with me. Just being in this big building within this enormous city made me feel as though I couldn't breathe. What was the technical term for fear of crowds? Massofolksophobia, perhaps. Though the train station was actually well lit, I had the impression of being in a dark, cavernous area, where a crush of people darted all around me like crazed bats. I alone seemed to have no idea where I was supposed to go. With purposeful strides, Tommy led the way, and we were soon outside on a noisy, smoggy street facing Madison Square Garden.

Surrounded by such tall buildings, I now had the distinct—though unoriginal—impression of being at the bottom of a canyon. Biting chill winds whipped my hair into my face, blinding me. The kitelike fabric of my dress was plastered against my thighs. I fully expected it to rise to neck level if I so much as took a step. This is what happens to me when I try to dress my age, I thought—should have stuck with the arrested-development look. Tommy all but shoved me into one of a half dozen cabs waiting by the curb. He gave an address to the dark, curly-haired cabbie, and we were off on a whiplash-inspiring ride.

Eight dollars later, we followed the receptionist at *Between the Legs* through a windowless maze of cubicles. She led us to a small meeting room, where she told us to help ourselves to coffee or tea. Tommy poured himself a cup of what appeared to be well on its way to becoming espresso, while I poured myself some orange pekoe tea. This room had three walls of fake mahogany paneling graced with large glossies of beautiful women shown from the shoulders up, and one glass wall. Employees walking by glanced with blank faces through the glass at Tommy and me. It gave me the childish impulse to draw mustaches and goatees on the photographs just to give passersby a better show.

The oval, oak-veneer table sat eight, and Tommy and I sat beside each other, facing the glass. Moments after we'd taken our seats, a tall, elegantly dressed woman entered, carrying a stack of papers. She appeared to be in her early forties. She hadn't dyed her long, white-streaked brown hair, which won me over immediately. She further impressed me with her sincere smile as she held out her hand to me. "Hello, I'm Susan Wolfe, also known as Butch Blake. We spoke on the phone earlier. You must be Ms. Masters."

Appalled, I rose and shook her hand, but stammered, "*You're* Butch Blake?"

"That's my professional name, yes." She then greeted Tommy, shook hands, and we all sat down.

For the next fifteen minutes or so, we discussed the situation with my cartoon and what should be done. She didn't hold it against me when I assured her that under no circumstances would I create cartoons for her magazine. To my surprise, she said that because they had published my cartoon without my consent, they were willing to pay me an extra thousand dollars in exchange for my signing a release to ensure that I wouldn't sue them. I agreed, and after reading and then signing the paper, she gave me a check for a thousand dollars. The meeting was pleasant, and I found myself liking Ms. Wolfe.

During a pause, I could no longer resist my curiosity and said, "Pardon me for asking, but doesn't it bother you to publish a magazine in which the bulk of the pages contain pornographic photos of naked women?"

"Printing men's literature simply happens to be my job, Ms. Masters. It doesn't carry as much prestige as, say, working for *The New Yorker*, but I wouldn't be editor-in-chief there, as I am here. I take it you don't approve?"

"It's not up to me to approve or disapprove of your job. It's just that I personally wouldn't wish to work for an industry that presents women as sex objects. One which caters to and encourages the prurient interests of men."

"You consider our magazine to be exploitative, but that's only one viewpoint. Mine is that beautiful bodies are always used in our society to sell products. Whether or not a model is willing to pose in the nude is a personal matter that should be up to the model to determine."

Her reply sounded rehearsed. This was no doubt her canned response to questions like mine.

She turned to Tommy, who had been quietly listening to us, and said, "Mr. Saunders seemed like a sincere, decent man. Obviously, I misjudged him." For the first time, her voice trembled slightly as she spoke, perhaps with anger at Preston for having conned her. "Do you have any idea who killed him?"

"Not enough to make an arrest at this time." He asked, "Have you ever heard of a group called Sisters Totally Opposed to Pornography?"

"As I told you when you asked me that over the phone, yes. But not until a couple of weeks ago. That was less than a week after the April edition hit the stands."

"The one that contained my cartoon?" I asked, just in case Tommy had missed the connection.

"Right. We received a soiled box on Monday, two weeks ago. This was glued to the lid." She rifled through her stack of papers and pulled out a small, pink paper that read:

Your publication has degraded and insulted women everywhere. Either you decide on your own to cease all publication of this filth, or we will decide *for* you.
Sisters Totally Opposed to Pornography

TEN

Where's My Thesaurus?

AFTER AN uneventful train ride home from the Big Apple, I was pleasantly surprised to find that Jim had beaten me home and had already picked up the children from next door. I was unpleasantly *not* surprised, however, to discover Karen and Nathan bickering. Nathan was insisting to Karen that the name of the song she was currently trying to sing was, "Hot and Cold," not "Heart and Soul."

"Tell him, Mom," Karen demanded. "Tell him it's 'Heart and Soul.'"

I glanced at Jim, who was watching the news, and wondered how it was that he was so adept at blocking out noise. Must be one of those Y chromosome things. "Karen's right, Nathan."

"That's cuz I'm always wrong!" he cried.

"Although," I continued quickly to circumvent his imminent tantrum, "'Hot and Cold' would make an excellent title for a song." To demonstrate, I sang, "Hot and cold. I had a lunch but it's covered with mold. I don't know why I didn't refrigerate it. Don't want to eat a bit of it, a bit of it."

Karen giggled at my lyrics and Nathan managed a smile. Jim turned off the TV and greeted me with a quick kiss. I asked him if he'd sing the bass part to my new song. Mostly thanks to Karen's "Oh, please, Daddy, oh, please," he agreed, and he and Nathan sang, "I'm a guy and I don't want to sing these notes cuz they're too high..." while Karen and I sang the soprano part.

Deb Nesbitt's chamber orchestra had nothing on my family's rendition of "Hot and Cold."

I WAS DELIGHTED the next morning to receive a job request for a personalized fax cover-sheet. The prospective customer was a technical writer who wanted to incorporate a humorous cartoon about writing on his cover sheets.

After several minutes of brainstorming, I settled on a caricature of Abraham Lincoln, looking frustrated as he sits at a desk with quill pen in hand and thinks: *Eighty-seven years ago, our forefathers... No. Four double-decades and seven years ago... No. Damn. Where's my thesaurus?*

Once the drawing was complete, I laid a black piece of paper on it cut into the shape of a large **X** and faxed this to him. That way, the customer could see enough of my work underneath the **X** to decide if he wanted it, but not enough to use it without payment. Minutes later, I received a fax that he "loved it." I responded that I was delighted and would send out the final fax to him the moment payment was received, and to please recommend me to his friends and associates.

That accomplished before 10 a.m., I now had two hours before Nathan's kindergarten bus arrived. I reflected upon the limited clues I'd managed to collect so far and my theories about Preston's murder. The one theory that seemed to be panning out was the idea that the "bad person"—to use Nathan's phraseology—was someone who knew Preston personally and knew he had submitted a cartoon to the magazine.

Preston had told me that drinking buddies at the country club had bet him he couldn't get the job as the cartoonist. Stephanie should know who those "buddies" were. This was Tuesday. I hadn't visited with her since Friday, and because her daughter and I had been shot at at the time, that visit had been less than leisurely.

I stopped at a flower shop and bought an arrangement of blue and white carnations in an *It's a Boy!* ceramic mug, plus a cute, cream-colored stuffed bear. I tried not to dwell on the thought that this cost me most of my earnings from the Abe cartoon.

Stephanie's private nurse answered the door and showed me to the sitting room. After a minute or two, Stephanie swept into the room. She had recently had her hair done and her makeup was perfect. In her loose-fitting caftan of an Indian-style print, it was impossible to tell she had recently given birth. She held out her arms to me and said, "Molly, what a nice surprise." Then she gave me a rather distant-feeling hug.

I gave her the gifts I'd bought, apologizing for not having gotten them to her sooner.

She examined the flowers. "Oh, my. You needn't have. We have so many beautiful flower arrangements." Then she grabbed the stuffed bear by both paws. "That's the wonderful thing about stuffed bears. No matter how many of them you already have, there's always room for one more."

She called, "Estelle?" then wandered into the hallway as I sat down. I gritted my teeth and counted to ten as I overheard Stephanie say, "Try to find someplace these can go where they won't be dwarfed entirely. Thank you so much."

"How's Michael?" I asked the moment she reentered, to postpone her from saying something offensive.

"He's fine." She eased herself into a chair across from me. "Absolutely precious."

"And Tiffany? Is she doing all right?"

"Fine. She and her boyfriend have decided to take things a little slower and just be friends for a while. She misses her father, of course, but she's being stoic. And, I told her as long as she stayed away from you, she didn't have to worry about getting shot at again." She paused. "I hope you're not offended. As a mother, you do realize that I am more concerned with my daughter's welfare than yours.''

"Steph, I don't mean to overstep my bounds, but if you *are* concerned about her welfare, don't you think you should consider taking her to a therapist?''

She sat up in her chair and gaped at me for a moment. Then she looked away and fidgeted with a fingernail. "You think my child is crazy?''

"No. I just think she could use some help to express and examine her feelings. Especially about her father's death. You say she's being 'stoic,' but why should she be? She needs to grieve, not bottle it up inside. It would be so sad if she grows up to be...'' another *you*, I thought, but said, "cold and emotionless.''

"There's plenty to be said for being cold,'' Stephanie said under her breath. "Coldness numbs the senses. Makes things hurt a lot less.''

"And also blots out joy and love. What's the worst that could happen if you took her to a good therapist?''

"The worst?'' she repeated with a sad chuckle. "She might learn to hate her mother.''

Her candor took me by surprise. Believing she'd expressed a valid concern, I had no ready response and changed subjects. "Can I see the baby?''

"No. He's asleep.'' She looked at me for a moment, then glanced at her watch and sighed.

"Are you interested in how my search for your husband's killer is coming along?''

"Why, of course. I assumed that was the reason you were here. Was I supposed to prompt you?''

I cleared my throat and fought down my typical reaction to Stephanie, which was to picture myself with my hands around her neck. If my efforts to learn more about the murder went as badly as my attempt to convince her to seek counseling, this entire visit would be a waste. My first task was to learn how much she knew. "What has Tommy told you about an organization called Sisters Totally Opposed to Pornography?''

"He told me something about Preston posing as Mike Masters and submitting a pornographic cartoon of yours to a contest. That he won the contest and, consequently, a bet against some friends of his at the club. Tommy also told me the...sorority had sent both Preston and you threats."

"Did you ever hear about STOP prior to Preston's death, or since then?"

"No."

"And did you know Preston subscribed to a magazine called *Between the Legs* behind your back?"

"*Between the Legs Behind Your Back* sounds like a publication for contortionists. But, yes, I knew about it. I allowed Preston to think he was fooling me by having it sent to a P.O. box. That at least prevented him from leaving copies on our coffee table."

"Did you know he'd entered the cartoon contest?"

"No, not until Tommy discussed all of that with me."

"And did you tell Tommy who'd made the bet with Preston?"

"No, I have no idea. It could be anyone at the Carlton Country Club, and they have hundreds of members."

"But Preston said he *won* the bet. So those particular friends should have paid him a thousand dollars apiece. That edition had been in print for more than a week before Preston was killed. He probably received an advance copy and would have had proof he won the bet for three or four weeks."

"Oh. Well, in that case, the thing to do would be to go through his bank records." She rose. "Come with me, Molly. We'll take a look in his library."

I followed Stephanie into a gorgeous room of polished oak and brass. An enormous desk ran almost the full length of the room. The room had everything anyone would want in a library—with the exception of books. The built-in bookshelves held mostly sports trophies and bric-a-brac. Preston apparently hadn't been much of a reader.

Behind the desk hung a lifelike portrait of Preston, looking downright regal in a maroon smoking jacket. Did people actually wear smoking jackets anymore? It seemed like such a cliché.

Ignoring my protestations to let me help, Stephanie pushed Preston's desk chair against the back wall and stood on the chair as she removed his portrait. My eyes widened. Here was the original "Princess and the Pea" stepping up onto a chair just days after giving birth. Was she disposing of Preston's portrait now that he was dead? I wondered. Then I realized there was a wall safe behind it. She handed the painting down to me, and I set it on the floor.

Stephanie quickly worked the combination and swung open the door. Then she pressed her index fingers on the opposite corners of the safe. The back wall of the safe popped open.

"Secret compartment," she said, glancing over her shoulder in my direction. "My husband tried to hide things from me. Honestly." She reached into the compartment and removed the contents: a stack of magazines and a few papers. She closed the compartment, stepped off the chair, and set the safe's contents on the desk. I glanced at the spines of the magazines. They were the last six editions of *Between the Legs.*

"Mrs. Saunders?" We both looked up. Estelle was standing in the doorway. "Michael is awake. He wants to nurse."

"Oh." She shot a nervous glance at me, then at the still-open safe. "Well." She crossed the room, then patted a hard-back chair near the door. "Sit right here while I'm gone, Estelle." Then she looked at me, still standing by the desk. "Go ahead and look through those papers, Molly, but don't touch anything in the safe." Her vision darted between me and Estelle. "I'll be right back." Her parting words betrayed such mistrust I couldn't help but smile.

Estelle rolled her eyes and returned my smile. Though plump, she was a pretty woman, some ten years older than I.

"Darn," I told her. "If only she hadn't left you to watch me. I was planning on stealing her blind."

Estelle laughed.

I studied the paper on top of the stack of magazines, which was a bank statement. The beginning balance was a little over twelve thousand dollars, and the final balance was over fifteen thousand. There were three deposits in the amount of one thousand dollars, each made a week to ten days before Preston died.

I looked at the sheet of paper underneath the bank statement. It was a contract detailing the terms of Preston's bet among him and three other men. In a messy scrawl, it specified that Preston had to supply indisputable proof—misspelled in the document as "indesuptable proof"—that he'd won the contest by next June; otherwise he would lose the bet and have to pay each of them a thousand dollars. Since they'd paid him, they had apparently agreed that his published photograph under the pseudonym Mike Masters was "indesuptable" proof. All four men had signed it. The names meant nothing to me; I jotted them down on a sheet of memo paper from the desk and pocketed it. Hank Mueller had apparently penned the contract, judging by his signature. The two other names were Richard Worthington and Chase Groves. Maybe one of these three men had killed Preston and had concocted this whole STOP thing to disguise his real motive.

Among the remaining papers was a document about the post office box number, which matched the address label on the magazines. The other papers were bank statements from the same account, which had been opened with ten thousand dollars a year ago. I scanned the statements, but nothing noteworthy jumped out at me. There were a few deposits and withdrawals most months, but no particular patterns that might indicate blackmail or that he was hoping to squirrel away great amounts of money.

I picked up the magazines by their spines, flipped through them, then shook each one, hoping something would fall out. Nothing. Not even one of those annoying advertisements on postcards. I then started to flip through one of the magazines, but stopped when I got grossed out by photos of a woman having an unnatural relationship with a beer bottle.

Had Preston really devoted a whole compartment in his safe just to this? A stack of dirty magazines and bank statements for one personal checking account?

I glanced over at Estelle, who looked half asleep, and tried to assess whether or not she'd want to give me, a total stranger, information about her employer. She'd been hired as a nurse, but was being used by Stephanie as her maid and girl Friday. If this were me, I'd not only want to blab, but to start vicious rumors. "Estelle, have you seen Stephanie open this safe before now?"

Her face lit up. "Just the one time. Right after that red-headed police officer left here last Friday. She was going through—"

"Here's my little angel boy," Stephanie announced as she waltzed into the library carrying Michael. "He's asleep again, but I thought you'd like a chance to hold him before I had Estelle put him down."

Quite unwittingly, my voice shot up a couple of octaves as I spoke admiringly to him and held his warm little body. That didn't used to happen to my voice. I hadn't squeaked or cooed even once the first time I visited my future in-laws and held Jim's new nephew—who peed on me. But as a mother, I found it impossible not to be enchanted by the presence of a newborn.

A minute or two later, I allowed Estelle to take the baby away. My usual nonsqueaking voice promptly returned as I showed Stephanie the handwritten contract and said,

"These are the names of the men who bet Preston he couldn't win the contest. Do you recognize any of them?"

Stephanie answered, "I barely know any of them, but they were all in Preston's regular golf foursome. They played eighteen holes every Tuesday afternoon, even in atrocious weather."

This was a Tuesday, and the weather was reasonably nice. Perhaps the three men had a tee-time. Then again, knowing how unfaithful Preston had been, maybe many of those Tuesdays had been used for extracurricular activities unrelated to golf. "I was looking at the bank statements here. It does look as though Preston received payments for his bet."

She looked at the statement, "Hmm. You're right. This was Preston's private account where he kept his mad money."

"It's got fifteen thousand dollars in it. You consider that *mad* money? That could cheer most people up in a hurry."

She shrugged. "He withdrew ten thousand dollars in cash from the account the morning he died. I found the withdrawal slip in his pocket."

She searched her husband's body? "Why did you search his pockets?"

After a brief hesitation, she flicked a wrist and said casually, "I really don't know. I guess old habits die hard."

Old habits! She was so used to searching her husband's pockets she couldn't wait to get his clothes back from the mortician? "What did Tommy say about the missing money?"

"I didn't tell him. I think it was a payoff to Tiffany's boyfriend to compel him to leave her alone."

"Why didn't you tell—"

"Because it looked bad for Tiffany. If she found out that Preston had given Cherokee ten thousand dollars to keep away from her, she might have come home in a rage and shot him."

"Shot her *father*? I still don't understand how you can possibly believe that of Tiffany."

Stephanie narrowed her eyes, not answering, and I had the chilling realization that I knew nothing about Tiffany's behavior at home. That maybe, all along, I'd resisted taking too close a look at Tiffany because she was someone I had trusted my children with.

Pushing that thought away for the time being, I continued, "I would think she'd have been more angry at her boyfriend for accepting the money. Did you ask Cherokee if he'd gotten money from your husband?"

"Yes, and he denies it."

"So what makes you think—"

"What else could Preston have done with the money? I checked his wallet and his pockets. There was no money on him at all when he died. And the time stamp on the withdrawal slip indicated he'd gone to the bank and driven straight home. The only scenario that makes sense is, while I was in the bathtub, he paid someone off, who shot him. It must have been Cherokee. Who else would have wanted to kill someone over a measly ten thousand dollars?"

"People have been killed for a pair of athletic shoes. Ten thousand isn't measly to most people in this world."

SOMEHOW, I had to get a tee-time at the country club, preferably with Preston's former golf partners. But as a mother, my priorities were steadfastly focused on my children. For me to be able to golf this afternoon, they needed someone to watch them. So I drove to school, signed in at the office, and dropped in on Karen's class.

As soon as I stepped inside the doorway, Karen leaped up from her nearby desk and gave me a hug—which, given her stature, meant she wrapped her arms around my waist. Her wispy, light brown hair now looked decidedly windblown, but she was the prettiest girl in the world in my eyes, now and always. Lauren's daughter, Rachel, also ran up to me to show me the tooth that had popped out during music class.

Their teacher was roughly my age, a delightful woman whose wild curls and messy desk could give the false impression that she was a scatterbrain. The antithesis of Nathan's teacher, she greeted me with enthusiasm and encouraged me to stay and type up a couple more of her students' stories, which we would then bind as keepsakes for each of them.

By a lucky coincidence, Karen told me she'd been invited to her friend Katie's house. I gave her my permission to go and said I'd call Katie's mom from the office as soon as I'd finished my typing.

Now I just needed to arrange for Nathan to go to his friend Jon's house—which wouldn't be difficult because Jon's mom would arrive shortly to walk Jon home from morning kindergarten, and she would remember her son had been at our house for the boys' last three get-togethers. Plus, during his last visit, Jon had managed to roll the bottom portion of a snow man through the back door and into our formal dining room. In other words, the woman owed me.

ONE OF THE PERKS of Jim's "temporary" assignment was a year's pass to the Carlton Country Club. After a brief search, I found the card with his membership number in Jim's nightstand, along with other ID cards he often kept in his wallet.

Both Jim and I love to golf, but this was an individual pass only, no family members. In fact, Jim loves golf so much that I'd once accused him of accepting this assignment purely because of the golf pass. He gallantly offered to let me use the pass instead of him…proof positive that my accusation was correct and I'd hit a nerve.

Now I needed to take Jim up on that offer.

I called the club and learned that there was a tee-time for a threesome at two this afternoon under the name

Mueller. I told the scheduler I was a single and he put me down to join the Mueller threesome.

I arranged for the children to play at friends' houses after school. I was all set, except for one thing: My conscience bothered me. Jim had apparently left his golf pass at home by mistake. My taking it without his knowledge was deceitful. I had to tell Jim what I was up to. I called his office.

"Hi, Jim?"

"Uh-oh. I hate it when you greet me that way. That little lilt to your voice when you say 'Jim' always means you're going to tell me something I don't want to know."

Time for a strategy change; to ease slowly into the subject of where I'd be this afternoon. "That shows what you know. I was just calling to say I love you."

"I love you, too. And?"

"And..." Damn! My mind was blank! "I ran over a camel on the Northway. It was going south in the northbound lane."

"What? Are you trying to tell me you wrecked the car?"

"Kidding." Babbling, actually. "The car's fine. I just wanted to tell you I was taking you up on your offer to use your pass to the Carlton Country Club."

There was a pause. Knowing Jim, he was probably searching his wallet for his golf card right about now. He said, "But the weather is finally getting nice. In six months I haven't been able to use that pass even once. I was hoping to get out there today myself. Besides, you said they were all a bunch of snobs and you'd rather play on the public course."

"No, all I said was I didn't want to belong to any club in which the Saunderses were members."

"You're hoping to investigate the murder, using my pass to get in, aren't you? Molly, where's my card? It's not in my wallet."

My stomach knotted. I shouldn't have called. My reasons for being willing to go to these lengths to find the killer were too complicated to explain in a two-minute phone conversation. "It must be around the house. When I find it, I'll give it back to you by, say, Saturday?"

"By, say, tomorrow, you're going to be on a flight to Florida!" He hung up on me.

ELEVEN

Fore!

I KNEW I was out of my financial league when I drove up to the clubhouse and saw they had a valet service. This ranked as one of the most absurd things I'd seen in a long time. Golf was a sport, after all, so theoretically golfers should expect to get some exercise. Being spared a walk across the parking lot was tantamount to taking an elevator to use a StairMaster at a gym.

I pretended I didn't see the valet signs and parked at the far end of the lot, only to have a young, muscular man decked out in white pants and a bright yellow mono-grammed shirt follow me in a golf cart and offer to help me get my clubs out of the trunk. When I declined, he gave me a look of disgust and said, "You do have a tee-time here at the Carlton Country Club, right?" His expression grew even more disgusted as he eyed my inexpensive bag and clubs. "Some...golfers get us confused with the public course across town."

I slung the strap of my bag over my shoulder and said, "Oh, I'm pretty sure this is the right place. This *is* the course with the cute little windmills and bridges, isn't it?"

He paled and said, "You're thinking of the putt-putt course on Route Nine."

"Oh, well, just the same, I'd better check in with the starter. I have a two o'clock tee-time."

When I tried to walk past him, he backed the cart directly

into my path, then glanced at a computer printout. He barked, "Are you Masters?"

"Yes."

"Get in. We have mandatory cart rentals. Your playing partners haven't arrived yet. You'll share this cart."

Apparently use of the valet service was also mandatory. He glared at me the entire time I loaded my bag onto the back and barely waited for me to sit down before taking off.

I regretted my earlier sarcastic reply. Alienating staff members was a lousy start to learning about Preston's foursome, and I had jeopardized my marital bliss just to find out if any of them had a motive.

I forced a smile and said, "I was just kidding about the putt-putt. I'm a really good golfer. In fact, they named a tournament in Augusta after me."

He did a double take, then finally cracked a smile and said, "They named the Masters after you, huh? Damn. You *must* be good."

"Not compared to my husband. Perhaps you've heard of him...British Open?"

He smiled broadly now. "Your husband's name is British Open?"

I nodded. "Friends call him Brit, or B.O. for short."

He laughed. He dropped me off at the clubhouse and asked whether I wanted my cart at the first tee or the practice range. Needing all the practice I could get, I opted for the latter. He was still chuckling as he drove away with my clubs.

Somewhat to my surprise, there was no doorman to the clubhouse. However, there was also no sign over the counter stating the price of a round of golf. They may as well have put up a notice that read: IF YOU HAVE TO ASK, YOU CAN'T AFFORD TO PLAY.

The man behind the counter, also wearing a yellow shirt, though I couldn't see his pants, greeted me and checked off my name for my two o'clock tee-time. I braced myself.

"That'll be a hundred dollars, ma'am, plus thirty for the cart."

I stifled a gasp. Talk about *greens* fees! I handed over my Visa card. Good thing I had deposited my check from the magazine. One hundred and thirty dollars for an afternoon of golf. And all for the privilege of playing with three men I'd never met who made thousand-dollar bets on cartoons. One of whom could well be a murderer.

Just as he was about to hand me my receipt, he hesitated and looked again at his schedule. "Uh-oh. It looks like there's been a slight mistake on your tee-time. You're supposed to go off at two-oh-eight. The scheduler put you down with Mr. Mueller's group at two, when he meant to put you with Mrs. Mueller's threesome, the men's wives." He gave me a sheepish grin. "I'm sure you don't mind waiting a few more minutes to golf with other women."

That explained why I had no problem arranging out of the blue to play in Preston's former group, who'd patronized this swank club for years.

I met his fake smile with one of my own, but my pulse was racing. If my group was changed now, not only had I angered my husband for nothing, but my investigation would come to a grinding halt.

"I'll stick with the original tee-time. I don't mind golfing with men. Some of my best friends are men. I even married one." He started to protest, so I continued, "I'll just tee off at two as scheduled, but if I'm slowing the group down, I'll drop back and join their wives. Could I get a small bucket of practice balls, please?"

He stared at the schedule, then at me. I tried to hold his gaze with confidence. My suggestion had been perfectly reasonable. But I was beginning to realize I was further out of my element than ever before. This was harder than pretending to be a teen. At least I'd once *been* one of those. I had never been wealthy, never pretended nor wanted to be a country-club jet-setter, let alone one who would fit in with an already male-bonded threesome.

"Look lady. Moving you to another group is in your own best interest. You don't want to play with those guys. They're out for blood. We don't want any more scenes."

"Excuse me?" Had the men gotten into a noisy argument, such as between Preston and his killer? "You mean the men argue sometimes?"

He chuckled. "Couple weeks ago, we nearly had to get the police out here to subdue the black guy. So what do you say we put you with the other ladies, hey?"

Yikes! "I'd still rather—"

He lifted up a palm. "Since this was our mistake I can't force you. But I gotta warn you. I *will* tell the marshal to keep an eye on you to make sure you're keeping pace." He handed me a gold metal token and said, "The ball machine and buckets are up on the range. You get fifteen balls per token. That'll be five dollars."

I shelled out another five dollars, a relative bargain. Great. So now I was going to have a marshal following me around with a cattle prod. Nothing like a nice, relaxing afternoon of golf with a possible murderer or two. First, though, I needed to learn more about the "scene" this counter-guy didn't want repeated.

"I read about Preston Saunders's murder. He was a member here, wasn't he?"

"Yes. Quite a tragedy." He reached for something under the counter. "Here. You might want to take a look at our course rules." He handed me a three-by-five card, along with a scorecard that showed the layout of the eighteen-hole course. "Note that we specifically state"—he pointed on my card—"no more than *two* practice swings. You're certain you won't slow down play, right? Because I'm serious about notifying the marshal."

"I'll golf just as fast as I possibly can," I replied testily. "You almost called the police to break up a fight among these men?"

He merely smiled and said, "Have a nice afternoon." Then he turned his back on me.

So much for getting information from him. I went outside, where the aroma of newly mowed grass failed to cheer me while I considered how much I hated this place so far. The basic attitude of the personnel was: Gimme your money and get outta here.

No moving walkways or rickshaws took me to the practice range. I decided to take a couple of my clubs and leave the cart by the path. Though there was room for about a dozen golfers, only four were currently using the range. They were all older men, decked out in full golf regalia: primary-colored Izod sweaters and short-sleeved shirts, perfectly pressed cotton slacks, brightly colored tams. How long could someone dressed like that last on a sidewalk in New York?

Having guessed this place would have a dress code, I had borrowed by husband's blue Izod sweater and wore tan slacks and a purple polo-shirt with a collar. Except for my not wearing a silly hat, I looked the part. However, my first two practice shots were worm-burners. My swing had better improve, *fast,* or I was in real trouble. I would be court-martialed; they would rip the little alligator off my sweater and send me home in disgrace.

Halfway through my bucket, I spotted the ''valet'' loading another bag onto my cart. My partners must have arrived. The set of clubs he was loading belonged to a handsome, powerfully built African-American man who looked to be in his early forties. This must be the ''black guy'' they had almost called in the police to ''subdue.'' A second golf cart with two other men drove up. They promptly got out of the cart and engaged the staff member in an animated discussion. Since they all turned their backs on me after a quick glance my way, it was a fairly safe bet that they weren't too thrilled with the prospect of my joining them.

If a staff member happened to mention my last name, I was in trouble. Having someone named Masters show up shortly after Preston had won a thousand dollars apiece from them by claiming to be Mike Masters would be quite a coincidence.

Before their discussion went any further, I trotted toward them and introduced myself as Molly, thanking them for so generously allowing me to join their group—as if I didn't know the scheduler had given them an unpleasant surprise. They were all smiles, and the staff member wandered off while the four of us were shaking hands.

Chase Groves was the African-American sharing my cart. He seemed quite nice, and I had a hard time imagining him publicly losing control. Yet I felt an instant dislike for Hank Mueller, a trim, middle-aged man with black hair and a mustache. He resembled Snidely Whiplash from cartoons—with a shorter mustache. His forearms had such thick hair I suspected his entire body was hairy as well. His deep-set eyes shifted to his partners as he shook my hand, as if to say, "One of you guys tell this chick she can't join us."

Richard Worthington was a potbellied, older man with a booming voice and a false cheeriness as he said, "Well, Molly. I sure hope we can keep up with you."

That was my cue to say that I hoped I could keep up with them, at which time one of them would suggest I join their wives.

"Thanks, Richard. I'm sure we'll all do our best."

He exchanged looks with Hank. The two of them got into their cart.

Chase then got into the driver's seat of our cart. Because I could not hit nearly as far as most men, my one hope of preventing myself from slowing play was to drive fast. So I said to Chase, "Is it all right if I take the wheel? I love driving golf carts with a passion. It's the only vehicle I know of where you can floor the accelerator and not get ticketed."

With a weak smile, Chase slid over and grabbed the bar that supported the car's roof. The starter waved us onto the tee-box and I followed the first cart, slamming on the brakes to jerk us to a halt just behind them.

We all got out. "Have you been golfing much, Molly?" Hank asked as he selected his driver from his bag.

"This is my first time out since last summer," I replied honestly.

"Oh, really?" Hank asked in a tone that made it clear he did not deem me fit to clean the spikes on his shoes. "Ah, look, Chase, Richard. Our wives have arrived. It's just the *three* of them playing today."

Again, I opted to pretend to be oblivious and scanned the fairway up ahead. At least the women were running a little late. If they got to the tee-box before the three of us hit our drives, there was no way I'd be allowed to stick with the men.

Richard cleared his throat loudly and asked me, "What's your handicap?"

If I admitted my handicap was higher than my age, he'd faint dead away, so I smiled and answered, "Two precocious children and a grouchy husband. Plus my left leg's shorter than my right, so I tend to hook my shots."

He didn't smile.

The men teed off first. They were going off the championship tees, which only the very best golfers were allowed to use. The three of them hit excellent drives. I would be hopelessly outclassed. I'd be lucky to stay within three strokes per hole of these men.

Knowing that after a ten-month layoff I'd be too rusty to use my driver, I grabbed my three-wood and trotted down the tiers to the women's tee. The men followed in the carts. To my chagrin, all three got out. They stood shoulder to shoulder at the edge of the women's tee-box.

No one spoke, but I could hear female laughter in the distance behind me. The wives were nearing. If I loused up my first shot, that would be it. The men would send me back to join the women and I'd never be able to ask about the bet they'd made with Preston.

"Keep your head down and take a nice easy swing," Hank Mueller offered just as I took my stance.

I hadn't taken a single shot and already he was giving me advice. This was so typical. Never would one man tell another man to "take a nice easy swing." Yet I'd probably golfed with more than thirty men over the years, and to the best of my recollection, every single one had given me advice, even those I could outplay.

The imaginary voice of that British announcer who's always whispering into the microphone prior to putts on TV now whispered in my ear. "The pressure is on Ms. Masters to make a good shot here. The gallery is holding its collective breath. Now, take a nice easy swing, and *for God's sake, don't screw up!*"

I took a ferocious swing. The ball went up, up...straight up. It dropped almost directly to my right, just a few yards off the tee, and splashed into some sort of mucky marsh where they were apparently cultivating water snakes or salamanders.

Though I wished the golf gremlins would come throttle me with my clubs till I was out of my misery once and for all, I turned and called to my partners, "Oops. That's an unplayable lie if there ever was one. I'll tee up another one and try again. Feel free to talk amongst yourselves."

"Say, Molly," Hank said, "I have an idea."

Before he could suggest I let them golf by themselves, I blurted, "How would you like to make a little bet?"

"A bet?" Hank repeated, grinning at Chase and Richard.

"That's right," I went on. "If I make a par on this hole, not counting that first shot, I get to stay in your foursome. If I don't I'll drop back and join the women."

Hank glanced at the sign on the women's tee, which showed it was 350 yards to the green. He chuckled and said, "Sure, Molly. Good luck."

Richard winked at Hank, who grinned and shook his head. Chase, however, gave me a reassuring smile. "Take as much time as you want."

If only I were at midseason form, I would stand a 10 or 20 percent chance of making a par. As it was, my odds were more like one in a hundred. I offered up a quick prayer to *puh-lease* either send down a bolt of lightning and electrocute me on the spot or prevent me from humiliating myself again. This time I hit the drive of my life: 220 yards, right down the middle of the fairway. I pretended not to be shocked, though that outdistanced the second-best drive of my life by at least twenty yards.

"There's a golf shot!" said Richard, using the tones of admiration that men use for sports talk and women reserve for cute babies.

"You got all of that one," Hank said.

"Nice shot, Molly," Chase said as I took a seat beside him.

I said, "Thanks," and floored the cart.

I couldn't gamble on continued shot-making of this caliber. When a miracle happens, you count your blessings, not demand that it recur immediately thereafter. I'd better ask some questions now, before we finished the first hole.

"So, Chase. I heard your usual playing partner, Preston Saunders, died recently. That must have been quite a shock."

Chase furrowed his brow, but replied, "You never expect someone you know to die. Especially not when they're only thirty-seven."

Up ahead, Hank and Richard had pulled off the path alongside my ball and were waiting for us. I eased up on the accelerator so I'd have more time to talk with Chase. "Did he die of natural causes?"

"Not unless you consider a gunshot to the chest a natural cause. But then, with Preston Saunders, you could consider that something of a natural consequence."

"What do you mean?" We reached the others. I stepped on the brake.

"The guy was a real SOB," Chase answered under his breath. "It finally caught up to him."

Despite my fine drive, my ball was farthest from the green, so according to golf etiquette and common sense, I had to go first. Richard hopped out of his cart and came over to me. "So," he said in his booming voice. "Looks like you're about one-thirty away. What club are you planning on using?"

Asking an opponent about their choice of clubs was not only bad form, but against the rules. He was trying to throw off my concentration. "My five-wood," I answered honestly but with a grin, realizing he had just made a tactical error. Trying to needle me was the best way to inspire me to play better.

I hit another wonderful shot. I was on the front edge in two strokes! Now all I had to do was two-putt on a totally unfamiliar green, with no practice. I looked at Richard, who was resting his crossed arms on his bloated belly.

He gave me a wink. That was Richard's second wink in the last five minutes. Maybe he had a facial tic. "Not bad. You left yourself one hell of a putt, though. Downhill. These greens are superfast, too." He walked back over to Hank, said something I couldn't catch, then they drove the short distance ahead to their balls.

Chase, who was waiting on our cart for me, was chuckling. He watched me start the motor, then said, "By golly, Miss Molly. You're trying to con us. You're fresh off the women's circuit, aren't you?"

I couldn't help but smile, my first sincere one since I'd arrived. He was really handsome, his dark skin accentuating his perfect teeth. "No, I'm a decent golfer, but that's all. I get the feeling your partners don't want me around, though."

"We've been playing together for a few years now. You know how it is."

"So the four of you were pretty close?"

A muscle in his jaw tightened. We'd already traveled the short distance to his ball, and he managed to escape the cart without answering. He took a long time selecting an iron. Hank, waiting near his own ball, called out, "Come on, Chase. Getting you to hurry is like pulling teeth."

Chase immediately hollered back, "Ah, ship it, Hank."

This seemed like their standard joke. Was Chase a dentist? And was Richard in the shipping business? Even if I didn't make my par, maybe I could talk to them at their businesses, if I could learn where they worked.

Chase hit an excellent approach shot and "stuck the green." Just then, up drove a skinny old man in a white cart with the word MARSHAL on the side in big black letters. I winced. *Not now! Please, don't blow my cover and say my last name!*

The marshal stopped, touched the brim of his pith helmet in a cowboy-style greeting, then spat out a wad of chewing tobacco. Perhaps he was taking his job title a tad too seriously. In a lazy drawl, he murmured, "How's it goin', Mr. Worthington, Mr. Mueller?"

"Fine," they answered simultaneously.

He nodded, then turned his cart around. For a moment, I hoped he would ignore Chase Groves and me, but then he looked back and called out, "How 'bout you, Mrs. Masters? Enjoying the course?"

"Immensely," I answered through my clenched teeth.

As the marshal drove away, Richard and Hank exchanged a look of surprise, then eyed me.

They both hit their balls onto the green. They shared a quiet conversation in their cart as they headed to the green. Discussing the coincidence of last names, no doubt. Once they realized my connection to Preston through my cartoon, that would be it for eliciting information from the two of them. Chase seemed infinitely more friendly, though. If he was indeed a dentist, I could schedule an appointment. I shuddered involuntarily. An unnecessary dentist appointment? Yeech! I had to be out of my mind!

Chase let me get behind the wheel again. He edged as far away from me as possible on the seat. Ignoring his body language, I asked, "Are you a dentist?"

"How'd you know that?"

"The joke that Hank made. I'm guessing that he's in the shipping business."

"Yeah. And Richard's an architect. How 'bout yourself?"

To avoid the subject of greeting cards and cartoons, I pulled up beside the other cart and stared at the green as if transfixed. "Richard was right. I've got quite a downhill lie."

All three men had putts ranging from twenty to thirty feet, but mine was just on the apron. This meant I couldn't mark my ball, but also meant the flag, called the "pin" for some reason, could stay in the hole for my shot. Sometimes the ball hits the pin and drops in. That had happened a few times for opponents of mine, but never for me.

They marked their balls and stood back. Hank flashed me a smile. "Looks like you're away, Molly."

As if I couldn't see that for myself. My ball was perched on top of a hill. If I misjudged the speed, it could easily roll clear across the green.

I went through the motions of lining up my putt, which meant getting down on one knee, holding up my putter, closing one eye, and leaning to one side and then the other. Truth be told, I've never so much as figured out what golfers are *looking* at when they go through these gyrations. But it was a nice stall technique that allowed me to ask more questions.

Donning a look of intense concentration while staring at the green blur of grass before me, I said, "This must be strange, playing with me when you were used to playing with Preston Saunders. Was he any good?"

"Yeah," Hank said. "He was a scratch golfer."

I gave an appreciative whistle. "You must miss him quite a bit, huh?"

Hank and Richard exchanged glances. Hank crossed his hairy arms and said to me, "It's hard to see, but the green breaks sharply to the left."

That was a clue to do the opposite and play for a break to the right. It was also a clue that they were suspicious about my relationship to Preston. If they weren't going to answer my questions, I may as well putt.

"Bombs away," I murmured and putted. The ball rolled to the left down the slope, then curved back slowly to the right...and dropped into the hole, dead center. "Yes!" I cried. "A birdie!" Two wonderful, long shots and now a great putt! Lightning had struck three times in the same spot! "You do consider this *within* par, don't you? I won the bet, right?"

"So you did," Richard grumbled. He winked at me again, but looked none too happy.

The men quickly got down to the business of making their own putts. They each sank their shots in two, parring the hole.

As we walked back to our carts, Hank asked, "Do you work, Molly?"

It struck me as pointless to lie, all the while trying to get the truth from them. Yet I might be able to avoid the subject of art. "I write greeting cards."

"Do you do your own artwork?"

So much for avoidance. "Mmm-hmm," I murmured. They froze. I pretended not to notice their reaction. No seasoned golfer would dawdle around a green under normal circumstances. Especially not at this course, where slow play was considered a more serious crime than murder.

"Say, Molly," Richard said. "Maybe I know your husband. What's his name?"

"Jim."

"*Jim* Masters?" Richard repeated, smiling at me, though his eyes were fierce. "And he's an artist?"

"No, he's an electrical engineer. Why?"

"So you're the artist in the family. Are you a cartoonist?"

"Yes." I returned my putter to my bag and got behind

the wheel, but the men were still standing, watching me. "We'd better get to the next tee, guys."

Hank grabbed a post on the cart. "Hold on a minute, here. Did you know Preston Saunders?"

"Yes, but only vaguely. He was just an acquaintance of mine. I went to school with his wife, but I've lived out of town until recently."

"So you sign your cartoons 'Masters.' Right?" Richard asked. He and Hank were really ganging up on me, but Chase was listening to all of this in silence.

"Right, but what does this—"

"That bastard," Hank snarled. "He ripped us off again!" On that note, the three men finally got into the carts.

As we drove to the second tee, I asked Chase, "Again?"

He said nothing and didn't meet my eyes. It occurred to me that I had about as much clout in this country club as a roasted marshmallow. There was nothing I could do to stop them if they refused to honor our bet. Chase had called Preston an "SOB," and Hank had called him "that bastard," but I still hadn't learned what Richard thought of him.

"The three of you don't seem to have liked Preston very much. Why? Did he cheat?"

Chase shook his head. "Golf brought out the best in him. That was the one time he never cheated."

He leaped out of the cart before I'd even braked.

The second fairway bent at almost a right angle around a lake. This formation is called a dogleg, though it resembles any mammal's leg, the green being the paw. From the championship tee, which would be the doggy's hip joint, it was 220 yards to the dog's elbow. The women's tee, closer to the green in acknowledgment of our weaker swings, was located forty yards away, about one-fifth of the way down the dog's thigh.

"We're going to cut off this leg," Richard told me.

"And they say golf isn't a violent sport," I joked.

Again, no one smiled. As Richard had foretold, all three men not only hit across the lake, but to the far side of the fairway where they would have only a seventy-yard pitch shot to the green.

"Chase, let Molly take the cart," Hank instructed. Chase grabbed his pitching wedge and his putter, and jogged along the path after Richard's cart, rounding the lake on the green's side. They were going to try to get to the green fast enough to give me the slip! Those welchers!

I floored it and headed to the women's tee. From this angle, there was no chance of my hitting over the lake to where the men were. My only hope was to come around the leg as fast as they did. I was not adverse to faking shots and throwing the ball up ahead of me, but they could still see me from the other side of the lake, and besides, I have a lousy arm.

It took me three shots till I was close enough to reach the green. Even though I'd practically played golf polo, barely stopping the cart to swing, the men were already putting. Chase watched for my shot and waved me on while Richard returned the pin to the hole. My ball stayed on the green, but it was too late. The three of them had already putted. Drat!

As I neared, they were having a conference, their heads together. Hank gestured angrily and Richard, hands in pockets, shrugged. Chase looked over at me. I felt like the tag-along little sister whom the older brother and his buddies were about to ditch.

Sure enough, Chase was wearing a guilty smile as he rejoined me. He said, "Molly, we just realized, you actually lost the bet, since you said you'd *make* par, not *within* par."

"What's the difference—"

"You got a birdie, not a par."

"Well, technically, but—"

"Each of our wives is playing just one group back. You can wait at the third tee and join up with them."

As he spoke, I considered my options. One: Leap onto

the cart and refuse to budge. (I'd have to get off to hit my shot at the next tee, though, at which time they would drive away without me.) Two: Insist we call the marshal to arbitrate our dispute. (He'd side with the men, not with an unknown female nonmember.) Three: Taunt them into yet another bet, which I had virtually no chance of winning.

I was stuck.

"But what about the cart and—"

While I spoke, he took out my clubs and set them on the grass near the cart path. "My wife will have a cart for you to share. It was nice playing with you."

They may have prevented me from talking to them during golf, but they'd never make me resign this easily. I still had questions for them. "Say, Chase, I haven't found a dentist here in town yet. Are you taking new patients?"

"Sure am. Just call my office and we'll get you scheduled."

He waved and drove off. I made a couple of haphazard putts, then kicked my ball into the hole and carried my clubs to the third tee to await their wives.

Maybe this would all work out in my favour. I would have an easier time getting women to drop their guard. They might know about "Mike" Masters's cartoon and the bet their husbands had made. Plus, it would be much easier for me to ask other women about a fight that had occurred among men.

TWELVE

Aft!

AFTER A SHORT wait, three women drove up in a pair of golf carts. Out of the first cart stepped a tall and shapely, absolutely stunning African-American woman. She had very short hair, which accentuated her remarkable large eyes and high cheekbones. Carlton was a small, predominantly white town. She and I traveled in different social circles, and I'd have remembered her had I ever seen her before. I rose from the bench and met her halfway to the cart path.

"You must be Molly Masters," she said with a melodic voice that bore a slight Jamaican accent. "Hello. I am Emma Groves, Chase's wife."

"How did you know my—"

"Hank Mueller called the clubhouse on his cellular phone. They sent someone out to contact us." She gestured with an open palm toward the two women behind her. "This is Hank's wife, Sabrina. And Kimberly Worthington, Richard's wife."

Perhaps the old adage about long-time married couples looking alike had some truth to it. Kimberly had some of Richard's physical characteristics: she was plump and elderly, though, unlike Richard, her hair was dyed blond. She also shared his loud, aggressive mannerisms as she pumped my arm vigorously and announced to the world how pleased she was to meet me.

And, as with Hank, I instantly didn't like Sabrina. The first thing she said to me was, "What does your husband do for a living?" She nodded politely when I told her, but the damage had already been done. She wore her thick, auburn hair in a pageboy flip that seemed straight out of an old yearbook. Her face, though attractive, had an unnatural sheen caused by either makeup or recent cosmetic surgery. It was hard to guess what age she was aiming to emulate, but she looked to be in her late thirties.

"What did you shoot on the first two holes, honey?" Kimberly asked me, pulling out a pencil to add my name to her scorecard.

"I got a three on the first hole and a seven on the second, though my seventh stroke was technically a kick."

"Whatever it takes, honey," Kimberly replied, grinning.

I checked over her shoulder, glad to see that she'd written my name as Molly, not Honey.

"Whoa," Sabrina said, lifting my ball retriever slightly from my bag, which, unasked, she was loading onto Emma's cart. "Look at this. She's going to be tough competition."

Emma whistled and shook her head. Though baffled at what my ball retriever had to do with my score, I replied, "I use that a lot. My clubs can double as divining rods, my shots find water so often."

"That experience will come in handy," Emma said. I marveled at how beautiful she was as she went on. "We subtract one stroke for each ball we find."

"That's how I got a five on the last hole," Sabrina said, poofing up her voluminous hair. "It was actually an eight, but I got three balls out of the lake. Care to join us in our friendly wager?"

Uh-oh. I'd had a bad enough experience betting with the men. "I'm...not much of a gambler."

"That's all right," Sabrina said with a shrug. "It's not much of a bet. Loser buys dessert." She smiled.

"Dessert?" I scanned for cracks in Sabrina's makeup, but saw none.

"The country club has a cheesecake that is out of this world," Emma said with a wide smile, which I returned. As with her husband, Chase, there was something immensely likable about her. I was as drawn to her as I felt repelled by Sabrina and Hank Mueller.

"That's the only reason I joined," Sabrina said, lighting up a cigarette as she approached the tee. "The pastry chef. He goes, I go. Speaking of which, we need to hit before that damned marshal gets on our asses again, so I'm going." She took a big draw on her cigarette, then rested it on the red marker that designated the women's tee. She could have just stashed it in her hair. In virtually the same movement, she stepped into her stance and swung. Her ball veered to the right of the fairway and hit a tree solidly. "Oh, damn," she said, shaking her head as she retrieved her cigarette. "That tree got in my way."

"Nice shot, Sabrina," Emma said. "I'd say you're a three-length farther down."

"Excuse me?" I asked, wondering what a "three-length" was.

"Hitting a tree is just bad luck," Emma explained. "You move your ball to where it would have been, had the tree not been planted in the wrong spot."

I smiled, thinking these women were my kind of golfers. "So when we miss putts, do we get to blame the cup for being in the wrong spot?"

Sabrina chuckled and took another long draw on her cigarette. "Why not? It's a good concept." I couldn't quite decide what it was about her that bothered me.

The rest of us hit our drives. Mine landed on the left side of the fairway some twenty yards ahead of Kimberly's. Emma and Sabrina dropped us off at Kimberly's ball, while they headed toward theirs on the opposite side of the fairway. Judging by how far Sabrina tossed her ball after picking it up, Kimberly would have been better off had she hit a tree.

Kimberly waggled her ample hips, brushed back a lock of her would-have-been-gray hair, then took an awkward swing at her ball, sending a divot of dirt and grass farther than her ball. She shrugged and stepped toward her ball, making no move to replace the divot. "Oh, well. We won't count that shot. Call it, 'ground under repair.'" She glanced back at the hole her club-head had left. "Sure needs repair *now,* at any rate."

I laughed. The phrase "ground under repair" actually referred to designated areas of the course where maintenance crews had recently dug up the turf. She hit a much better second shot, though that would have been her third by anyone else's count.

My ball went just fifteen yards with my next swing. Kimberly immediately called on my behalf, "Ground under repair!"

The four of us finished the hole and awarded ourselves scores none of us actually earned. Hoping to learn about the men's relationships, I asked at the next tee-box, "Do your husbands make wagers during their round, too?"

"Constantly," Sabrina answered, rolling her eyes while poofing her hair—reminiscent of Mae West, except with auburn tresses. "They bet money, not pastry."

"Major money?"

"No, just fifty dollars a round."

That was odd. Why the enormous bet about my cartoon, then?

"They're ruthless about it," Kimberly said. "It's not the money, it's that macho 'Mine's bigger than yours' thing."

"Kimberly!" Sabrina admonished, letting out a smoker's wheeze as she laughed.

"If they're that serious about small bets," I said, trying to sound casual, "I wonder how they'd handle something larger."

"Chase would step on someone's face to win a big bet," Emma said, a hint of anger seeping into her voice.

"So would Hank," Sabrina said. "And he'd be wearing cleats at the time."

"Richard's the same way. Which is probably why they never bet more than fifty on anything." Kimberly paused. "Then again, Richard knows I'd kill him if I ever found out he bet a lot of money. So who's to say he's telling the truth about the amounts?"

She glanced at her two friends, who both looked thoughtful for a moment, then agreed that was a good question. Kimberly chuckled and wagged a pudgy finger at me. "Come to think of it, we missed quite an opportunity with you, honey. You could've spied on 'em for us."

Imagine that, I thought to myself.

Sabrina narrowed her eyes at me. "Did they make any bets while you were with them?"

There was no reason to admit that *I'd* made a bet to avoid being forced to join this current group. "No, but I was only with them for one and a half holes. They told me they've been golfing together for a number of years now." I paused. "Since they're so competitive, they must get into quite a few arguments. Or are they all good friends?"

Kimberly shrugged and looked at Emma. "Do men even *have* friends?"

Sabrina abruptly turned on a heel and said over her shoulder, "Let's not talk about this now. Who's up?"

Just what was it that Sabrina suddenly didn't want to talk about? I wondered. The men's friendships? Her husband, Hank, had changed subjects at almost the same exact point—right when I'd asked about the friendships among the four men. Yet the three men had seemed to be good friends, so the trouble must have been with Preston. Now I was getting somewhere. But if I asked too many questions they'd get suspicious. The last thing I wanted was to get bumped back again, this time to a group of strangers.

This hole was a par three, the theory being that the golfer

hits the drive onto the green, then two-putts into the hole. We all hit decent shots, landing within a few yards of the green. Emma was farthest from the hole. She hit a lousy second shot that went clear over the green. She immediately reached into her pocket and dropped a second ball, saying, "Mulligan toss, girls," as she hit this one onto the green.

"Yes!" Sabrina said. She and Kimberly promptly picked up their balls and threw them onto the green.

This was more than a little unusual, but I merely watched them in silence. A "mulligan" was a term commonly used by weekend golfers—a flubbed shot was ignored and the golfer merely hit a new one. I'd never heard of a "mulligan toss," though. Was I supposed to compliment them on the accuracy of their throws?

"She's taking a mulligan, so now all of us get to throw our balls forward," Kimberly explained to me.

Never having been one to argue with a gift horse, I followed suit and got an excellent bounce and roll. I wound up making a par, counting the toss as a stroke.

The women's casual attitude about golf gave me an idea for a cartoon. A man, sitting on the ground with a bent golf club in one hand, rubs a huge bump on his head and glares at a woman. The woman says to him, "I *know* you're supposed to yell 'Fore,' but that's when your *ball* goes *forward*. This time my *club* went *backward*, so naturally I yelled 'Aft!'"

Sergeant Tommy would no doubt call the cartoon sexist.

The next hole had a lake to the left of the fairway, which my ball just missed. After hitting our second shots, we scanned the water, and Sabrina pointed to someone's lost ball that looked to be well beyond reach.

"What do you think?" Sabrina asked, lighting another cigarette. "Too far?"

"Link hands, girls," Emma said by way of reply. "We shall give it a try." With the flourish of a fencer unsheathing a sword, Emma extended the longest ball retriever I'd ever seen. We linked hands in a human chain to support her as she leaned out over the water. Moments later, we cheered as she pulled up the dripping ball.

"This is why we always try to fill our foursome," Kimberly told me. "We can lean farther out with four than three." She patted her hips and added, "Good ballast."

Minutes later, we'd finished up the hole, but to my surprise, Emma drove us right past the next tee. "We are skipping this hole," she explained. "Trees and traps everywhere." We came upon their husbands near the green. "Driving through, gentlemen," she called to them with a wave. Apparently the men were used to this hole-skipping, for they showed no reaction. She said to me, "They are so anal when it comes to golf. 'Do not touch your ball. Do not talk while I am hitting.' You would think it was brain surgery, for all the fuddy-duddy reverence they attach to it."

I smiled at the word *fuddy-duddy*, which sounded amusing in the midst of Emma's careful, accented diction. "I heard your husbands were involved in quite an altercation recently."

She stopped the cart. "Who told you that?"

"The guy at the counter."

"It was all Preston's fault. We had no recourse."

"We?"

She pursed her lips. The other cart pulled up behind ours. All three women headed to the next tee at once. "This hole's got a really wide tee-box," Kimberly called back to me. "We all go off together."

My stomach was in knots as I wondered who "we" was—had Emma been part of this fight that all but required police intervention? My best course of action to learn more was simply to continue to befriend Emma.

Again, teeing off simultaneously was a new one, but I was willing to try, though I had visions of a midair ball collision or, worse, getting hit in the head by Sabrina's club. The four of us teed up in a line, then Kimberly called out, "Okay, ladies. On the count of three. One...

two...three." We all swung, and, to my delight, I hit my second-best drive of the day, my ball outdistancing the others by at least thirty yards.

"Nice shot, Molly!" Emma cried. "Maybe we should play best ball on this hole." The others immediately murmured their approval, and Emma turned toward me. "Do you object?"

"Not at all," I said, though this was yet another golfing first for me.

The three unused balls were scooped up, and Emma was elected to hit the second shot on my ball. She hit it well, but a little to the left of the green, where it rolled into a sand trap.

Fortunately, it wasn't my turn next. It once took me ten strokes to get out of a trap on a par three. When we neared the green, Sabrina hopped down into the trap.

"Need my water bottle?" Kimberly called to her.

Sabrina shook her head. "I brought mine." She poured water on the sand near our ball. My eyes widened and I had to look away momentarily to keep from laughing. If the marshal were to see the club's pristine sand being treated like this, he'd charge us with destruction of private property. Sabrina formed a sand mound, then picked the ball up and set it on her hand-crafted sand tee. One swing later, the ball was resting a few feet from the cup, and Kimberly confidently and briskly knocked it in. We exchanged a round of high-fives.

By playing only the one ball, we had caught up with the group ahead, which was just starting to tee off. Emma "you-hooed" at them and they waited as she drove up and asked if we could play through. They complied, though they shot us less-than-charitable glances, and we headed down to the women's tee.

All of us but Kimberly hit good drives, so she picked hers up.

"So, Emma," I said as we drove through the fairway, "how long have you lived in Carlton?"

"Five years," she replied.

"Did you know Preston Saunders very well?"

'Yes.'' She gave me a look that implied, "the stories I could tell,'' but she said no more. She got out of the cart, grabbed an iron, and hit with newfound power, as if she'd visualized that the little white ball was Preston's head.

To establish camaraderie, I immediately said when she returned to the cart, "I didn't care for Preston."

"You knew him?" she asked, sounding quite surprised.

Not wanting to reveal my cards till I'd seen hers, I answered casually, "His daughter baby-sits for my children."

Her expression suddenly grew fierce. "As far as I am concerned, that man—'' She stopped abruptly as Sabrina's and Kimberly's cart neared. "Here comes Sabrina. I try not to speak about the lawsuit when she is near."

"Lawsuit?" I repeated, but Emma's flawless smile had returned as she waved at the others. My mind raced. A lawsuit brought by her against Preston, maybe? Or vice versa? Either way, how could Sabrina be involved?

"Did you see how far I just hit?" Emma asked the others, pointing down the fairway. "That little speck of white next to the green is Anthony."

While our playing partners complimented her, I muttered in confusion, "Anthony?"

"Yes. I sometimes name my balls, but only when they behave. My husband, Chase, on the other hand, says, 'What a piece of crap' every time he hits a bad shot. So last Christmas I got him a box of balls with the words *Piece of Crap* imprinted on them."

Though the other two women had to have heard this anecdote before, we all laughed. We shared a short cart ride to my ball, but when I asked, *"What* lawsuit?" Emma told me in a calm, sincere voice that we would have to "discuss this some other time." Soon the four of us had finished out the hole.

"That's enough golf for me," Kimberly announced. This

was very unexpected, as we were only on the eighth hole of our eighteen-hole course.

"Me too," Sabrina echoed. "Enough of this golf cart. I'm hittin' the dessert cart."

"How about you?" Emma asked me.

Chatting over cheesecake would be my best bet for getting the women to talk about their husbands. "I could go for some dessert now."

"Good. We'll give ourselves holes-in-one from here on," Emma said. "I suppose one day I should at least *look* at the back nine."

Though having someone drive by is always distracting, Emma gave the occasional disgruntled golfer a wave, and they smiled and returned the gesture. I asked her how old her son was and learned he was just ten months younger than Nathan. At my suggestion that we get the boys together to play sometime, she surprised me by inviting Nathan and me for lunch at her house on Thursday.

I accepted, but silently worried whether or not I would even be here two days from now. If Jim had his way, the kids and I would be in Florida by then. Our original agreement gave the police until Friday night to solve the murder, provided I stayed out of it. My only violation—at least the only one Jim knew about—was this afternoon of golf. That was just a minor breach. I may have ruffled a few feathers where Preston's former partners were concerned, but none of them had tried to kill me. Not even once.

To appease Jim, my best course of action was to demonstrate I intended to live up to our agreement by making plane reservations for Saturday morning. Then, just in case Jim disagreed about how severe this breach of mine had been, I would schedule as many appointments as possible between now and then to make it appear I was too busy to get into any trouble.

Yet another reason for me to go ahead and schedule a visit to Dr. Chase Groves. And if Emma and I never got another opportunity to discuss the lawsuit she'd mentioned, I might be able to get Chase to talk about it.

Having settled on a plan, I used the public phone outside the clubhouse rest rooms and dialed Chase Groves's office. All the while a couple of waitresses nearby were grousing about their children. Just as the receptionist answered the phone, a blond waitress said in a half shout, "You think that's bad? Wait till your son gets to be mine's age!" I had to cover my free ear. Chase happened to have had a cancellation, so I managed to set an appointment for tomorrow morning. Not wanting to keep the others waiting, I made a mental note to get plane reservations for Saturday as soon as I got home.

I joined the others at our table, a square butcher-block top surrounded by four tall wing-backed chairs in gingham floral prints. The tables were staggered in such a way that the overall effect was more one of sitting in a conversation nook in a living room than being seated in an enormous restaurant.

Our waitress was the strawberry blonde who'd been complaining about her son. She looked to be a few years older than I. She would have been pretty had her frown lines not been quite so chasmlike. She brought the others the drinks they had already ordered. She quickly set each glass on the table, sloshing out some of Sabrina's margarita in the process, then turned on a heel without acknowledging me.

"Excuse me," I called after her. I had to rotate completely around in my seat, then kneel so that I could peer at her over the top of the wing-back. This was probably not the most dignified manner in which to get someone's attention. At least my chair didn't topple over backward. "I'd like an iced tea, please."

She turned and glared at me. "I'll get it for you just as soon as I'm done with my other tables."

My companions were smiling at me as I settled back into

my oversized chair. "It must be me. This is the second surly waitress I've had this week."

"Oh, it's not you, it's *me* she doesn't like," Sabrina said, clicking her tongue.

"Oh? Do you two have a history?"

Sabrina nodded. "There's a regular flood under our bridge. You see, Lindsay is my brother's jilted girlfriend."

"Your *brother* dumped her? And she has a grudge against *you?*"

"We were all just kids," she said with a slight shrug. "Lindsay and I were seniors in high school, back in Ohio. My brother was just sixteen at the time."

She paused. Emma and Kimberly were only half listening to her. They must have already heard Sabrina Mueller's story. Leaning back in her chair, she flicked her wrist in a mannerism that reminded me of Stephanie. That, I finally realized, was why I had taken such an immediate dislike to her; the two women had such similar body language.

"Now that I think about it," she continued, "my friendship with her, with Lindsay, was just the typical rebellious teenager-type thing. She was not exactly wild, but she was certainly from the wrong side of…well, you know what I mean."

I nodded, gritting my teeth. I wondered if Sabrina would even want to be having this conversation if she'd realized how many tax brackets she was speaking down to at that very moment.

"She used to come over to my house after school." Sabrina leaned closer to me and whispered, "We smoked dope together."

By now, Emma and Kimberly, who were sitting next to each other, began their own separate conversation. I, too, was beginning to lose interest in Sabrina's tale, but hoped it would soon be winding to a close.

"Then my brother started hanging around with us, too," she went on. "It never occurred to me that he might actually be attracted to…someone like her. I mean, it was one thing to be friends with her, but quite another to..." She shuddered, letting her voice trail off.

"To make a long story short," she continued, "she got pregnant and refused to get an abortion. As you can imagine, it would have ruined Preston's life if he'd had to marry her at sixteen. And, after all, it *was* her fault. She was old enough to have known better than to let herself get pregnant."

My jaw had dropped at the name. "*Preston?* Your brother's name is *Preston?*"

She raised an eyebrow. "That's right. Preston Saunders." She gave a sad sigh. "I suppose you heard his name on the news, if not from our husbands. He was killed last week."

THIRTEEN

Déjà Vu All Over Again

IT FELT AS IF the air had been sucked out of the room. My mind raced. Sabrina was watching me in silence, an expression of perplexed concern on her face.

For a moment, I had a terrible thought: What if Cherokee Taylor was Preston's illegitimate son? Tiffany might've unknowingly fallen for her half brother.

But simple arithmetic put that theory to rest. Preston had been thirty-seven when he died. If he got a girl pregnant when he was sixteen, his child had to be twenty or twenty-one. Cherokee was eighteen.

At least this new information cleared up a question my interrupted conversation with Emma had given me: Emma simply hadn't wanted to deride Preston in front of his sister. "Actually," I said, trying to summon some semblance of normal behavior, "I'm friends with...I know Stephanie Saunders. I went to school with her." That would be the very same Stephanie Saunders who'd failed to mention that one of the *three* names on the list of Preston's bettors was *his brother-in-law!*

"Oh?" Sabrina said, raising her very plucked eyebrows in surprise.

Emma and Kimberly's private conversation beside us came to an abrupt halt. They both turned to face us.

Emma asked, "You attended Carlton High?"

"Yes, I did." I couldn't resist adding as a private joke,

"Seems like it was just last week. Time sure flies." I returned my attention to Sabrina. "So Stephanie is your sister-in-law."

She grimaced. "Don't remind me."

"The two of you don't get along?"

"A major understatement. When Hank's business brought him here, in the same town with that woman..." She focused on the ceiling for several seconds, as if searching for strong enough words. "Well, I almost left him rather than make the move."

"Knowing Stephanie, I can understand that."

Emma and Kimberly were still paying strict attention to us, so I asked, "Do either of you know her, too?"

"Oh, honey," Kimberly said with a snort, "it's impossible to belong to the Carlton Country Club and not know Stephanie Saunders. She doesn't play golf; she just plays Queen Bee."

At that point, Lindsay, the apple of a very young Preston's eye, returned with my iced tea. No one spoke as she set my glass down.

Sensitized by my new knowledge, I noticed every painful detail about her appearance. The cheap dye-job of her strawberry-blond hair. The short black dress uniform with puffy quarter-sleeves. The white apron, stained with what looked like a thumb-sized smear of chocolate sauce. Black fishnet stockings. Maybe management had thought the uniform would appeal to its wealthy clientele. And apparently they were right, because the place was doing a good business. Yet here was a forty-year-old woman dressed up like a French maid, taking dessert orders from Sabrina Saunders Mueller, whose family had apparently disowned her and her illegitimate child.

If Lindsay knew we'd been talking about her, she didn't let on. Emma and Kimberly both ordered cheesecake, then excused themselves to use the rest room. My appetite was gone. I ordered a chocolate parfait, figuring if anything could restore my appetite, that would do the trick.

The moment Lindsay walked away with our order, I asked Sabrina, "Does Stephanie know about Preston's child?"

She paused, then gave a little shrug, "I would assume so." Her vision drifted in the direction of the bathrooms, as if she were anxious for her friends to return. She frowned. "Now that Preston's gone, Stephanie will want to cut off all of my contact with the baby."

Confused, I furrowed my brow, then realized Sabrina had changed gears and was now talking about Michael Saunders, Stephanie's baby.

Sabrina took a halting breath. Almost in tears, she muttered, more to herself than to me, "Hank and I have always wanted to be parents, but I can't have children. Yet that bitch Stephanie gets pregnant. There's no justice."

This subject brought back painful memories. Ten years ago, Jim and I had been heartbroken when I had a miscarriage of my first pregnancy. We'd already told the world our wonderful news and had begun decorating the nursery. Long afterwards, I felt hollowed out, as if I'd lost my uterus and my heart along with that baby. The miscarriage happened to coincide with Lauren's wedding and caused us to cancel what would have been my first return visit to Carlton in seven years. It felt like punishment for my sin against Lauren when she and I were eighteen.

But Sabrina was not someone I was comfortable sharing my feelings with, so I merely murmured words of condolence. She assured me that she had learned to accept her childlessness, though these words contradicted her previous ones. As she spoke, she periodically pushed on her hair, and suddenly I recalled having seen that hair someplace prior to today.

"I remember seeing you now at the funeral." At the funeral service, I'd noticed an auburn-colored hairdo in the front row, but hadn't seen the face that went with it. Now that I thought about it, I *didn't* recall having seen Hank. "I must have seen your husband there, too, and had forgotten."

She whipped out a pack of cigarettes from her pocket and selected one, her hands trembling slightly. "No, Hank wasn't in town that day."

He missed his wife's brother's funeral? That was rather heartless. Which reminded me: Emma Groves hadn't been there, either, though I now recalled having seen Chase there.

In an unexpected demonstration of prompt service, Lindsay returned with our desserts. Sabrina, I noted, didn't even look up the entire time Lindsay was at our table. I took a spoonful of my parfait, trying to shrug off a tinge of guilt at the thought of how intensely my children would have relished this dessert that I could take or leave.

"You must be the aunt whom Tiffany stayed with for a few days last week," I said. "Tiffany's my children's favorite baby-sitter. I had no idea she had a half brother or sister in town."

Sabrina grimaced and took a pause from the cigarette she was inhaling along with her cherry pie. "She doesn't. I ran into Lindsay for the first time in…two decades last year here at the club. But, unfortunately, I suppose, I asked her about her son. She'd had a little boy. She said he died in a car accident."

"Oh, how horrible!" Then I paused, trying to make sense of this news. Her son had died, yet minutes ago Lindsay and another waitress had been complaining noisily about parenting. Then I realized that this affair with Preston had taken place more than twenty years ago. She'd most likely had another child or two since then. "How old was he when it happened?"

"She didn't say. She just spat out at me, 'He died in a car accident,' and turned her back on me. As if the whole thing were *my* fault." She shook her head indignantly, then glanced straight ahead and smiled. I was slightly startled to see Emma already seated in her chair. The tall, curved wing-backs had blocked my peripheral view.

"There you are," Sabrina said, as Kimberly returned to the table, too. "You were gone so long I was starting to think you fell in."

"We were adding up our scores." Emma laced her fingers and flashed one of her stunning smiles at me. "The four of us tied. According to our rules, that means we buy for the person on our right. So thank you for the cheesecake, Molly."

I RANG the doorbell at Stephanie's house. Estelle, the nurse, answered. She gave me a smile that showed she remembered me and said, "Hello. Mrs. Saunders is upstairs." She glanced behind her shoulder, then whispered, "You wouldn't happen to know anyone looking to hire a private nurse, would you? I could start right away."

"No, I don't. Sorry. I'll let you know if I hear of anything." This gave me the opportunity to speak to Estelle in private and complete our conversation from this morning.

I stepped inside and said quietly, "When I was here earlier today, you started to tell me about another time when Stephanie was going through her safe."

She nodded and whispered, "I got the feeling she was searching it as a result of something the policeman had said to her."

"What did he say?"

"I really don't know. I was upstairs at the time and couldn't hear. But when I came down, I saw—"

"Molly, hello," said Stephanie as she headed down the spiral staircase. "I thought I heard the doorbell." Wearing purple super-stretched pants and a matching knit top, she was not dressed to her usual standards. I almost outclassed her in my preppy-putter look, having come straight from the club. Stephanie smiled at the nurse. "Estelle, I didn't realize you were still here. I thought you'd already left to get those supplies Mikey so desperately needs."

"I was just on my way out," she answered. She curled her lips at me to show her frustration with her employer, then said to me, "*Will* I be able to get anything for you, too?"

"Uh, no." She had hit the word *will* so hard it could only have been meant as a clue. She was trying to tell me Stephanie had searched the safe for Preston's will. "But *thank you* for asking."

Estelle nodded and went out the door.

So Stephanie apparently referred to a copy of Preston's will. She might have suddenly become worried she hadn't been named the sole beneficiary. Perhaps Tommy had inquired about another relative, such as the Muellers.

"It's been so long since I had a baby," Stephanie said to me, letting out a sigh of deep exhaustion and sweeping some errant tresses into place. "I'd forgotten how they go through diapers." She turned and headed for the kitchen. "I've got to get some lemonade. Mikey nurses constantly. It sucks the fluid out of me so fast I feel like a wrung-out sponge."

I followed, realizing this was the first time I'd been in the kitchen since I'd seen Preston's body. I eyed my surroundings for signs of the previous violence. The rug was now spotless as was the oak kitchen floor where Preston's body had lain.

Stephanie strolled to the refrigerator, showing no signs of the hesitancy and queasiness I felt. This particular part of her home had been where her husband had died a horrible death. Yet she seemed utterly unfazed. There was something dreadfully wrong.

All along, I had tried to blame shock for her odd actions. She definitely wasn't in shock now. The only other explanation I could come up with chilled me: that Stephanie had killed Preston.

She filled a beautiful, hand-blown indigo-colored glass with lemonade from a matching pitcher, which she returned to the refrigerator. After taking a long sip, she said, "Oh.

I'm sorry. Would you like some lemonade? It's fresh-squeezed. That Estelle is an absolute wonder. I've offered her a permanent position."

I shook my head and sat down at the oak, country-style kitchen table. "Okay, Stephanie. Explain to me why you didn't tell me Hank Mueller was Preston's brother-in-law."

"Was that important?" An infuriating smirk crossed her lips.

"Oh, cut the crap, Stephanie. I've known you too long to fall for the blond-bimbo routine. What are you trying to pull on me, and why? You'd better clue me in fast or you're on your own."

She pulled out a ladder-back chair across from me and, in what looked almost like a swoon, slid down onto it. "What do you mean?" she asked, appearing to be quite shaken by my words.

"I'll tell Sergeant Tommy everything I know. And I won't do one more thing to try and vindicate Tiffany, which, as you might recall, is how you suckered me into this whole mess in the first place."

Stephanie pursed her lips so tightly they looked white despite her lipstick. As if she were making a supreme sacrifice, she eventually said, "I neglected to tell you, because it was our own private business."

"If that's the best you can do, I'm going straight to Tommy Newton with everything I know."

Stephanie clicked her tongue in annoyance at me, leaned back in her chair, and crossed her arms. "Preston and Hank Mueller disliked each other, intensely. Preston felt forced to keep up social appearances. They were both excellent golfers, and when the Muellers joined the club where we were already members, Preston realized it would have been uncouth not to invite him to play a round or two together. Once they did, I suppose they enjoyed themselves. Although, personally, I think golf is the world's most idiotic sport. Grown men thwacking away at a tiny little ball, chasing it for miles. Honestly, Molly. Why ever do you do it?"

"Most sports are comprised of 'thwacking at' or 'chasing' some sort of ball. Let's just get on with your story, shall we?"

She gave a lazy sigh. "At any rate, Hank joined Preston's regular golf group and they went to the club every Tuesday. Even when their game was snowed out or rained out, they met for drinks."

"Who belonged to the foursome before Hank joined last year?"

"It was some older fellow. He dropped out of the group six months prior to Hank Mueller's arrival in Carlton." She gestured casually with one hand. "Had a heart attack or moved away. Whatever."

"Why did Hank and Preston dislike each other?"

She widened her eyes, but said only, "Personality clash."

"That's it? A 'personality clash'? A *clash* that was so severe you neglected to even mention to me the two men were in-laws?"

She smiled at me, took a long drink of lemonade, and murmured, "Mm-hmm."

"Oh, come off it, Stephanie! That excuse is utter nonsense, and we both know it!"

"'Come *off* it'?" She rolled her eyes. "You sound like a child, Molly. No wonder you managed to blend in with my daughter's friends so easily."

I balled my fists on my lap, rapidly losing my self-control. "Tell me the truth, for once! Why do you suspect your daughter of killing her own father? Did she confess to you?"

"Of course not," she snapped, glaring at me. "I *told* you why. Because Preston said 'Tiffany,' before he died."

So now *she* was angry at *me?* That did it. "Was that before or after you searched his pockets?" I asked loudly. "Before or after you dragged him into the kitchen? You want to know what I think, Stephanie? I think you killed him." By now I was shouting, and Stephanie's gestures for me to quiet down only increased my anger. "I think you were so fed up with his unfaithfulness you shot him. You invented this thing about him saying 'Tiffany' before he died, and you called me because you knew I have a soft spot for your daughter."

"Keep your voice down, Molly," Stephanie finally growled at me.

She had a legitimate reason to hush me, not wanting me to wake the baby, but I was too enraged now to care. I shouted, "All that I've done is muck up Tommy's investigation, when it was you all along! I've loused up my marriage for you! Because my husband was right about you all along. He was right about everything! And I've been a damned idiot, thanks to you!"

Stephanie was now staring into her lap, her cheeks crimson. For a moment, the silence rang in my ears, but then I heard a small whimper behind me and turned. Tiffany was standing in the kitchen doorway. One look at her face told me she had overheard much of my tirade.

"Oh, no," I moaned, rising. Her short hairstyle and oversized, grungy clothes made her look painfully waiflike. I hadn't stopped to realize it was after four; high school let out at half past three. "Tiffany. I didn't know you were home. Everything you've just heard was said out of anger. It wasn't—"

"I *did* shoot him," Tiffany said, crying.

Stephanie rose and rushed over to her, wrapping her arms around her daughter. "Don't listen to her, Molly. She's just trying to protect me."

"Preston wasn't my father," Tiffany sobbed. "Hank Mueller is my father."

"What?" I cried, confused now to the point of desperation. "You're saying your uncle is your father?"

"How did you know that?" Stephanie asked Tiffany in a harsh whisper.

"Aunt Sabrina told me. Last year."

Stephanie grabbed Tiffany by both shoulders and said

firmly into her daughter's weeping face, "Sabrina had no right to tell you. I would have told you myself if I had any idea you'd find out that way."

Tiffany was shaking her head and sobbing loudly. Stephanie raised her voice and said, "Tiffany, that was just a biological fluke. Preston is your father in every other sense of the word." She cast a sideways glance my way, then returned her attention to her daughter. "Preston and I were already engaged, and I'd just found out he'd..." She stopped, studying her daughter's face. Stephanie shrugged and said gently, "Hank was just a one-time fling when I happened to be vulnerable. I had cold feet about the marriage, and Hank and I were drunk. That all happened before Hank had even started dating your Aunt Sabrina. It was a bad mistake on our part, which your father, *Preston,* and I put behind us a long time ago."

Though I said nothing, I had a rare moment of appreciation for what Stephanie had just done. Stephanie must have found out that Preston had cheated on her when they were engaged. That was why she'd been receptive to Hank's advances. She'd omitted this detail because she didn't wanted to smear Preston further when speaking to Tiffany.

Tiffany, still shaking her head and crying as if she hadn't heard a word Stephanie had said, leaned past her mother's shoulder to look at me. Tiffany moaned, "He said he was going to have Cherokee arrested. So I killed him. I—"

"Then where's the gun?" I interrupted. "How did you get hold of it in the first place? And who was that shooting at us from behind the bushes?"

I paused. Stephanie released her grip on her daughter as both she and Tiffany looked at me. Tiffany's sobs quickly began to subside as we all realized the same thing.

"Damn." I punched my thigh and cried, "You idiot!" meaning me. "I got so angry I'd forgotten about that." I turned to Stephanie. "You weren't the murderer. You were in the house when the person shooting at us ran away." I looked at Tiffany. "And you were with me. So unless you hired someone to shoot at us..."

Tiffany shook her head, dabbing with a tissue at her eyes and tear-streaked cheeks. "No, I didn't hire anyone. I just claimed I shot Daddy because what you were saying to Mom made sense. And I couldn't bear to let her go to jail."

My knees were shaking. I sank back into the chair, struggling to regain my composure. "Don't mess around with making false confessions, Tiffany. You can get into big trouble that way."

Stephanie, too, was horribly shaken. She pressed her temples with the heels of her hands for a moment, then she combed her fingers through her hair and turned toward Tiffany. She gently touched her daughter's face and said, "Look at me, Tiffany. I had nothing to do with your father's murder. Nothing. Don't let anyone"—she turned her head to give me a quick glare and repeated pointedly— "*anyone,* convince you otherwise." She took a deep breath. "Heaven knows this is a dysfunctional family, but show me one that isn't. And this is all we've got. The three of us are going to get through this as a family."

For a moment, I thought she was including me in the trio, but then I realized to my relief that she meant Michael.

"Stephanie, I'm sorry I falsely accused you. It's just that your reactions have been so bizarre. I can't figure out why you've done a single thing you've done since this all started. I wish you could explain it to me."

"I wish I could, too, Molly." She managed a sad smile. "I'm going to check on the baby. And if he's still asleep, I'm going to join him." She turned to leave and said, "Tiffany, why don't you show Molly to the door, please."

This was my chance to say something to Tiffany, to compensate somehow for my horrible gaffe in not checking to make sure she wasn't within earshot. But I was at a loss for words. If only that had been the case a few minutes earlier.

We trudged silently to the front door, which Tiffany

opened for me. She glanced down and said, "Oh." Then she called over her shoulder, "Mom, we got another package."

Stephanie changed courses at this news, heading toward us instead of up the stairs. "It must be another baby gift," she said happily.

The package that Tiffany had retrieved from the porch was a cube of about six-inches, wrapped in brown paper. The dimensions weren't the same as the ones I'd seen from STOP. Yet something, maybe the brown wrapping, made me—to quote one of my favorite quips from Yogi Berra—feel it was "déjà vu all over again." So I said to Tiffany, "Can I see that?"

Without waiting for Tiffany's answer, I snatched the box from her. It had a typed address label, to Mrs. Preston Saunders at the complete mailing address. No markings indicated how the package had arrived. There was no return address. My heart pounded. I sniffed at it and held it up to my ear.

Both Tiffany and Stephanie looked at me as if I were insane, but made no comment.

"Were you expecting a package?" I asked.

"Let me have that, Molly," Stephanie said, reaching for it. "We've been getting baby gifts from acquaintances in other parts of the country. I'm sure that's—"

I held it away from her.

"Give that to me, Molly. It is mine, isn't it?"

"I'm sorry." I backed out the door wrapping my arms around the package to prevent them from even touching it. "I know this is crazy, but the label reminds me of the one I got from STOP. I'm taking the box to Tommy Newton to make sure it's safe before anyone opens it."

Stephanie put her hands on her hips and glared at me. "Pardon me for pointing this out to you, Molly, but you received dog excrement, didn't you? If that's what's in this box, it would certainly be distasteful, but hardly dangerous. Now give me my package. This minute."

I shook my head, muttered "Sorry," and took it to my car. The two Saunderses stood staring at me in the doorway as I drove off.

I could only guess at how Tommy would treat me when I gave the package to him.

FOR ONCE, Tommy merely listened when I barged into his office at the station house and set the package on his desk. He agreed that it was "better to be safe than sorry," and told me to wait in his office while he had it X-rayed.

After a long wait in Tommy's tiny office, I grew bored and impatient. I made use of the time by making my flight reservations for Saturday morning. That bought me just a little more than three days to solve this thing, or I'd be stuck in Florida till the police figured it out. If they ever did. By the time my flight arrangements were completed, it was almost five thirty. Next I decided to call my husband at work to do some marital damage control. To my surprise, the receptionist told me he'd left for the day a half hour earlier.

I called home and he answered on the first ring.

"Jim," I said quickly, feeling a little on edge. "Is everything all right?"

"If you call my being married to Nancy Drew all right, I suppose so," he answered testily. "Where are the kids?"

"At Jon's and Katie's houses. I'm picking them up at six."

"I'll go get them now."

"Why? I'll get them on my way home."

"Because I want to explain to them why they're flying with you to Florida tonight, that's why."

My stomach knotted. "I didn't even golf with Preston's foursome. I barely even *met* them. So please don't be upset with me."

"We'll talk about it when you get home. Are you about to leave?"

This was not a prudent time to let on that I was currently

having a possible explosive device analyzed at the police station, so I just said that yes, I'd be leaving here soon.

But several minutes passed. By the time Tommy finally returned, I was in the process of writing a note stating that I couldn't wait any longer so please call me at home. Out of the corner of my eye, I saw him heading toward me carrying some kind of a long, bouncy tube by the middle. As he neared, I realized it was a "party snake," those springs that pop out of peanut cans to scare the living daylights out of some unfortunate peanut lover. That must have been what was in the box. I felt only slightly vindicated about having snatched it from Stephanie. Though she wouldn't have enjoyed something springing out at her, it was actually a less onerous—and odorous—practical joke than dog doo-doo.

Tommy's first words to me were, "Good thing you were there to intercept the package." He lifted up one of the ends of the spring and revealed a cap with some twenty razor blades embedded in it. "The perp put this device on both ends. Damn thing may not have killed Stephanie, or whoever opened it. Sure could've caused major cosmetic surgery, though."

"Jesus," I whispered.

"Tell me again how you found this?"

"It was by the front door. Tiffany actually found it. That's all I can tell you. Listen, Tommy, this has been a long, strange day, and my husband's already mad at me. I've got to get home. Okay?"

He let me go, and I drove home, my heart pounding.

As soon as I arrived, Karen and Nathan ran to meet me at the garage door. "Mommy!" Karen cried. I gasped as I saw what she was holding. "This package was by the door." I swept it out of her hands and stumbled back against the wall as she continued happily, "Nathan and I wanted to open it but Daddy said we had to wait for you. So can I open it now?"

The package was identical to Stephanie's.

FOURTEEN

Lose the Big White Fish

"THE PACKAGE was addressed to Ms. Molly Masters," I said to Lauren. "The other one was to Mrs. Preston Saunders. What does that tell you?"

Lauren stared into her coffee mug for a moment, then met my eyes. She tilted her head a little, a gesture that was her own unique shrug. Her round, pretty face looked pale, her soft brown eyes rife with worry. "The person who sent it knows your first name, but not Stephanie's?"

"Or wants everyone to think so."

My brain refused to relinquish the image of Karen holding that hideous package. Over half an hour ago, Jim had taken the box away from me, not wanting me to handle it once I told him about Stephanie's package. He drove off, saying he was taking it straight to Sergeant Newton himself. Seeking comfort and adult companionship, I then went to Lauren's house, bringing Karen and Nathan, who were currently playing upstairs with Rachel.

For the hundredth time I rose to glance out the window to see if any lights were on at my house to indicate that Jim had returned. He hadn't, so I sat back down at Lauren's kitchen table. Our kitchens had identical white-pine cabinets, wood-grain Formica countertops, and brick-pattern linoleum floors, but her house was a mirror image of mine. Long ago I had adjusted to everything being in the exact opposite direction. But now I felt disoriented to the point of dizziness.

"Whoever did this is sick," Lauren said. "Imagine having razor blades springing out at—"

"Stop." I held up both palms. "My children almost opened that thing. I don't want to think about it."

She winced slightly in an unspoken and unnecessary apology. "What are you going to tell Jim when he gets back?" she asked gently. "Are you going to leave immediately for Florida?"

I shook my head. "I know he'll never understand this, but I just can't *do* that. This maniac almost hurt our children. I'll be constantly looking over my shoulder, regardless of how far we run, till the creep's locked up. Now he or she is after Stephanie, too. I can't help but feel it's my fault."

"*Your* fault? Preston's the one that got you involved by printing your cartoon. Then Stephanie *asked* you to look for the killer."

"I realize that. But even if it isn't rational, I feel that if only I had stayed out of the investigation, Preston's death would've been the end of it. Plus, if the person wanted to hurt Stephanie, maybe Tiffany was the real target that time we both got shot at."

Lauren leaned on her elbows and met my eyes. "Let me see if I've got this straight. You feel you've endangered the Saunders family by doing what Stephanie asked you to do. That by trying to catch the guy, you've actually only egged him on. Therefore, you're going to stay and egg him on further. Is that right?"

I sighed and checked out the window again. My house was still dark. I returned to my seat. "It does sound stupid when you put it that way. The point is, though, I really believe I can outsmart this horrid person and get him or her behind bars. I'm giving myself till Saturday morning, when I've got the flight reservations."

Lauren raised her eyebrows but said nothing.

"I can't even tell you how desperately I don't want to be visiting my parents at this particular time. Here I'll suddenly be arriving with their grandchildren and no husband because someone's supposedly trying to kill me as a result of my cartoon being in a porno mag. They're going to think they raised a complete ditz.''

"Your parents know you, Molly. It's not like your personality's going to shock them at this late juncture. Come on, Molly. What's really going on with you?''

I dropped my face into my hands for a moment, then met her eyes and said, "Having you know me this well isn't always such a pleasant experience.''

She smiled a little, but waited patiently for me to answer her question.

"It's...the prospect of my running away from Carlton again when the going gets tough. It's you dating Tommy. It's the—''

"Oh my gosh," Lauren interrupted. Her face had paled a little. "You're worried about what happened between you and Howie. That's ancient history. And Howie was largely to blame." She reached across the table and put her hand on top of mine. "How many times can I tell you I've forgiven you till you believe me?''

My heart was pounding. I hated rehashing this, but it was bothering me and wouldn't go away on its own. "I know you've forgiven me. But I can't forgive myself. Howie was your fiancé. And I was flirting with him at our graduation party. I'd like to blame it all on Howie and the alcohol, but on some level I was aware of what I was doing. You two broke up because of catching me and him in his car that night.''

She laced her fingers and leaned on her elbows. With the bright overhead lighting of her brass chandelier, I could see the tiny lines in her face. "Yes, that's why we broke up. That was all very painful and I hurt over it for a long time. But, Molly, my wounds have been healed for a much longer time, and it's got nothing to do with what's happening to you now."

"Right. Except that it's shaped my self-image. I don't get to be a person who never broke up her best friend's wedding. I don't get to be someone who never left her hometown without so much as a return visit for seventeen years. But now, I *do* get to be a thirty-five-year-old woman who stays and fights when I get threatened. Who encourages her two dear friends from high school to date each other, and who would never make the same mistake. I need to do this thing. I need to stay."

The doorbell rang.

"That's probably the pizza," Lauren said quietly, rising.

But when Lauren opened the door, I heard Jim's voice. I rushed to the front of the house to greet him and gave him a sustained hug.

"I've been checking," I told him, "but I didn't see you come home."

"I figured you'd be at Lauren's and came straight here," he said. His chest vibrated against the side of my face as he spoke.

"What was in the box?"

"Same type of spring," Jim answered, still holding me against his body and rubbing my back. "Sergeant Newton says you can buy one of those at more than a dozen stores in the area, but he thinks he can trace the box."

"The box?" I pulled away to meet his gaze.

"Both boxes had unusual metal reinforcements on the seams and on the tops and bottoms. Otherwise the razor blades would have cut right through the cardboard, of course."

"Of course," I repeated, though I hadn't thought of that before.

Hank Mueller! He was in the shipping business. If only I'd asked what the name of his company was. Unless they had some obvious name in the phone book, such as Mueller's Mailers, I'd have to get it from another source.

I could ask Chase Groves during my dental appointment in the morning.

Provided I wasn't on an airplane by then.

THE MOMENT we got the kids tucked in bed, I pulled out all the stops with my husband. I told him we needed to talk, and we locked the bedroom door behind us. He sat on the edge of the bed. So that he couldn't avoid looking at me, I knelt in front of him, rested my arms on his thighs, and said, "Jim, I can't leave for Florida this way. It's like...the sermon last Sunday, how the priest talked about Jesus telling his followers to 'look at the log in your own eye before you look at the speck in your brother's or sister's eye.' I can't—"

"We're talking about you being shot at and receiving spring-loaded razors," Jim interrupted. "That's hardly a speck in someone's eye."

I began again. "I know. But I can't run away from Carlton like I did before, when I assumed everyone hated me for breaking up Lauren and Howie."

"But that—"

"Don't tell me it's not the same thing. I'm well aware of that. The biggest difference is that now I have you and the children. And I desperately don't want to lose you. But if I leave now, if I let myself feel I've been driven from this town one more time, I'm afraid I'll lose *myself*. I feel as if I'm reliving one of the worst times of my life." The very worst time, we both knew, had been during my miscarriage. "Please, Jim, this is just too hard to face alone."

Jim caressed my face and said softly, "Okay. I'll take some time off work. I won't leave your side."

I pulled his hand down and wove my fingers through his. "Thank you. But the hard part is *I'll* have to. I'll have to leave your side to solve this thing."

Jim closed his eyes in frustration for a moment. "So what am I supposed to do?"

"Be there afterward, when I work it out for myself."

He stared at the wall beyond my shoulder and shook his head. "Let you risk your life. Then welcome you back with open arms *if* you live through it." He sighed, then looked at me. "I don't know if I can do that."

"Can you try? Please?"

We left the question dangling and made love.

IT RAINED on Wednesday morning—the perfect weather for a dentist appointment, and I was in Chase Groves's office in downtown Schenectady as scheduled. The dental chair was especially comfortable. If it weren't for the dental assistant's hands in my mouth as she cleaned my teeth, along with my concentrated efforts to prevent her from sucking my tongue into that damned spit vacuum of hers, I'd have been downright comfy.

As I sat there, my thoughts, unlike my tongue, wandered freely. Jim and I had compromised that I wouldn't leave until Saturday morning—Jim convinced me that if I were to stay beyond that, he'd wind up with bleeding ulcers. He also took the rest of the week off to keep an eye on me.

Okay, so I didn't tell him my dental appointment was with a key suspect in the case. Nor did Jim know of my plan to visit Hank Mueller's Mailers, or whatever his business was really called. My plan had to do with a cartoon I'd drawn for a friend in Colorado.

I'd received a letter from my friend, back before I'd ever heard of *Between the Legs*. Was that really just two weeks ago? I'd been so carefree and innocent then. At any rate, my friend was depressed because the book she'd written had been rejected by editors at two different publishing houses. The editors had written personal replies, stating why they felt her book didn't "quite work." In both cases, their reasons were just plain stupid. I knew that, because, seemingly unlike the editors, I'd *read* her book.

To cheer up my friend, I had drawn a cartoon of a man sitting in an editor's office. The editor hands him a thick stack of manuscript pages, titled *Moby Dick*. He stares at the editor in dismay as she tells him, "Lose the big white fish, Mr. Melville. Make it a purple dinosaur. Then we'll talk."

Originally I had planned merely to color in my cartoon and mail it to her, but I now needed an excuse to use Hank Mueller's shipping company. Although it felt ostentatious to do so, I had taken it to a frame shop first thing this morning. My theory was that it would be at least marginally reasonable for me to ask to speak to Hank Mueller personally about special metal-reinforced packaging to protect the glass of the frame. Then I could ask him one-on-one about his relationship with Preston.

It also occurred to me that just as soon as this murderous maniac was behind bars, I was going to sit down and ponder how, if I'd spent half as much energy being kind to my dear husband as I did finding devious ways to circumvent his desire to protect me, our marriage might be stronger. But it was already Wednesday morning. Right now I had only three days to catch this person, and I intended to devote my mental faculties to that, and that alone.

The dental assistant finally finished cleaning my teeth and Chase Groves reentered the room, carrying my X rays. When I'd first arrived, he had briefly examined my teeth and gums, then laid the standard not-flossing-quite-regularly-enough guilt trip on me.

He said quietly to his assistant, "Go ahead and get that thing taken care of. I can handle everything here myself."

"Are you sure?" Though she was standing behind me and I couldn't see her face, her voice sounded incredulous. So was I! Why was he sending her away?

"It's fine," Chase answered her. "Just be back in time for my next appointment."

I was going to be *alone* with him? I'd never so much as *heard* of any dentist being completely alone with a patient. Wasn't there some sort of governing American Dental Board to insist that dentists always have witnesses? It's not like patients can see for themselves what's going on in their mouths, for heaven's sake!

He gave me a smile and sat down. The two of us were alone now with his numerous pain-inflicting instruments. From my vantage point he looked gigantic—a defensive lineman turned dentist. He put on a pair of rubber gloves. His hands were huge, his forearms strong. He could crush my face with one squeeze.

"Turns out it was lucky you managed to get an appointment on such short notice. Looks like you've got a cavity."

"I've got a cavity?" It hadn't even been a year since my last appointment. My real dentist hadn't said anything about a burgeoning cavity. "Are you sure?"

"'Fraid so," he said, showing me one of the inch-square pictures of my teeth. "See that little spot there?" He pointed.

I looked, but all I could see was that my teeth looked truly unattractive lipless and with translucent gums. "Not really."

"Well, it's there, all right," he said, taking the X rays away. "Don't worry. It's just a small one. Besides, you're lucky. Normally you'd have to make a second appointment, but the cancellation slot you fit into this morning happened to be for ninety minutes. I can get you taken care of right now, and save you the inconvenience of a second office visit."

"Oh, goody," I muttered.

"Do you want nitrous-oxide gas, or Novocain?"

"Gas," I repeated in dismay. My real dentist never offered to asphyxiate me.

"Very well, I'll—"

"No! That was a question, not an answer." I couldn't allow myself to be slipping off into la-la land while trying to question him. "I said 'gas' because I was surprised. But I like Novocain."

"You *like* it? That's a first." He held up a foot-long needle.

Though I felt faint, I replied, "Oh, I think needles and pain are one of those small steps we take to build moral character, don't you?"

"Mmmm," he murmured, slipping on his mask. It was one of those disposable masks sold in hardware stores. The white paper contrasted sharply with his dark skin. "Open wide."

I eyed the syringe. For all I knew, that could be full of poison. This was, after all, the same man rumored to have recently gotten so out of control that personnel at his golf course considered calling the police. "Wait!" I cried. "I, uh, can't do this right now. I just remembered. I have to...eat soon. The Novocain will numb my mouth." I tried to push away the tray suspended over my chest so I could scoot out of the chair, but Chase put a restraining hand on my shoulder.

"Relax, Molly. Maybe we should use nitrous oxide after all."

"No! It's not just that, it's—"

"Cold feet." He sat back and lowered his mask, letting it rest against his neck. "I understand. You weren't expecting to have a cavity drilled today."

"Exactly." I felt a surge of relief, surprised that I'd escaped this threatening situation so easily. "I'm not mentally psyched up for it."

He nodded. "It's a small cavity, so you can schedule another appointment anytime within the next month or two." He studied my eyes. "Or would you rather I recommend another dentist? One whose office is closer to Carlton?"

He was graciously giving me an "out." He realized I didn't trust him to drill my tooth. He seemed like such a nice person. Suddenly I was overwhelmed with guilt for having scheduled this appointment with the sole intention of investigating him.

"On second thought," I heard myself say, "I may as well get it out of the way."

"You're sure?" he asked, putting his mask on again.

I nodded. *Please. Dear God. Don't let him be a homicidal maniac!* Of all the ways I didn't wish to die, death by dental work was right at the top of my list.

Even if he'd killed Preston, surely he wouldn't give me a poisonous injection. That would be impossible to get away with. Nonetheless, I had to dab away a sweat mustache. I opened my mouth, wondering if I was about to die.

"You'll feel just a slight pinch." Then he jabbed me with the needle.

"The Novocain will take just a couple of minutes to take effect," Chase assured me.

Provided it *was* Novocain. "Let me ask you something," I blurted, realizing this was my one opportunity to talk to him sans drool. "Where does Hank Mueller work? I have some glass I need to ship."

"He owns the Ship-it franchise."

Figured. There were at least ten SHIP IT! shops in the Albany area alone. "So how could I find him to discuss my project personally?"

"Unless I'm mistaken, he spends most of his time at the shop on Route Nine."

He scratched the side of his nose. The motion must have been similar to watching someone yawn, for my nose began to itch. I scratched both sides, remembering how drills always made me feel the need to sneeze.

"Say, Molly," Chase said. "How well did you know Preston Saunders?"

"Not very well, like I said yesterday. He'd been over to my house a number of times, picking up his daughter, who baby-sits for my children. Why?"

Chase became engrossed with rearranging the silver instruments of oral torture on his tray. "You seemed inordinately nervous about my drilling your cavity. I wondered if Preston had said something to you."

Chase seemed to be implying that Preston might have warned me not to let Chase drill my teeth. Maybe this had to do with the legal matter Emma had started to tell me about yesterday. I took a gamble and asked, "You mean about his lawsuit?"

His face tightened. "So he *did* tell you." He sighed. "I hope he also told you it was a complete scam."

"Your good fwend Pweston bwought a phony lawsuit against you?" The injection had indeed been Novocain, thank God, and was starting to take effect.

Chase nodded.

"That must have made you fuwious."

"Let's see if the anesthetic is working yet," Chase said. He reached inside my mouth and did something with a pointy instrument that I couldn't feel at all.

"Ouch!" I feigned pain to stall for time, hoping to learn more about his relationship with Preston.

"You felt that?" he asked, surprised.

I nodded.

"Hmm. I'll give you a second half dose, just to be safe, then give it another minute to work."

I clenched my fists in frustration, and opened my mouth while he gave me a totally unnecessary second shot. My mouth felt painfully dry, all of my saliva having already been vacuumed away to who knows where. When he'd finished, I licked my lips in a failed attempt to wet them. It felt as though I were licking pork chops. Taking a sip of water with four-inch-thick lips was out of the question, though.

He certainly was not going to tell me about a possible malpractice suit while he was moments away from drilling into my tooth. I cleared my throat, then said, "I enjoyed pwaying wiff your wife yesterday. She's vewy nice."

"So you got to talk to each other quite a bit?" he asked.

"Not weewee, but she invited me ova fa wunch tomorrow."

"That's nice. Let's check the Novocain again." He again did something with his pointed instrument in my mouth and asked, "Did you feel that?"

"Yeah."

He chuckled. "Amazing, since I didn't touch you at all that time. Let's get it over with, shall we? I promise. You won't feel a thing."

True to his word, I didn't feel the drill, but smelled the awful, eye-watering scent of burning tooth as he worked. The procedure took only a minute or two, then he prepared my filling at the counter in back of the room.

I ran my tongue along the hole, glad that I seemed to be alive and well. Preston's death probably brought a timely end to a legal case against Chase—one that had apparently inspired an ugly altercation at the Carlton Country Club. Yet I decided to cross him off of my list of suspects. Maybe it was flawed logic, but I just couldn't see him trying to slash my face with razor blades, then filling my cavity. That would be similar to building a chimney atop a house you'd tried to demolish.

"Who do you think killed Pweston?" I asked.

He glanced over his shoulder at me. Just for that moment, he let his guard slip and I saw raw hatred on his face. He turned his head again, and muttered, "I don't know. But I'd sure like to shake the person's hand."

WITH NO FEELING in half of my face, I could not bring myself to go into SHIP IT! and try to have an intelligent conversation with Hank Mueller. On the other hand, I had Jim waiting for me at home, and I'd assured him I would be back by lunchtime. Not that I was allowed to *eat* in this condition.

After pondering the matter for a few minutes, I drove to Carlton High School and wove through the parking lot to search for José's junky Ford Galaxy. It was there. I parked and sat in my car, carefully redoing my drawing of the messenger that I'd given to Tommy Newton. My work was especially slow, since I periodically interrupted myself to look into the rearview mirror to make sure both halves of my face were still present and I hadn't mutated into the hideous drooling beast I felt like.

The results were far superior to my first rendition. I jotted José a note on the margin, asking him please to show this picture around to all of his friends and acquaintances, and to call me if he had any information about the subject's whereabouts. In case of rain, I stashed it inside a discarded peanut butter-scented sandwich bag I'd found in my backseat, and carefully wedged this under José's windshield wiper. Then, not having the luxury of time, I massaged my lips as I drove to SHIP IT! My mouth was getting a tingling sensation, and I practiced enunciating. By the time I arrived, I could hear some improvement in my speech.

Though the young female clerk seemed put out that I insisted on speaking directly to the owner about my precious picture, she also seemed to have no trouble believing that I was an eccentric. She disappeared through a doorway at the back of the store and returned moments later with Hank Mueller.

Hank was wearing slacks but no jacket or tie, the top button of his shirt open and his sleeves rolled up on those hairy arms of his. The overall effect seemed as carefully orchestrated as a campaign poster: Here's Hard-working Everyman, at your service. Yet with his hawk nose and dark, deep-set eyes, he too closely resembled a cartoon villain to have succeeded in politics.

I contorted my facial muscles in what I hoped was a smile. "Hi, Hank. How are you?"

"I'm fine." He studied my face. "Did you get hit in the mouth or something yesterday?"

"No. Excuse my speech. I've just been to the dentist, where I lost most of the feeling in my face, along with much of my dignity."

Again, I tried to smile, but he winced as he watched me. I began again, slowly, "When I heard you owned this place, I remembered I had a picture I've been meaning to ship, but didn't know who I could trust to do a proper job."

His eyes lit up. Nothing got results as fast as the ol' ego-massage. "Ah. Well, you've come to the right place. I'll show you my design. It's revolutionized the shipping industry, if I do say so myself." He put his hand on my back to escort me to a display case that was all of two steps away.

The display helped to demonstrate their patented design for "So lightweight! And yet so sturdy!" metal reinforcements inside a Cardboard! box.

It was indeed precisely the type of box that Jim had described as holding the bladed springs Stephanie and I had received.

"Oh, good," I said, looking at a photo in the display of an elephant standing on one of SHIP IT!'s boxes. "I see it's elephant proof. They seem to step on a lot of packages shipped through U.S. Mail."

Hank chuckled and began his spiel. Midway through, it occurred to me that Hank Mueller could not possibly be so stupid as to use packaging material that pointed directly to him. He was being set up.

After he'd finished his routine and I'd murmured what felt like a sufficient number of appreciative remarks, I said, "Preston Saunders ran an export business. Are your companies affiliated?"

Hank shook his head. "We used to be their main contractor. Not anymore."

"Come to think of it, I should have known your companies weren't affiliated. You'd made a remark about him 'ripping you off again.'"

He merely watched me. His brow was furrowed and his jaw and fists were clenched. He looked like the quintessential villain, but with his black hair and mustache combined with his craggy features, that didn't take much. Maybe I could get him to open up by using an us-against-Preston tack. "You were right, by the way," I said. "That was my cartoon he won the contest with, not his. He took my drawing and submitted without my knowledge or consent."

"Sounds like Preston Saunders, all right. I hate to speak ill of the dead, but his questionable business tactics almost put my company under. That's why I moved here. To keep a closer eye on what he was doing to my franchise." He slicked back his hair with his palms. "Let's get this picture ready to go, shall we?"

FIFTEEN

Putting on a Shine

I WAS SLIGHTLY leery of letting Hank Mueller handle my picture in his current mood, but he was surprisingly gentle with it. He packaged up my picture himself, allowing me to watch every stage. It turned into a grand production, especially when the foam peanuts children love and mothers detest were added by a big machine that resembled a coal chute.

To set up Hank Mueller, all someone would have to do was get hold of a couple of his boxes. As he totaled my charges, I asked, "Does your company have to do all the packaging yourselves, or do you sell your boxes as well?"

"We can do it either way. Do you have some exact dimensions in mind?"

"Actually, I was wondering about a pair of boxes you might have sold here recently. They were cubes, about six inches or so each direction."

"Doesn't ring any bells for me." He turned toward the clerk, who was standing nearby. "Becky?"

She shook her head. "We have several stores in the Albany area, you know. Could've been bought at any of them."

I nodded and thanked them, but felt deeply frustrated. There had to have been tremendous animosity between the two men. Preston had damaged Hank's business. Hank had impregnated Preston's fiancée. Preston had raised Hank's only child as his own.

Here was the man who had the motive and the opportunity. He *had* to be guilty. Yet there was no getting around one question: How could anyone run a large franchise successfully, but be so stupid as to incriminate himself by using his own, patented boxes?

The person setting him up had to be someone who knew about Preston's bet over my cartoon. So if it wasn't Chase or Hank, that left Richard Worthington. An architect. How was I supposed to spy surreptitiously on him? Tell him I wanted him to design an addition for my *parents'* house? Maybe tomorrow's luncheon with Emma Groves would give me some ideas.

I paid my staggering shipping and handling fees and left the store, and nearly collided with Tommy Newton, who was about to enter. We both jerked back a little in surprise.

"Aw, jeez, Molly!" he cried as the glass door swung shut. "When the hell are you gonna learn to stay out of police business!"

I feigned indignation. "I was just mailing a package."

His face was rapidly turning redder than his hair. "Uh-huh. And Al Capone was just a choir leader." He stared at me. "What's the matter with your mouth? Someone smack you?"

"No, I just—" I stopped, realizing the mention of a dental appointment would tip Tommy off to my visit to Chase.

"You just...got a shot of Novocain, right? And was Chase Groves your dentist, by any chance?"

If only Tommy were this successful at analyzing the murderer's behavior, my children wouldn't have handled a box of spring-loaded razors. To escape the weight of his glare, I glanced around. The store next to SHIP IT! was a doughnut shop.

Giving his arm a friendly squeeze, I said, "How 'bout I buy you coffee and a doughnut, Tommy?"

He shook his head. "I hate doughnuts."

"Fine." I turned on a heel and headed for the restaurant door without waiting for his response. "We'll make it a muffin."

Tommy grumbled, but followed me inside. It was a bargain-basement establishment—scuffed-up linoleum floors and a crumb-laden counter where one middle-aged woman stood, looking bored. All four small tables were empty. We sat at one and Tommy tried to order me a cup of coffee. No doubt he would have enjoyed watching me dribble scalding hot liquid down my chin. Though it cost me two blueberry muffins—how anyone could "hate" doughnuts but love blueberries was beyond me—he eventually cooled off. He even agreed he may as well give me the scoop on Preston's malpractice suit against Chase to save me a trip to the library and its newspaper microfilm.

Preston had claimed Chase gave him permanent nerve damage when he'd drilled too deep while replacing an old filling. That, however, was as much information as I could extract from Tommy. When I mentioned, casually, that Preston's death must have brought a timely end to that lawsuit, Tommy said, "Chase was in Cleveland last Monday. He didn't do it."

En route to the school bus stop the next morning, rain drummed steadily on the hood of my Gore-Tex coat. It was another of those dreary East Coast days when the world looks like an enormous black-and-white photograph. And an ugly one at that. Damn, I missed Boulder's blue skies; I had never known how brilliant a shade of blue the sky could be till I moved to Colorado.

"Eww! Sick!" Karen cried as Nathan pulled a soggy earthworm out of a puddle on our driveway.

"How come you say everything's sick?" He held the dripping worm up in front of Karen's face, who shrieked. Nathan giggled. "It's just a wet worm."

"The bus will be here any minute. Please put the worm down, Nathan, and—"

"Bus!" Karen interrupted as the shoosh of air brakes resounded from the corner where the yellow bus was just now turning. She took off at a dead run.

"Slow down!" I demanded, afraid she'd slip on the wet pavement. "There's—"

"Wait for me, Karen!" Nathan turned, called, "Here, Mommy," and flung the worm at me. "Have a nice day."

Startled at suddenly having a worm pitched to me, I jumped back, said something along the lines of, "Gilll," then had to peel the lower life-form off the sleeve of my jacket.

Worm in hand, I waved good-bye, then dropped it onto the mud in my mother's garden. Plants seemed to die en masse in my presence. Now when Mother returned in June, I could tell her I'd made an earnest effort to plant *something,* at least.

I went inside, ready to set a plan into motion for getting information from Richard Worthington, the architect. From my brief stint at pretending to be with *20/20* I knew that people were willing to answer all kinds of questions posed by a stranger's voice over the phone, provided that voice was supposedly affiliated with a recognized institution.

The laundry room was the least likely room for my husband, currently sleeping late, to stumble into accidentally. I grabbed the portable phone and climbed on top of my dryer for a seat. With a quick prayer that Jim wouldn't wake and realize he had no clean underwear and that the Worthingtons wouldn't have Caller I.D. installed on their phone, I dialed.

"Hello, is this Mr. Richard Worthington?" I asked, holding my nose and using my breathiest voice—which took some doing, considering I couldn't breathe this way.

"Yes it is," he answered, his voice just as booming over the phone as it was in person.

"My name is Elsa Vanderkind. I'm doing a very brief phone survey on behalf of the NRA."

"The NRA?"

"Yes," I replied, panicking slightly as I realized I suddenly couldn't remember what the initials stood for. "The National Right to Armament. What types of guns do you currently own, sir?"

"A three-fifty-seven Magnum. Double-action."

Aha! He *did* own a gun. "Have you, or any member of your family, had an occasion to fire your weapon within the last three months?"

"No."

"Would you say you felt very strongly, somewhat strongly, or don't care about your Constitutional right to continue to own your weapon?"

"Very strongly."

"Thank you very much, sir." I promptly hung up and hopped off the dryer.

That had all worked out quite nicely. Though I was fairly certain that when Tommy had talked to me just after Tiffany and I had been shot at, he'd said the weapon in both shootings was a .22, not a .357. And I suddenly realized that NRA stood for National Rifle Association.

Drat! This is what happens when I try to sleuth before drinking my first cup of coffee.

Richard Worthington was now my top suspect. Forty-eight hours and counting from my flight to Florida. Though Tommy was sharp and a good cop, I couldn't shake my fear that he would never solve this thing on his own and we'd be stuck in my parents' tiny condo for months.

I tried to block out the ever-louder ticking clock by sketching some ideas for greeting cards. Recalling yesterday's exploits, I drew a man wearing an expression of terror as he sits in a dentist chair and stares at a parrot perched in the corner of the office. The parrot is squawking, "Open wide. OWWW!! Open wide. OWWW!! Open wide..."

Then I paused to consider marketing strategy. The cartoon might work as a postcard reminding patients about upcoming dental checkups. Any dentist willing to send such a card would have to know the patient pretty well. I worked up a second drawing as a companion card for newer patients. This one showed a woman with rays of light beaming from her wide smile and another woman shielding her eyes. Underneath was the caption, "Time to put a shine on your smile!"

The phone rang. I glanced at the clock, surprised to discover it was already almost ten and that Jim was still in bed. But then the poor man hadn't been sleeping well of late. I answered the phone on the first ring.

"Molly," said a male voice. "I was like, verklempt, even, that you came to me for help."

"Oh?" My mind raced. Whom had I asked for help that would say something so weird? *José*. I had put the drawing of the messenger on his windshield yesterday. "How are you, José?"

"Filthy, homeslice. How 'bout you?"

Say, what? How was someone supposed to respond nowadays to being called a dirty piece of pizza? "Oh, the same, more or less."

"Kooky. You're not, like, gonna believe this, but I'm with Roke at the mall and—"

"Aren't you supposed to be in school right now?"

"We decided to bump study hall. Anyways, Roke and me were just lampin' outside of the Java Bean, when in walks this, like, reality-impaired dude with a shaved head. And Roke and me both think he kind of looks like the guy in your drawing."

I hopped to my feet. This could be the break I'd been waiting for! "Where is he now?"

"Havin' a cup of java at the Bean. Cherokee's keeping an eye on him."

"Okay. I'll be right there. If he tries to leave, do your best to stall him."

"No *problemo*, dudette." He hung up.

I dialed Sergeant Newton's office, but got his machine. I hung up, not willing to wait through his recorded greeting. I hollered upstairs to Jim that I was going to run to the store and I'd be right back. Then I dashed to my car before Jim could respond.

I broke every speed limit driving to the mall, but fortunately kept control of the car despite rain-slicked roads, and pulled into a space. I hadn't taken the time to put on a coat, and now had to ignore the rain soaking into my sweatshirt and jeans as I ran to the main entrance.

Having just opened for the day, the mall was fairly quiet except for piped-in instrumental music. The Carlton Mall had been built a couple of years after I'd left town, so I was not familiar with its layout, and it was enormous. I ran across the parquet floor to the nearest "You Are Here" map, located between two huge white ceramic-tile planters.

Though I'd been there once or twice, I had no recollection of where the Java Bean was located, not even whether it was on the main level or upstairs. Under normal conditions, the maps were very easy to decipher, but nothing slows any task like trying to do it quickly. The Java Bean sold bags of coffee blends, so was it under "Restaurants" or "Specialty Stores"? Restaurant. Blue color-coded. That meant it was on the second floor.

I found it on the map at last. The shop was at the very opposite end of the mall. I charged up the stairs, taking the steps two at a time while jamming my keys into a back pocket of my jeans.

When I finally reached the doorway of the restaurant, I was sweaty and out of breath. I gasped for air and scanned the little shop and restaurant. The coffee aroma was overwhelming and made my mouth water. The restaurant was shaped in a long rectangle, with coffee and its paraphernalia sold along the left wall and a single row of small, aquamarine tables lining the right wall. A long sales-counter island in the middle formed a divider between the two sales functions. Two old women, getting a refill from a waitress, were at a table near me. José and Cherokee were sitting in the far corner with a young man with a shaved head. Even sitting down, Cherokee was a good inch taller than this companion, though that may have been an illusion caused by Cherokee's curly hair.

José's back was turned. He was so thin and wiry I could see the bumps of his backbone wrinkling the fabric of his white T-shirt. Cherokee and their companion were facing me. The man certainly looked like the messenger, all right. He had the same thick eyelids and crooked nose. Without the blue hair it was hard to be certain. The three of them seemed to be chatting pleasantly, though I'm sure the phrase "chatting pleasantly" would never have crossed their young lips.

I swept back my damp bangs and tried to get one last deep breath. Forcing myself to ignore my pounding heart, I walked casually toward their table. I had not taken three steps when both Bald Head and Cherokee looked up and saw me. Cherokee, who had never gotten a good look at me sans disguise, registered no reaction.

Bald Head's eyes widened, however. He stood up so fast he knocked over his bentwood chair. Just as the thought, *He's trapped; I'm in front of the exit* flashed through my brain, he bolted toward me. Before I could even react, he gave me a straight-arm that sent me flying backwards. I landed on my bottom, right on my keys. Momentum carried me partway into a backward somersault. I managed to get an arm down to break the impact of the back of my head hitting the linoleum floor. The waitress, carrying a pot of coffee, gasped and whirled around, sending a stream of scalding coffee onto me, most of which hit my right shin.

All at once someone screamed. A woman's voice cried, "Are you all right?" A male voice said, "Molly?" But my attention was focused on pulling on the hem of my jeans to separate the searing, wet fabric from my skin. In the process, I rolled onto my knees.

I gestured blindly and wildly at the entranceway. "I'm fine. Just catch him."

Through vision blurred with pain, I recognized José's retreating form as he tore after Bald Head. Someone with a strong grip had grabbed my upper arm to help me up. "Don't worry," said a deep voice. I craned my neck to see it was Cherokee. "José's a track star."

"The guy might be able to identify Tiffany's father's killer," I said.

Cherokee instantly released his grip on my arm and raced after José. The waitress took Cherokee's place, though she was so preoccupied with gushing out apologies for the spilled coffee that she was more of a hindrance than a help. The two elderly women had risen, and chattered at once about "that awful boy," and "Did you know him? Is he your son?"

My *son?* Oh, fine. In one week I'd gone from being a teenage impersonator to mother of a twenty-year-old.

Though I was certain the imprint of my key was permanently tattooed on my behind and my shin still smarted, I was not seriously injured. I ignored the women and limped out into the center area in time to look across the wood-and-metal railings and see José tackle Bald Head halfway across the mall from me. Cherokee was just a few strides away from the other two and sat on the guy's legs to keep him down.

My burned leg was killing me. Forcing myself into a rapid step, lunge, step, lunge, I made my way toward them. A salesman from a men's-suit store leaned out of his nearby shop, surveyed the scene, and said to me, "Don't worry, ma'am. I'll call Security."

My first words, when I reached the boys, were to the prone Bald Head, who was struggling to free himself under the weight of both José and Cherokee. "Hey, jerk-face," I yelled, panting, "that hurt! Don't you realize the police have been looking for you for the last ten days?"

"Yeah, I know." He struggled again. "Tell these baboons to get off my back so I can breathe."

"Sure. Just as soon as you answer my questions. What's your name?"

"Dayton."

"What's your first name?"

Though the side of his head was flat against the floor he managed to affix a fierce glare on me. "That *is* my first name, *Mike.* Last name's Smith. Lookit, lady. I'll talk to you once I stand up." He panted and barked back at Cherokee, "Hey you. Get off me or I'll fart in your face."

Cherokee grimaced and let him go. Dayton jerked free from José's grip as well and rolled over, rubbing his shoulder as he sat up. His face was bright red. He glared at me and said, "Whatever crap was in those boxes, I had nothing to do with it, okay?" I smiled at his unintentional pun as he continued, "I'm no idiot. I figured they prob'ly contained drugs, but the guy gave me a hundred dollars apiece to deliver the pair of 'em, and I needed the money."

"What guy?"

He rose. "It was some grungy-looking black dude," Dayton answered. "Met him in a bar. We were shooting pool and got to talking."

"Did he tell you his name or where he lived?"

"Just said his name was Bob. We arranged to meet at the park last Monday morning. He gave me the boxes and a hundred-dollar bill; told me he'd give me the other hundred after I got the two signatures to prove I'd made the deliveries."

"Two signatures?"

"Yeah. Mike Masters and Preston Saunders."

"And what happened when you went to the Saunderses' house?"

"Nobody answered the doorbell. So I went away and had a smoke, then I came back after about a half hour. This time a man answered the door, said he was Preston Saunders, and signed for the package."

A half an hour later? Would Stephanie have been in the bathroom all that time? I asked Dayton, "What did he look like?"

"Tall. Kinda old. White hair."

That fit Preston's description, all right, though only a

person younger than twenty-two or so would call a thirty-seven-year-old man "kind of old." "Then what?"

"I was supposed to meet up with the guy at the Java Bean and show him the signatures, but he never showed. Then I heard on the news about Preston Saunders getting shot, so I split. Till I found out my ol' lady filed a missing-persons report. I got back in town yesterday."

"Yesterday? Did you deliver a second package to my house yesterday?"

Dayton shook his head. "I haven't seen that black guy since he gave me the first two boxes. If I ever find him, I'm sure as hell not going to do another delivery for him."

"What's your address, Dayton?" I asked.

"Fourteen sixty-eight Groves Road," he answered quickly. That was a fairly major road that ran the length of downtown Carlton. I borrowed a pen from Cherokee and jotted down Dayton Smith's name and address on a facial tissue I'd found in my pocket.

Where was a security guard? Surely there couldn't be many disturbances at a few minutes after ten in the morning keeping them occupied. "Dayton, the boxes didn't contain drugs, so you don't have to worry. It's extremely important that you tell what you just told me to the police. They need to find the man who hired you."

"Yeah, sure," he said with a shrug. "No problem."

Hmm. He skips town, barrels me over to get away, then claims he'll just go complacently to the police. He was planning to bolt. *Where was Security?* "The three of you stay right here. I'll go get someone from Security to contact the police."

Cherokee, who was the tallest and bulkiest of the three young men, crossed his arms and stared at Dayton. José grinned and gave me a little salute, ignoring the shock of straight, black hair that had fallen into his eyes.

Security personnel, I knew, were stationed in a booth near the stairs by the south entrance. Which was, of course, assuming I could *find* south, considering that my internal compass played "Wheel of Fortune" with me on a regular basis. It would be faster to get the nearest salesperson to call Security. I darted into the men's-clothing store next door. The salesman who'd said he'd call Security was now deeply involved in showing someone a sports jacket.

"Excuse me," I said, not bothering to disguise my aggravation. "Did you—"

A male voice shouted my name from the open space of the mall. I whirled around just as the same voice cried, "He's getting away!"

I ran out of the clothing store. All three boys were out of sight. They had to have run into JCPenney. By repeatedly asking sales clerks if a young man or two ran by this way, I eventually found a very angry José and a distraught Cherokee by a JCPenney exit.

José flicked his hair out of his eyes and panted. "Lost him. There was a Fatty Arbuckle blocking my way down the escalator."

Cherokee said, "The three of us were just standing there, and then he goes, 'I got some unpaid parking tickets.' Then he Audi Five-thousands."

"He ran away?" I translated.

Cherokee nodded.

"Did he go outside?" I asked José.

He shrugged. "Maybe. Could still be hiding out inside."

I put a hand on each boy's arm. "Check the parking lots for a motorcycle. He drives some sort of a dirt bike."

They dashed outside, charging off in opposite directions on the sidewalk. I asked every shopper and sales clerk I came across if they had seen a young man with a shaved head, but had no luck. I made my way to the opposite side of the mall, figuring that was where Cherokee and José would likely meet up at some point.

Several minutes later, José and Cherokee trudged in, red-faced and winded. José shook his head. "No motorcycles out there at all."

"Yeah," Cherokee said. "We got to get to our English

class now, but we'll help you look for a while longer if you want.''

"No. I'd hate for you to miss English, of all things. Should I write your teacher a note, explaining why you're late?''

José let out a guffaw, but then smiled sweetly. "Nah. We'll take our chances.''

I thanked them for their Herculean efforts. They left for school while I located a public phone. I would have to call Sergeant Tommy and try to explain all of this. At least I had Dayton's name and address. Then again, I'd simply taken his word. With his outstanding "parking tickets,'' that information was worth almost as much as the facial tissue I'd written them on.

Once again, I got Tommy's machine, instructing me to leave a message or press One to get transferred to the dispatcher.

"Tommy?'' I began, opting to leave a message. "This is Molly. I saw the messenger at the mall. He says his name is Dayton Smith and he lives at Fourteen sixty-eight Groves Road. He says a grungy-looking black dude paid him a hundred dollars to deliver the packages to me and Preston, but then he couldn't find the black guy again to get the other hundred. There's more, but the thing is, he's gone now. I was trying to get a call in to you when he ran away. So, that's about it. Good luck.''

By the time I made my way to my car, I was limping badly. However, sitting down on my bruised behind didn't feel much better. This was my just desserts for letting him get away, I decided as I drove toward the exit.

The light was red. I stopped behind a van, then scanned in my rearview mirror for vehicles pulling up behind mine, hoping against logic that I would spot Dayton's motorcycle. Two cars were approaching. I did a double take at the driver in the second car, a bright red Subaru. Was that a bald head, or just a pink, skin-tight hat?

My view was partially blocked by the vehicle between

ours. I yanked the parking brake on and stepped out of my car to look into the Subaru.

It was Dayton. His jaw dropped at the sight of me. He threw his car into reverse and pulled a squealing U-turn.

SIXTEEN

Think "Horses"

DAYTON SPED diagonally across the parking lot. The license plate was caked with mud. I couldn't make out a single number. I gave in to a stupid impulse to run after him for a short distance, then charged back to my car and got in. One vehicle was in front of me, another was behind, and a traffic island plus two cars in the adjacent lane prevented me from turning. I was stuck in the middle like the filling of one big, automotive panic sandwich.

I turned and gestured wildly for the driver behind me to back up. It was one of the old ladies from the coffee shop. She gave me a wan smile and answered me with a gentle hand gesture that said, "No, dearie. We're supposed to go forward now."

I growled in frustration, then shook my steering wheel so hard the airbag would have inflated, if my car had had one. I scanned the island wondering if I could drive over it, but it featured a steep cement planter that held daffodils. "Sit here and wait for the World's Slowest Traffic Light but, hey, at least there are some *damn daffodils to look at!*"

At last the light turned green. My tires squealed and shot out a spray of puddle water as I pulled a U-turn and sped toward the entrance opposite this one, in the direction Dayton had driven.

I screeched my Toyota to a stop as I neared the rear mall entrance, seeing no sign of the red Subaru. This entrance was at an intersection in which Dayton could have gone any of three directions. He had escaped.

I went home. Jim, wearing a red flannel shirt and blue sweatpants, was sitting at the kitchen table, idly pulling on his mustache in an unconscious habit as he read the paper. Though he had excellent eyesight, he always furrowed his brow when he read, and I flashed on the first time I'd ever seen him: at the CU library when he was a junior engineering student and I was a sophomore in journalism. He had no mustache to pull on back then, but was fidgeting with the ends of his hair that reached past the collar of his denim jacket. I was with two girlfriends, and one whispered to me as we neared him, "What a cutie." Just then, he looked up, did a barely detectable double take at me, and returned to his reading. My girlfriends and I passed his table, but my friends, both of whom had boyfriends, dared me to go talk to him. I never could resist a really good dare. So, with butterflies in my stomach, my cheeks burning, I crossed the room and said...

"Hi. What are you reading?"

"The sports section." His vision stayed riveted on his newspaper. "The comics are on the counter by the microwave."

I sighed. I pulled out an oak chair across from him, but wasn't sure I really felt like sitting. For one thing, I had too much adrenaline to sit, and for another, my tailbone was still very sore.

He looked up at me, then scanned the kitchen counters in confusion. "Didn't you get anything at the store?"

"Almost, but it got away."

He grimaced, but said nothing and waited for me to continue.

I kicked one leg of the chair with my sneaker. "If only I'd insisted Cherokee and José sit on the guy till Security came...."

Jim groaned. "Who's this 'guy' that the other two people didn't get the chance to wrestle to the ground for you?"

"The messenger. You know. The one that brought the box of dog poop."

"Oh, of course." He rubbed his forehead. "And who are Cherokee and José?"

"They're just kids. Friends of Tiffany's."

Jim refolded his newspaper and stood up. "What's Sergeant Newton's number?"

"Why?"

"Since you're staying till Saturday, I want to call him and ask if he can put you into protective custody for the next two days."

"You're kidding, aren't you?"

He merely met my gaze.

The phone rang. I beat Jim to the phone and answered.

"Molly, what is going on?" Tommy Newton hollered over the phone by way of a greeting.

"You got my message, I take it?"

"Where's this Dayton Smith guy now? That address you gave me was totally bogus. There *is* no One-four-six-eight Groves Road."

Damn. "He drove away from the, um, south exit of the Carlton Mall in a red Subaru with an unreadable license plate."

"What do you mean, unreadable?"

"He'd deliberately plastered mud on it. I'm not even positive what state it was from. That probably wasn't really his name, either. He said he had some unresolved run-ins with the law. He also told me that last week his live-in girl friend or his mother, whatever an 'old lady' is these days, filed a missing-persons report on him."

"Last week? We haven't had any MPRs filed last week. Come down here, Molly."

"Down where?"

"To the station house. You need me to send an officer to pick you up?"

"No, I can drive. I'll be there in a few minutes." I hung up and this time went to the coat closet for my raincoat.

"Where are you going now?" Jim asked.

"The police station. Tommy probably wants me to fill out a report or something."

"I'm coming with you." He started to grab that navy blue, chicken-feather coat of his.

"Nathan's kindergarten bus will be arriving in forty minutes. You'll have to stay here to meet it. I probably won't be back in time."

I gave him a parting kiss, but he looked miserable. I hated to see him so worried about me. But I was already feeling more than enough guilt; I couldn't take on more now for having caused my husband to be so concerned. He asked me to take the Jeep. "Its tires are better on slick roads than the Toyota's." Too bad he hadn't convinced me to drive his car earlier. The Jeep might have managed to plow up and over the daffodil garden.

As I backed down the driveway, I suddenly remembered I had forgotten to help out in Nathan's class for the second Thursday in a row. My luncheon date with Emma Groves was an hour from now, and I was supposed to bring Nathan to meet her five-year-old. This was like being in the middle of a tidal wave. All I could do now was try to keep my head up.

"HARD TO BE consistent when you lie," Tommy said. We were in the cramped, messy quarters of his office once again.

I studied Tommy's face, wondering if he meant the general "you," or "You, Molly, are lying to me." Tommy, apparently sensing how bad I already felt, was more talkative and friendly than normal. On the other hand, his current openness might merely be an act he thought was encouraging me to "spill my guts." During the past forty minutes, I'd already spilled all the guts I thought I had. If I was withholding even one piece of information that might prove to be a clue, it was certainly unbeknownst to me. He continued, "Usually, when a suspect gives you an alias, it's one he's used before. Name'll be similar to his real one, or it's his nickname. Here, your guy says his last name is Smith, so you figure, his first name really is Dayton. Or maybe his last name's Dayton. His nickname's Dayton. But I've checked the computer records, and nothing. DMV's got nothing for motorcycles or Subarus owned by Smiths or Daytons. Same thing with the address. Right street, wrong number or wrong street, right number. Again, nothing. Either this Dayton fellow lied about having some past brushes with the law and is completely clean, or he's one smooth operator.''

"Did you check unpaid parking tickets?" I asked quietly.

Tommy ignored my question and asked, "So the only physical description Dayton gave you of the man he claims paid him for the deliveries was 'a grungy-looking black man'?''

"Dude, actually. But, yes. The only black man I know of who knew Preston was Chase Groves. I'm sure Preston knew others who might have borne a grudge against him, but how would they know about the cartoon?''

"It wasn't Dr. Groves," Tommy said. "Like I told you yesterday, he was in Ohio at the time Preston was killed. By the way, how's your tooth?''

"Fine. Thanks for asking.''

"The way you keep popping up, talking to our chief witnesses, I could make a pretty good case for obstruction of justice.''

Oh, great. So now he was threatening to put me in jail. No more Mr. Nice Cop. Considering my friendship with his new girlfriend, I wasn't totally without power, either. "How are things going between you and Lauren?''

"Fine. Thanks for asking.'' He pointed a thick, slightly freckled finger in my face. "Stay away from the Saunders family today. No phone calls. No visits. That's a direct order. You break it, and any judge in this country will agree with me 'bout obstruction.''

"Why? Are you going to arrest Stephanie?"

"Don't see as I have much choice. She's the one with the obvious motive and opportunity. There's an old saying, 'When you hear hoofbeats and neighing, think horses, not zebras.'"

I'd heard the expression before on a TV show—the experienced doctor giving that advice to an intern. At the time, I'd grumbled, "Yeah, but this is television, Doc. You'd better think pink wooly mammoths, dancing the mambo." Tommy had made a valid point for real life, though. "But what about the person who shot at me and Tiffany? That couldn't have been Stephanie."

"That's been the only puzzling piece of evidence. Kept me from arresting her this long. But she could have just hired someone."

"Why would she do that? Why would she hire someone to shoot at me and her own daughter?"

He made a face as if he thought my question was idiotic, but answered, "So she could establish an alibi for the second shooting. To make it look like someone else murdered her husband."

I shook my head. "Stephanie adores Tiffany. She just plain wouldn't have taken the risk that the person she hired might accidentally shoot her daughter. Even if her instructions had been to fire a couple of shots into the air then run away, she couldn't have known for sure the person would follow her instructions."

He leaned back in his chair. "Which is exactly why it was a good ploy for diverting suspicion from herself."

"The murder weapon was a twenty-two, right?"

He nodded. "And, by the way, Richard Worthington's three-fifty-seven Magnum is his only gun."

His only *registered* gun, I silently corrected. I rose. "I've got to get going. I won't contact the Saunderses, but just for the record, I think you're wrong. She looks guilty...but that's partially why I think she's innocent; because she has tried to look guilty."

"She looks guilty 'cause she is. Like I said, Moll. Think horses." He stood up. "Better yet, leave the thinking to me."

I chuckled, but managed to resist giving a sarcastic reply.

In defiance of Tommy's recent advice, I sat thinking things over in my car for a minute before starting the engine. If Stephanie had indeed hired the person who shot at me and Tiffany, she may well have hired the "grungy-looking" black man who'd paid Dayton to deliver the boxes. For that matter, anyone could have hired him as a go-between.

But a more puzzling question was: Why had Tommy told me in advance he was going to arrest Stephanie? That was out of character for him. Perhaps he *wanted* me to warn her, to see if she'd act guilty and try to leave town. If so, his logic was flawed. I was not about to contact Stephanie and risk obstruction-of-justice charges for someone I disliked and mistrusted.

I drove home, planning to rush in and explain to Jim that Nathan and I had a lunch date. However, when I pulled into the driveway, Jim was sitting in my Toyota, engine running. We rolled down our windows, and he called over the motor noise, "I called the police station just now. Tom said you'd left. There's been an emergency at work. Nathan's inside. I'll be back as soon as I can."

After wishing him well, I collected Nathan, scooped up my dentist drawings to leave them with Emma for Chase's feedback, and drove to Emma's house. She lived in a newer section of town called Northern Knolls.

Despite the development's name, the land there was flat. This was one of the nicer parts of town, though not quite as affluent as I might have predicted for country club members. The homes were mostly two-story structures, white or gray the most popular color of exterior paint, on well-maintained, half-acre lots. The Groveses' residence looked the same as their immediate neighbors', except it was the only one painted yellow with maroon shutters and trim.

When I first rang the doorbell, I suffered a momentary anxiety, wondering if she would remember the arrangements we'd made two days earlier. Emma opened the door and greeted me warmly. She was wearing sandals and a simple yet elegant cotton dress with a pattern of black leaves against a brown background slightly lighter than her skin. Her nice clothes reminded me I'd forgotten to change from my jeans and sweatshirt.

Her son, Joshua, was adorable. He'd inherited his mother's wonderful smile and had big brown eyes. A bundle of energy, he hopped the entire time Emma and I introduced the children to each other. I made a big deal of the fact that they'd go to the same school next year, thinking this might give them some common ground. The moment I stopped talking, Joshua said, "Come on, Nathan. I got a race track in my room. And *two* monster trucks."

Nathan, though typically shy, said, "Cool!" and dashed up the stairs with him.

"Nathan?" Emma called. He stopped on the top landing and looked back at her. "I made a Chinese dish for your mother and me. It has chicken and almonds in it. Would you like some, or would you rather have a peanut-butter-and-jelly sandwich?"

"Go for the sandwich, Nathan," Joshua advised.

"I'll take a peanut-butter-and-jelly sandwich," Nathan answered earnestly. "But no jelly. Just put peanut butter on bread. Can I still get a fortune cookie?"

"I have no fortune cookies, dear. Not even for your mother." While Nathan scrambled into Joshua's room and shut the door, she winked at me. "I hope you will forgive the oversight."

"Ah, well. Those fortunes are hardly ever worth reading, anyway. 'You will inherit great wealth and a large car.' Personally, I think it would be way more interesting if those cookies would give some more immediate fortunes, such as 'Leave your waitress a good tip—she's packing an Uzi.' Or 'There's something stuck between your teeth.'"

Emma laughed. We decided to give the boys a chance to play for a few minutes. Emma took me on a brief tour of the main level, which was nicely decorated in attractive yet comfortable furniture. It was dust free and recently vacuumed, though there were occasional marks and fingerprints that indicated a child lived here. We settled into comfortable seats in the living room.

During a conversational pause, I pulled out my drawings from my purse. "Before I forget, could you show these to Chase tonight? I'm not going to try to pressure him into buying them himself, I'd just like his feedback on whether or not he thinks they'd be worth trying to market to dentists."

She looked at the drawings and chuckled. "You design advertisements?"

"No, greeting cards."

"What a wonderful occupation."

She gave me such an engaging smile I didn't feel like arguing with her, though in truth my "occupation" did have one serious flaw—it paid less than any other vocation, with the possible exceptions of preschool teacher and migrant farm worker.

"So," Emma said, "Tell me what it was like to return to Carlton. You said you were gone for seventeen years, is that right?"

"Right. Just after I graduated until this past fall. It's not too bad, I guess. I miss my friends and my home in Boulder. My husband, Jim, and I are looking to rent a place here. My parents will be coming back to Carlton soon, but we don't know how long Jim's assignment here will last."

"Are you anxious to return to Boulder?"

"Sometimes. One wonderful thing about Carlton, though, is I'm living next door to my childhood best friend again. On the other hand, it's certainly been difficult returning to my childhood nemesis."

"Oh? And who is that?"

"Stephanie Saunders, though her name was Geist when I knew her. Before she married Preston."

I straightened in surprise as she let out an angry growl and punched the couch on either side of her. "I am so sick of hearing that man's name. He got exactly what he deserved."

"You think he deserved to be murdered?" I asked quietly, uncomfortable in the face of her unexpected reaction.

"As long as I live, I will never forget how I felt when, out of the blue, I got a call from Preston's lawyer."

"*You* got a call?"

"He asked to speak to Chase, but Chase happened to be out of town. So I asked what the call was in reference to, and he said in this...incredulous tone, 'This is about Mr. Saunders's malpractice suit against Dr. Chase Groves.'" She grimaced and shook her head. "I called Chase out of his meeting—"

"Meeting?" I repeated, trying to sort out whether this out-of-town visit was the trip to Cleveland that gave Chase an unshakable alibi, according to Tommy.

"Yes. He was at a convention in Cleveland. Chase knew nothing about the suit either. Needless to say, he was most upset. Apparently, last December, Preston had gone to my husband to have him replace an old filling. Now, mind you, Preston was the one who insisted on the appointment. He claimed he wanted the filling removed because he had heard some nonsense about old fillings being poisonous. Preston had been a patient of my husband's for a couple of years by then, and a golf partner for even longer. Preston mentioned to my husband that he had read an article about some lady suing her dentist, claiming permanent nerve damage from a filling. That the dentist's insurance covered everything, so the whole lawsuit business was 'no skin off the dentist's nose.' Chase, of course, pointed out to Preston that the dentist could easily lose his practice in a case like that. Chase had to drill Preston's tooth just a little for the new filling, and..."

"Preston claimed to have permanent nerve damage as a result?"

Emma nodded and gritted her teeth. "In the past four months or so, he made not one mention of any tooth pain, let alone an impending lawsuit, during their weekly get-togethers at the club."

I shook my head. "Chase must have gone through the ceiling."

"Oh, yes. We confronted Preston at the club the very next day."

Aha! The altercation the employee at the country club had said nearly required police intervention. But how could that be? "Which next day? Didn't you say Chase was in Cleveland?"

"He was so upset he flew home. All Preston had to say about the matter was it was nothing personal. Just a legal matter for their lawyers and my husband's insurance carrier to dicker over."

"How awful," I murmured, but all I could think was that Chase's alibi that he was in Cleveland at the time was now suspect.

"Did he return to his convention?"

She shrugged. "Yes, a few days later, though he had missed everything. He could not concentrate, in any case."

So why return at all? Or did he need that Cleveland convention as an alibi? Maybe he really stayed in town through Monday, the day Preston was killed.

Suddenly I recalled Tommy's words about how pieces of the truth filter into suspects' stories. That's when it hit me. Maybe I'd crossed Chase off my list of suspects too easily, blinded by his elegance and charm. If I could be a twenty-year-old student, Chase could be a "grungy-looking black dude."

Perhaps Dayton had known the name of the black man who hired him after all. Dayton had said he lived on Groves Road. As in Emma and Chase Groves.

SEVENTEEN

There's Something Stuck
Between Your Teeth

WHILE EMMA called the children to the table, a realization struck me with the force of a Mack truck: I had brought my son to the home of a possible murderer!

None of this necessarily meant Chase had killed Preston. Yet here was Dayton, or whatever the messenger's real name was, telling me a "grungy-looking black dude" hired him. All Chase would have to do was put on some worn-out clothes, go hang out at the bar till the right type of person wanders in—Dayton—and hire him. And here was Chase claiming to be in Cleveland, yet so angry with Preston less than a week before the murder, Chase had flown home.

Though it felt as if I had swallowed a bowling ball, I did my best to eat a respectable amount of almond chicken. In the meantime, Nathan and Joshua giggled over their peanut butter sandwiches.

After a tense hour, I managed to drag Nathan away from Joshua and explain that I needed to "get some things done around the house before Karen gets home."

It had started to drizzle again and the windows instantly fogged up. We stayed at the curb and let the engine and the front and rear defrosters warm up. Though the passenger seat was empty, Nathan had taken his usual seat directly behind me. I automatically asked him if he'd had a good time with Joshua. While Nathan was answering that yes, he'd had "a really good time," I decided I would call Tommy the moment we got home.

"Josh said he was going to go to my school next year," came Nathan's sweet, disembodied little voice from behind me. "I hope he's in my class. Then I won't be the only one who's different."

"What do you mean?"

"Josh is different 'cause he has brown skin. I'm different 'cause I'm the only kid in my class from Colorado."

My eyes welled with tears. It struck me as both profound and heartbreaking that my six-year-old would know that the color of someone's skin should be no more differentiating than what state the person happened to have been born in. And here I was, minutes away from turning in Josh's dad as a possible murderer.

The Jeep's windows weren't entirely defogged, but I backed down the driveway in a hurry to get home and report to Tommy. Oddly, someone in a green Mazda pulled out from two houses down just as I did. Maybe I was just being paranoid, but instead of heading for the housing-development exit, I turned right at the next block just to make sure the car wasn't following me. It turned, too.

"Mommy? When Karen's ten, how old will I be?"

"Eight." It was possible the car behind me was simply visiting a friend who lived down this street. I took my second right.

"Why will I just be eight?"

The green Mazda turned as well. I took a left and another right, zigzagging through Northern Knolls.

"Why, Mommy?"

The car was still behind me. I silently strung a slew of swear words together. We were being followed.

"Why, Mommy?" Nathan asked again.

"Uh…" Age. He'd asked about his and Karen's ages. "You'll always be two years younger than she is."

The green Mazda had sped up a little to keep pace. The driver was a black man.

"That's not fair! I don't want to be younger!"

Oh my God! I'm being followed! My child's in the backseat! Drive safely and don't panic!

Nathan was in tears now and kicking my seat.

My pulse raced. I desperately needed Nathan to be quiet. "Stop crying! You'll appreciate being younger when you're older!"

My answer gave him pause, but then he cried, "You like Karen best! That's why you made her get born first!"

"Not now, Nathan! Mommy needs to concentrate on her driving."

"How come you keep looking in the mirror?"

"Because...because there's something stuck between my teeth."

Please. Dear God. I scanned for people out in their front yards. If I could find anyone outside, I could pull into their driveway and ask them to call the police. No one was in sight. Two p.m. on a rainy Thursday afternoon. They were probably all at work or watching soaps.

"Are you lost again, Mommy?"

"Yes," I snapped back, then realized that was the truth.

"I think we go this way," Nathan pointed at an intersection.

I followed his instructions. He was right. We were back on the main drag that would take us out of Northern Knolls. The car behind me sped closer still. I sped up as well. This time the Mazda had gotten near enough for me to recognize the driver. It was Chase Groves.

He beeped his horn at me and waved. I waved back, rationalizing that if I behaved normally, he wouldn't realize I suspected him of murdering Preston. My taking circuitous routes through housing developments in the process of being lost was normal behavior for me, sad to say.

We neared the exit of Northern Knolls. The light was red. "We turn left after this light, don't we?"

"Yes," Nathan answered.

I'd already known this, but letting him feel he was helping me find my way home had proven to be a good distraction for him. The last thing I wanted to do now, though, was lead Chase to my house. I would drive straight past it, to the police station a mile beyond our home.

Chase stopped behind my Jeep for the light and gestured for me to pull over. Oh, right. Like I'm really going to risk that!

Then again, my son was in the car. I couldn't take any chances of Chase trying to run me off the slick roads. Instead, I could try to gain some distance on him by getting him to leave his car, then I'd speed away. I cranked down my window, gave the "okay" sign, and gestured at the wide shoulder up ahead.

I pulled over, holding my breath. *Please don't let him shoot at me!* He stopped right behind me and got out of his sporty-looking Mazda into the drizzling rain. He was wearing a bulky leather jacket. His right hand was in his jacket pocket. If that hand was holding a .22, I was doomed. I called out the window, "Stop following me, Chase! My son is in the car and you're scaring me!"

He froze, but then took another couple of steps, his hand still in his pocket. "Wait, Molly. I just want to tell you something."

I gunned my engine and sped away, pulling in between two cars. I breathed a sigh of relief and watched him through my rearview mirror. He held both palms up in a gesture of helplessness, then pivoted and headed back to his car.

"Who was that, Mommy?" Nathan asked nervously.

"My dentist. I probably have a cavity he wanted to tell me about."

"Maybe he wants to help you with that thing stuck between your teeth."

"Yeah, that's probably it." We drove up a steel hill. I stared into the mirror. To my horror, Chase had gotten back into his car and was now speeding to catch up to us. Defying the rain and the steep hill, he crossed the double yellow line and passed two cars. *Oh, shit!*

Recollections haunted me of a horrifying incident that took place in Denver. A woman who'd temporarily rescued a kidnap victim drove to a police station, only to be shot herself and the victim recaptured in the police parking lot.

"Um, that reminds me. We're going to pay a visit to my friend Sergeant Tommy and ask him about his dentist." Though I'd tried my best, my voice sounded tense and unnatural.

Nathan craned his neck and peered out the back window. "The dentist is waving at us."

"Sit back down!" I took a deep breath and tried to calm myself. "He's just being friendly."

Alarmed by my mood, Nathan said nothing as we zoomed past the turnoff for our house. The police station was straight up ahead. Chase's car was now just three cars back from mine. I got into the left-turn lane for the station.

A steady stream of traffic blocked my way. Chase pulled up directly behind me. He clasped his hands together in mock prayer, then gestured at me to pull over to the right of the road.

There was a small gap between cars and I gunned it. We squeaked through, though the cars hit their brakes and honked.

"What's wrong, Mommy?" Nathan asked.

"I think my dentist's mad at me. We're going to talk to Sergeant Tommy about it." I shed my seat belt and opened Nathan's. "I'm carrying you in so we can go really fast."

I ignored Nathan's protests and pulled him between the bucket seats and into my lap—no easy matter, but I wanted to shield him with my body. I watched the street, my heart pounding. Chase was still in the turn lane.

I leaned on my horn. A black, elderly officer came out. I opened my door and clutched Nathan against my body and ran toward him.

I whirled around and pointed with my chin just as Chase pulled a U-turn. "See that green Mazda?" I cried to the officer. "It's been following me for the last five miles. Driver's name is Chase Groves."

"Okay, ma'am. I'll pull him over and see what's going on."

Tommy, who must have heard my honking, met us in the lobby, where I finally felt it was safe to lower Nathan to his feet. I told Tommy I needed to talk to him privately for a couple of minutes. He said he'd get someone to keep an eye on Nathan for me. He located a female officer, who pulled out a game of Trouble from a cabinet and sat with Nathan outside Tommy's office.

Tommy listened patiently as I told him I was being chased by Chase Groves and how Chase had suddenly discovered Preston was suing him. When I finished relating my theory that Chase hadn't returned to Cleveland but had stayed in town to kill Preston, Tommy shook his head.

"Couple days ago," Tommy said, "Dr. Groves told me all about that lawsuit. Also 'bout how he'd flown in, confronted Preston, then flew back out the next Friday. So I called his sister in Cleveland. She verified the whole story."

"And you're just going to take his sister's word for it?"

"Hers and the airline's. He was on a flight from Cleveland to Albany on a Monday, a week before Preston died. He was also on the following day's flight *back* to Cleveland, just like he said. *And* he was on his scheduled return flight from Cleveland a week later...the day *after* Preston died."

I hesitated, but only for an instant. "So? That doesn't tell us anything."

"Us?" Tommy growled.

"Who's to say he didn't take another round trip in between those flights? He flies into town that weekend, goes into a bar looking for someone to make the deliveries that made STOP look guilty. He hires Dayton, maybe follows him so he knows the boxes were delivered, then kills Preston and returns to Cleveland so he can be on his Tuesday flight home.''

''Checked that already,'' Tommy said, mangling a paper clip absentmindedly as he spoke. ''Checked the passenger lists for all the round-trip flights between Cleveland 'n' here that week. Chase Groves wasn't on any of them.''

''So? He used an alias! You think if he went through this much trouble to concoct this elaborate scheme of dog-poop deliveries that he'd just get tickets under his own name?''

''He'd have to have paid cash for his tickets,'' Tommy argued as his mangled paper clip broke. ''Credit cards or personal checks would have listed his name. There were no passengers, none, from Friday through Sunday who paid cash in Cleveland for a flight to Albany.''

''Maybe one of his relatives paid for the flight. Or he drove. Or went by train.''

Tommy rested his elbows on his desk and glared into my eyes. ''Molly, you are the most stubborn person I've met in my life. Listen to me. Chase Groves did not kill Preston Saunders. He was in Cleveland.''

''How can you be so sure? He just followed me halfway across town! Why would he do that unless he knew I was going straight to the police?''

He rubbed his forehead. ''Answer me this, Molly. Half of the town knew about his beef with Preston. So what was he going to gain by preventing you from talking to us, huh?''

My cheeks grew warm. That was a good question, and both of us knew it. ''Maybe he thought Emma told me more than she did. Maybe he confessed to her.''

Tommy sank his face onto his hands in frustration.

''Well?'' I said, my voice shooting up with my own frustration that more than matched his. ''That's plausible. Why else would he chase after me like that?''

He straightened. "I don't know. Possibly if you'd given him a chance to tell you, you'd have found out."

I stood up and grabbed the doorknob to leave. "Or possibly, if I hadn't driven off like I did, I would be dead by now."

As I opened the door, Tommy said, "Just one more thing you may want to know, Molly."

I turned and waited. Tommy was now leaning back in his chair, arms folded across his chest. "That sister of his who says Chase was with her on Monday? Don't be too quick to accuse her of lying."

Tommy waited for me to take the bait. While part of me knew better, the defiant part of me couldn't resist. "Now's when you tell me she wouldn't lie, right? She's a judge or policewoman or someone you're sure wouldn't lie, even to save her own brother."

"She's a nun."

I winced. I couldn't help it. Tommy gave me such a smarter-than-thou smile, I retorted, "Oh, right. Like nuns don't ever lie? It could happen."

I marched up to Nathan, who was in the process of winning his third straight game—bless her—from the policewoman. After waiting for the last couple of rolls of the die and Nathan's victory, we left. The patrolman who'd, upon my urging, raced after Chase was now chatting with the woman behind the desk in the lobby. They stopped talking when I passed, and I had the distinct impression they'd been talking about me.

Okay. So maybe I'd made a mistake. Maybe Chase wasn't guilty. But then why follow me all over the place and pull me over? Were my brake lights out?

Just in case, the moment we got home I had Nathan help me check my brake and signal lights. They were fine. Jim still wasn't home from his "office emergency," but Karen's bus would arrive in a few minutes. In the relative quiet, the question of why Chase followed me ran through my brain. Asking him myself was too embarrassing even to consider—"Hello, Chase? Sorry I called the police on you. Did you have something important on your mind?" Instead, I decided to call Emma and thank her for lunch, and perhaps see if I could glean some inkling about why her husband may have followed me.

I dialed Emma and was shocked when a deep voice answered that sounded a lot like Chase. My first instinct was to hang up, but I thought twice and said in a squeaky voice, "May I speak to Emma, please?"

When she got on the line moments later, I said, "Hi, Emma? It's Molly. I just wanted to thank you for lunch. I had a nice time."

"Oh, you did, did you?" There was such unmistakable, seething anger in her voice that my palms began to perspire.

"Yes. Really. Thank you. I guess Chase is there, so he probably told you about his trying to talk to me earlier, right?"

"Yes, indeed. He told me. About that. About how you sent a police officer to arrest him. An African-American follows you in his car, and you leap to the conclusion that 'the black guy did it.'"

"It isn't that, Emma. I *didn't* ask the officer to arrest him, just to find out why he'd been following me. A mutual acquaintance of ours was recently murdered. Given the circumstances, any woman would panic being followed by a man—white or black. I had no way of knowing why Chase was following me, so I—"

"He wanted to invite you to my birthday party tonight, Molly. He had only thought to invite you after you mentioned our lunch at your dental appointment. He spotted your car in the driveway, and decided at the last minute to see if you could come."

"Oh," I said quietly. I nodded at my daughter, Karen, who'd just burst through the door and was trying to tell me how cold and wet she was.

"And, by the way," Emma continued, "despite the fact

that you humiliated him, he wants to buy your cartoons. Call him at his office.''

She hung up.

I set the phone down gently, and Karen studied my face and asked, ''Who was that on the phone, Mom? What's wrong?''

Bewildered and horridly embarrassed, I hung my head. ''Nothing,'' I said quietly. ''I just made a sale.''

EIGHTEEN

We Must Look at zee Evidence

AFTER HANGING up with Emma, I sat in quiet contemplation. Chase Groves might have had a printed invitation for me, which he'd been keeping safe from the elements in his pocket. That could marginally explain why he'd kept his hand in his pocket and why he wanted to see me in person rather than simply call me at home. And then perhaps he'd followed me to explain or apologize, thinking I must have needed help because I was so agitated.

Still, Chase Groves had made some fundamental mistakes in following me. As I'd tried to explain to Emma, any woman traveling with her young child in the car would feel threatened when followed by some man she'd just met, regardless of his race. Especially when that man was on the woman's short list of possible murder suspects.

The phone rang. The moment I answered, Jim said, "Are you all right?"

"Pretty much."

"Where were you?" His voice was rife with worry. "I thought you were going to be home. I called several times and nobody answered."

"I was out making a fool of myself during a luncheon date with a former potential friend. But I'm home now. How are things going at work?"

"Never mind that." He sighed. "I can't take this. When you didn't answer, I thought...are you planning on going out again?"

"No."

"Good. I've got to…things are a mess here. The system crashed and there's…I can't come home right now, but I can't concentrate."

Jim was not easily rattled. Now suddenly he couldn't complete his sentences. I'd never heard him sound this scared. "I'm planning to stay home the rest of the day."

"Good. Just…call me if you have to run out for any reason. Okay? So I'll know where you are?"

I agreed, empathizing. On several memorable occasions my imagination had run rampant with fear that Jim had gotten into a traffic accident when we'd merely miscommunicated.

Interfering with my thoughts was Karen and Nathan's spirited debate about which one of them was ignoring the other. The correct and obvious answer being "neither," this was a particularly lame-brained argument to have to listen to. They compounded my aggravation by drifting into whichever room I entered. They finally quieted when I put on my unplugged headphones, which I've conned the children into thinking blocks all noise.

Despite my desire to direct my brain waves elsewhere, my mind went right back to my suspicions about the murder. I'd already crossed off Hank Mueller for being too obvious, but what about his wife? Could Sabrina have wanted to frame her own husband for murder? No. Having a convicted murderer as a spouse would drop her too far in social standings. That left Richard Worthington. But if he had a motive, I hadn't discovered it yet.

It felt as though I had overlooked some major, obvious clue in all of this. If only I could discover that clue, I could stay "safe at home" as Jim wanted, yet solve this thing, as I so desperately wanted.

To help me sort out my thoughts, I sat down in the living room and doodled a drawing of Hercule Poirot in a room with a toppled, empty birdcage. There are claw marks on the rug and feathers around the room. Around him sit a circle of elderly people, plus one very guilty looking cat. Hercule is saying, "And now, *mon ami*, we must use zee little gray cells. We must look at zee evidence."

The doorbell rang. Fortunately, the children were out of the room so they didn't notice that I, headphones and all, had heard it ring. Karen was in her room. Nathan, wearing his red Bart Simpson raincoat, was on the back deck, hammering tacks into a short two-by-four he'd found.

I opened the door. Stephanie! She was supposed to be in the process of being arrested. Now what? Did she want me to hide her?

She mustered a smile. "I am so sick of being cooped up in that house. Estelle has Mikey. I know I should probably have called first, but I was so anxious to get out I just took off. May I come in?"

Oh, sure, I told myself. Tempt Tommy to arrest me as an accomplice. But, there was no place better to start re-hashing possible overlooked clues than by talking to Stephanie. "Come on in." I scanned the empty street for police vehicles before shutting the door.

She hung up her London Fog overcoat on the brass rack on the entranceway wall, and we settled into seats in the living room. Stephanie was not the sort of person simply to drop in on anyone, least of all me, without an ulterior motive. Nonetheless, I went through the ordinary motions of offering her something to drink and asking about the baby, determined to let her settle in and then glean as much information from her as possible. In the meantime, Karen gave one peek down the stairs, saw it was only Stephanie and not a friend of hers, and went back to her room and shut the door.

Stephanie asked, "Have you talked to Tommy lately?"

"Why do you ask?" I responded, avoiding the question.

"Just a feeling. He's going to arrest me, isn't he?"

"Is he?"

She picked some lint off the armrest of her chair. "That's twice now you've answered me with another question. That's not like you. You're usually so blunt."

"Am I?" I asked automatically, then shrugged in apology. "I'm turning over a new leaf."

"Well, turn it back," she snapped. "It's annoying and I'm in a hurry. Who killed my husband?"

Surprised at the unexpected question, I answered simply, "I don't know."

In a rare display of frazzled nerves, she pounded the tops of her thighs and said. "Then think, damn it! I don't want to get arrested! Tell me what your best clues are."

Not wanting to repeat the awful scene at the Saunderses' house when I'd allowed Tiffany to overhear, I excused myself, summoned Karen, and insisted she play out in the backyard with her brother. When the sliding glass door was safely closed behind them, I returned to the living room and reclaimed my seat.

"I don't know who killed Preston," I admitted to Stephanie. "Just as soon as something starts to make sense, it winds up only making everything more confusing than ever. So be straight with me. Why did you search Preston's pockets?"

"I'm minutes away from getting arrested, Molly. You're wasting my precious time." She rolled her eyes. "But I do owe you an explanation. The truth is…" She pursed her lips and averted her gaze. "He was leaving me for another woman. He'd told me he would stick around to help me through the birth, but that afterwards he would file for a divorce."

I was completely taken aback, though now I chastised myself that I should have known. It went a long way toward explaining Stephanie's hard-heartedness regarding Preston's death. "Who was the other woman?"

Though her cheeks were flushed and she fidgeted with a cuticle, her voice was steady as she said, "I still don't know. That's why I was searching his pockets. I thought if

I could find a name or phone number in his pocket, I'd also find out who killed him—an angry husband or jilted lover.''

"But you told me his last word was 'Tiffany.' That you were afraid she might have done it. Why would you have immediately decided the killer was actually his mistress's lover?"

She flicked her hand at me impatiently. "Okay, okay. So I told one little fib. I never really suspected Tiffany. She's the main beneficiary of Preston's estate, once she's of age. Preston was probably afraid for her life."

"You *lied* about suspecting your own *daughter* just to get me to help you?"

"Molly, this is no time for quibbling. Yes, I lied to you. I'm sorry. There. All better?"

"No! You owe one hell of an apology to Tiffany!"

She pursed her lips.

To prevent myself from slapping her, I dug my fingers into the cushions of the couch and gritted my teeth. "What about the bank withdrawal slip for ten thousand dollars? Did you lie about that, too?"

"Of course not. Why would I lie about something like that?"

I counted to ten, then asked, "And you really did ask Cherokee if Preston had paid him off?"

"Yes, and he was quite indignant about it. He denied that he would ever have accepted money to stop seeing our daughter. I believe him. Especially because Preston had been trying to hide money from me. He'd probably withdrawn the ten thousand intending to get it to his girlfriend, but the killer stole it."

"So you don't have any idea who the other woman is?"

She shook her head. "Frankly, at first I thought it was you."

"Me?" I shrieked. "Why would you think such a ridiculous thing?"

"I found a long, straight brown hair on his jacket, so I knew she was a brunette. He'd refused to tell me, claiming

I'd freak out if I heard who it was. So you were the brunette person it would have bothered me the most to have run off with my husband.''

That was either a back-handed compliment or a front-handed insult, but I chose to ignore its implications. ''Well, you were absolutely wrong. I would never cheat on Jim. Certainly not with Preston. I didn't even *like* him.''

''I realize that now.''

''*Now?* When exactly did you *stop* suspecting me of being the other woman?''

She blushed and said quietly, ''Shortly after you came to my house. You showed no emotional reaction to seeing Preston's body. I knew then you couldn't possibly have been in love with him.''

''So you really called me over there to find out if I was his lover?''

She gazed out the window for a moment, stalling for time, trying to compose herself. In a sad voice, she quietly began, ''Molly, you have to understand. Here I was, my husband of fifteen years about to leave me. An hour after he'd supposedly left for work, I'm in the tub for fifteen minutes when I hear shots, rush downstairs, and there he is, dead on the floor. There was no doubt in my mind who the prime suspect was going to be. I had gone to sleep every night for months fantasizing about killing him.''

She leaned toward me and met my gaze. ''I desperately needed help. If I'd told you the truth about everything, you'd have just suspected me, too. So once I realized you weren't his mistress, I told you the fib about Tiffany, hoping you'd uncover something. But it didn't work.'' She burst into tears. ''M-mm-molly, oh, Molly! I'm going to go to jail! To jail! Me! For a murder I didn't commit!''

I groaned, still knowing in my heart that despite her life-long pattern of lies, obfuscations, and half-truths, Stephanie did not kill Preston. I rose, grabbed a box of tissues from the kitchen counter, and handed it to her. She blew her nose, then curled her lip at the tissue and glanced at the brand name on the bottom of the box then set it on my coffee table with a look of disgust.

The woman was truly amazing. Faced with the prospect of being whisked off to prison at any moment, she still had the time and moxie to be disdainful about the quality of my facial tissues. I paced, trying to block out my annoyance so I could think. Long, straight brown hair. That let out Preston's ex-girlfriend Lindsay and Emma Groves.

"The morning Preston died," I said, "he came over here and showed me the magazine. He told me he was on his way to work."

Stephanie nodded. "I didn't know anything about the magazine at that time. I assumed he was already at his office."

"So why would he suddenly withdraw ten thousand dollars, and return to his house? Maybe someone was blackmailing him, someone who'd called him on his car phone and arranged to meet him there, then killed him. Is it possible he was being blackmailed?"

"Yes. It would be impossible for me to tell from his financial records. As I said, he was moving money all over the place, trying to hide it before the divorce. But if it *was* blackmail money, Molly, why kill him? Why kill the goose laying the golden eggs?"

I sat down on the couch again. "Maybe it was someone whose primary intention was to kill him, and just hoped to get some money from him first. Someone to whom ten thousand dollars would seem like an enormous sum. Like his former girlfriend, the waitress at the club."

Stephanie's expression changed to one of pure shock. "What former girlfriend?"

"Lindsay. The one who had Preston's baby when they were teenagers. She could have overheard about the—"

"Whatever are you talking about, Molly?"

"Don't you know that Preston fathered a child when he was a teenager?"

"That's absurd," she scoffed, accentuating her words with a toss of her hair. "Who told you that?"

"His sister. Sabrina Mueller."

"She's lying. Preston couldn't have fathered anyone's child. He was sterile."

Astounded, I muttered only, "What?"

"We tried for years to have a baby. Eventually, when Preston finally agreed to see a fertility expert, we learned the problem was with his sperm count. We spent thousands of dollars on artificial inseminations with Preston's sperm that failed. So finally we used an anonymous donor, and that's how Michael was conceived. As a matter of fact," she continued, her features tightening with anger, "that was something Preston pointed out to me. I asked him how he could leave me when I was about to have our baby. He said that 'it' wasn't really his baby anyway." Her eyes filled with tears and she said evenly, "So trust me. Preston has not fathered *any* children, let alone illegitimate ones."

I let this information sink in for a minute, thinking I needed a chart to keep track of who had what child with whom. Claiming 'it' wasn't his child after Stephanie had endured countless fertility procedures! No wonder Stephanie wasn't forthcoming with the truth about her relationship with Preston. No wonder she could waltz through her kitchen without a second thought about her husband's death. At the moment, I agreed completely with what Emma Groves had said earlier this afternoon: Preston got exactly what he deserved.

But was this the whole truth? Or had Stephanie returned to her typical creative augmentation of facts? Thinking out loud, I muttered, "It seems strange to me that his own sister didn't know that Preston was sterile."

"There was never a lot of communication in that family. The Saunderses are not exactly the Waltons. That may be news to you, but it certainly isn't to me."

Karen slid open the back door and called, "Um, Mom? Nathan hammered a board to the deck. And we—"

"It was an accident!" Nathan cried, on the verge of tears.

"We can't get it off," Karen continued.

Momentarily forgetting about Stephanie, I dashed out onto the deck. At first try, I was unable to pull up the board and lectured Nathan that he'd broken our rules about using only preapproved nails on preapproved boards and had damaged the deck Grandpa had built.

Nathan, however, cut me off and handed me the hammer. "Here," he sobbed. "Hit me in the head with the hammer. I'm the stupidest person in the whole world. You should put me on time-out for the rest of my life!"

"Oh, for heaven's sake, Nathan! You're not stupid, you just used bad judgment. You may lose hammering privileges as a result, but you'll be allowed to leave your room."

He put himself on time-out, marching tearfully past Stephanie and Karen in the living room, then up the stairs. I called after him, "It's not that bad, you know. If worse comes to worse, we can always build a permanent picnic table on that spot."

He slammed the door.

Stephanie, who'd been watching all of this without comment, now rose. "Well, I should be going." She smiled at Karen. "Sorry I kept your mom tied up for so long. How's school going?"

"Fine."

Stephanie nodded, then turned to me. Her eyes brimmed with tears, yet she smiled. "It's time for me to go home and let myself be you-know-whated by you-know-who. I'm truly sorry for all that I've put you through the last two weeks. Thank you for your help. I'm sure you tried your best."

I felt so sorry for her. For all of Stephanie's numerous faults, she was innocent and shouldn't be going to jail. I rose, too, and in the most startling personal revelation to date, I gave Stephanie a heart-felt hug, which she returned. Then she composed herself and left.

Karen, who'd been watching all of this with great interest, looked up at me as I shut the front door. With wide eyes, she asked, "Is Tommy Sergeant going to arrest Tiffany's mom?"

"I'm afraid so, sweetie."

"Did she kill Tiffany's father?"

"No."

"Then how come she's getting arrested?"

"It's hard to explain."

Karen, showing no signs of her brother's relentless persistence, let that answer suffice. So, in one of life's unfairnesses I'd yet to resolve, I turned my energy away from her and to resolving Nathan's current crisis. I carefully pried the board off the deck. The resulting nail holes were barely visible. His recent behavior of coming down harder on himself than I would as authority figure was a relative new one on me. This was one of those times I wished there were an eight-hundred number with a parenting adviser at my disposal.

By the time I went upstairs, Nathan had stopped crying but was curled up in bed, his pale green comforter pulled over his head. I told him his time-out was over, that he was "hangin' up his hammer" till further notice, and that we'd help him fill the holes on the deck and write a letter to his grandparents explaining what happened.

Half a minute later, an inspiration hit me. I grabbed the portable phone and locked myself in the bathroom for some privacy while I called our family doctor's office. I told the receptionist I had to ask Dr. Harris an urgent question, and that I would hold for however long it took till he could get to the phone. After a few minutes, he got on the line and I asked, "Is it possible for a man to become sterile after he's already fathered a child?"

"Certainly, that's possible." His voice sounded deeply concerned. "There are some...sexually transmitted diseases, for example, that can lead to sterility in certain circumstances."

He obviously thought there were sterility problems in my own family, but I needed to get off the phone. "Thanks. You've been a big help."

"How's Jim?"

"He's fine. I'll let you get back to your patients now." I hung up and quickly dialed next door. She answered.

"Lauren. Thank God you're home. Can you watch Nathan and Karen for an hour or so?"

"Sure. What's up?"

"I'm going to go speak to a waitress named Lindsay at the Carlton Country Club. I have a hunch she may be Preston's killer."

"You're *not* going to go talk to the murderer! Molly, for God's sake! Have *Tommy* go to the club and talk to this woman!"

"He won't listen to me after I just cried wolf about someone else I suspected. And I don't even know for sure that this person really is Preston's ex-lover, let alone his murderer. Besides, I'll be at the country club, where there's a zillion people around."

"What if you're right about her and she takes you hostage?"

"With what weapon? Her tray? She'll be waitressing."

She let out a long sigh. "Send the kids on over. But call me as soon as you know everything's all right."

I thanked her, then called Jim. I got his machine and left a message that I was going to the Carlton Country Club and would be home in less than an hour.

MY THOUGHTS raced ahead of me as I drove to the club. Lindsay may or may not have given birth to Preston's child. If the father had been someone else, she may have tried to con the Saunders family into believing otherwise for money. Either way, having overheard the men making their bet on my cartoon, she might have hatched a plot to exact her final, ultimate revenge.

It all began to make sense to me as I pulled into the

entrance. By framing his golf buddies, Lindsay would get back not only at Preston, but also at the rich country-club members she so disdained.

The lot was surprisingly full, considering the weather conditions. Despite this, the valet service was operating, though the valets wore clear plastic ponchos over their uniforms. Once again I drove past the service and parked. And once again the same young man met me in a golf cart.

I decided not to waste any time and quickly got into the seat. He grinned and said, "Hey, if it isn't Ms. Masters. How's B.O. doing?"

"He's fine, thanks." Someday, probably soon, my poor, dear husband will have some perfect stranger come up to him and say, "Hey, B.O. Is your VD all cleared up?" Then Jim would kill me, and Tommy would have a whole new murder case to investigate. "I don't have a tee-time, I just need to speak to the waitress who took care of our table Tuesday afternoon."

"Tuesday afternoon?" he repeated, stopping our cart at the awning that covered the length of the front walkway. "You mean Lindsay Mintoff?"

"Yes. Is she a friend of yours?"

He shook his head. "You're not gonna find her here. She quit last night."

"Really? Why?"

He shrugged and said, "Claimed she got a better job someplace else."

I got out of the cart, saying, "Maybe I can speak to the manager and get her phone number."

"We don't give out employees' numbers or addresses. Corporate policy."

"Huh. Oh, well. I'll just use the bathroom, then. Thanks for the lift."

I rushed to the public phone outside the rest rooms. In a town this size, how many Mintoffs could there be?

According to the local directory, the answer was none. Then I looked through *The Capital District Directory* and found an L. Mintoff listed as living in downtown Schenectady.

The door to the men's room creaked open behind me. An instant later, a deep voice boomed, "Well, look who's here. Miss Molly Masters."

I turned. It was Richard Worthington, who was weaving so badly he looked like he was trying to navigate one of his own private Seven Seas. He was wearing a red sweater, red knickerbockers, and plaid socks—a drunken, beardless Santa Claus out for a round of golf.

"I was s'posed to be golfing today," he explained, donning a goofy smile, "but the rain took care of that."

He put a beefy hand on my shoulder. Was I supposed to sway with him or support him?

"My wife says you were a lot of fun to golf with. I apologize if we treated you abruptly the other day." He gave me a wink.

If?

"Just to show there are no hard feelings," Richard said, slurring his words, "how's about I buy you a drink."

"No, thanks. I don't drink that much."

"Well, so you can just drink a little."

I reconsidered his offer. A conversation with Richard could prove enlightening, especially with alcohol loosening his lips. I said, "Okay, but only one," and followed him to the bar.

"What'll it be?" Richard asked me, snapping his fingers for the bartender.

"I'll have a Shirley Temple."

"That's a kiddie drink. Whatsa matter? You a wimp or something?"

"No, but if it bothers you, I'll have the bartender put it in a dirty glass."

That was an old joke, but Richard laughed heartily and ordered my drink, repeating my line about the dirty glass, at which the bartender forced a smile.

"It's a shame about Preston Saunders," I told Richard

as I watched the bartender spray soda pop into a glass with one hand and pour grenadine with his other hand. "I understand he made a lot of enemies, though."

Richard nodded. "All he cared about was money. Money and his looks." He leaned toward me and said, "Now, if it were me doin' him in, I'd have gone with fire."

"Fire?" I repeated as the bartender set my glass in front of me.

"Set his beloved Benz on fire, or his house. Get him with the ol' double whammy, so even if he lives, he'd have lost money and gotten maimed."

"You wouldn't have simply...shot him in the chest, huh?"

He shook his head emphatically. "The face, maybe, but not the chest."

"What reason would you have had for killing him?"

He widened his bloodshot eyes and tried to put on, I suppose, a somber appearance, but because such an expression required sobriety, he merely appeared to be airing out his lower lip. "None. I didn't care for the bastard, but, hey, that's no reason to start shooting people, right? We can't have just the ten or so people in this world we really like be all there is. Who'd be left to clean the toilets, right?" He laughed and jabbed my upper arm.

If we'd been at my house, the temptation to bop him in the face with my toilet-bowl brush might have been overwhelming, but now I said nothing.

He took a gulp of his amber-colored drink. "I will say this for Preston. Hell of a golfer. Beat the three of us damn near every time we played. Only time I remember him losing was right before he suckered us into that bet over your cartoon. We were playing double or nothing, too, so that one bad round cost him six hundred. Says he can win this cartoon contest. He bets us three grand and, Christ, the guy draws stick figures, you know? Should have guessed something was up."

For the first time, I voiced a question that had nagged at

me all along. "It wasn't that good a cartoon. I can't imagine why he'd be so confident as to bet that kind of money on it."

Richard snorted. "Once we paid up, he admitted he had an inside track. Said he was boinkin' some editor at the magazine."

Rage seeped into me. At least, up until now, I had believed that I'd won that contest fairly. To find out now I'd cheated to win a contest I never intended to enter in the first place was so infuriating I wanted to spit on Preston's grave. "Was her name Susan Wolfe?"

"Yeah. That's it. Says he'd met her on a business trip several months ago. That it was 'the real thing' this time."

NINETEEN

Is That Too Much
to Ask?

DAMN! The mystery long-haired brunette was Butch Blake, editor-in-chief of *Between the Legs*. And she'd been so likable, too. "He was in love with her?"

"Claimed to be," Richard answered, giving me another of his winks. "'Course, Preston had a pot in every port." He looked thoughtful for a moment. "A broad in every port. Port in every pot. A—"

"What about Lindsay, the waitress who used to work here? Did he have any feelings for her?"

Richard laughed. "Oh, yeah. He had feelings, all right. Hated her. Know what I heard? She'd had his son when he was just a pip, I mean a pup, himself. Rumor was the kid died, though."

I rose, took a couple of gulps of my Shirley Temple, and set it back on the bar. "Thanks for the drink, Richard."

"'S all right." He gave me yet another wink. "Goin' home myself in a shortly."

"You're not driving, are you?"

"No, no. Wife's meeting me here any minute. Good talking to you, Missy Masters."

I marched to the public phone, got the number for *Between the Legs* from information, and dialed, charging the costs. When Susan Wolfe was on the line, I growled, "You and Preston Saunders were having an affair. That cartoon contest was bogus!''

After a brief pause, she replied, "No it wasn't. Your cartoon would have won anyway.''

"You expect me to believe that?''

"Please, Ms. Masters. This could cost me my job. I admit, I made some poor decisions. I should have disqualified your entry when I saw Preston's name as the contact person. He convinced me not to. He assured me he was your agent. I had no reason not to believe him. I'm telling you the truth. All of our contest entries were atrocious, except yours.''

"Preston was going to leave his pregnant wife for you.''

"She was pregnant?'' she cried. After a pause, she said in a voice choked with emotion, "I believed every lie. About his being your agent. About his wife being a self-absorbed shrew who loved only herself. The only time I *didn't* believe him was when he said he was leaving his wife for me. The one time he was telling the truth.''

Actually, the part about the self-absorbed shrew was accurate, too, but my loyalties were with Stephanie now. Especially considering that Preston's lies had led Susan to believe I was said shrew until recently. I believed Susan, though it seems odd for her to be telling me, a virtual stranger, all of this. Perhaps she just needed to get it off of her guilty conscience.

"I loved him,'' Susan blurted. "I'm so sorry.''

In the corner of my vision, I spotted Kimberly Worthington entering and heading toward her husband at the bar. I pivoted so she wouldn't recognize me. If I didn't get going soon, I'd never get the chance to talk to Lindsay Mintoff. "I've got to go. Good-bye.''

I hung up and dashed out the door before Kimberly could delay me. As I sped to Schenectady, my heart was pounding. I needed just a few minutes to think this all out, but I didn't *have* a few minutes. There was a traffic snarl up ahead caused by some road construction. "All I want is for the world to go away and leave me alone for fifteen lousy minutes!" I said to myself. "Is that too much to ask?" There was potential for humorous greeting cards in this someplace: a woman cries to the heavens, "All I want is to be perfect all the time and be adored by everyone I come into contact with. Is that too much to ask?"

But while pondering the precise language for the card, my previous words, "fifteen minutes," suddenly rang a bell. That was it! Stephanie said she'd been in the bathtub for only fifteen minutes when Preston was shot, yet Dayton had claimed to have gone there a first time, right after leaving my house, and no one answered the door. "The Postman Always Rings a Couple of Times," I said to myself, mentally putting what I hoped was the final missing piece of this puzzle into place.

I was surprised when a glance at my watch showed me it had taken only twenty minutes to reach Lindsay's home. It was a dilapidated residence in the city. She answered the buzzer. She had a couple of blue, ribbon-shaped plastic clips in her strawberry-blond hair. Though she wore a lot of makeup, her clothes were decidedly casual: gray sweatpants cut off at the knees, a white *Just Say No!* T-shirt.

She looked me up and down, maintained her stance in the doorway and said, "I saw you at that damned club, right? Whatcha want?"

"I wanted to ask you a couple of questions about your son."

"What he do now?" she asked.

I was right! Her son was still alive! She must have lied about her son's death to make Sabrina and Preston feel guilty. I was pretty sure I knew who her son was, too. I took a calculated gamble and said, "Dayton's gotten into some serious trouble. May I come in?"

"Suit yourself." She whirled around and hollered, "Dayton? There's someone here to see you."

Not to mince words, the place was a pigsty. Not only was it in dire need of a good cleaning, but a dose of air

freshener wouldn't have hurt either—the place had the
aroma of a moldy ashtray. Lindsay watched me shove aside
some clothes and take a seat on the nearest chair. "Let me
introduce myself. I'm—"

"I already know more than I need to know about you
and your type. You're all the same." She gestured with
sweeping arms at her humble abode. "Welcome to how the
other half lives. Just tell me what you've got to do with
Dayton."

"He's gotten himself into a lot of trouble with some
people I know."

"What kind of trouble?"

"He tried to kill me."

She laughed heartily. "You can't be serious. Just last
week he won ten thousand dollars on one of them slot
machines in Atlantic City. Why would he go try 'n' kill
you, just when our luck's finally changing?"

I studied her face. Her expression was guileless. In that
instant, I decided my theory had been slightly off base. That
she truly didn't know where her son had really gotten the
money. "You told him you overheard Preston Saunders
making that bet with his golfing buddies, didn't you?"

She tossed her hair back haughtily. "The man can't ac-
knowledge his own flesh-and-blood, but makes thousand-
dollar bets over porno cartoons. All of you people think
you're so much better than everyone else. You sit in that
stinkin' country club and drink your hundred-dollar bottles
of wine and make me pick up your scraps to keep alive. If
it weren't for my boy, I don't know what I'd do. He's all
I've got in this world. But he's worth any six of you and
your friends." She hollered over her shoulder, "Dayton?"

Something partially hidden by the phone on the far side
of the coffee table caught my eye and I craned my neck to
get a better look. It was a copy of *Between the Legs,* the
edition that contained my cartoon. Lindsay must have
bought the magazine out of curiosity when she overheard
Preston using it to collect on his bet.

In the meantime, Lindsay padded down the hall, threw open a door, surveyed the room, let out a surprised "Huh." Then she returned to me, saying, "He must have gone out."

I rose, realizing how lucky I'd been that he wasn't home. I needed to get out of here, *now*, and go sic some policemen on him. "He should really be here before we continue this discussion. If he comes home please tell him that...I was looking for him."

She put her hands on her hips and stuck her chin out. "Don't you be spreading rumors 'bout my boy. I know how you and your rich friends like to gossip. He didn't do a thing to you."

"You're probably right. My mistake."

I hustled myself out the door and trotted down the cracked, dirty cement steps out front. I got in my Jeep quickly and started the engine. The streets were busy now with rush-hour traffic, but I managed to slip into a gap right away. I would head straight to the police station again and tell Tommy this time I knew for sure who the killer was: Dayton Mintoff.

After driving only about half a block, I tensed as I heard a noise that sounded for all the world as if it had come from the backseat. Just as I started to look over my shoulder, Dayton popped up from the floor. I screamed.

He held a gun to my head and said, "Quite a scream, there, Mike. You just about busted my eardrum. Now keep your eyes on the road and keep driving. We're gonna find us a nice secluded spot."

My first impulse was to dive out of the car and take my chances with the pavement. But Dayton immediately vetoed that by pressing the gun to my temple.

My second impulse, which I had to battle against with all my might, was to give in to my fear and turn into a blubbering idiot. I looked at my watch. Just after four thirty. Jim wouldn't be suspecting anything was up for another forty minutes or so. My eyes welled despite my best efforts.

So this was it. I was going to die. This Dayton character had been smart enough to outwit the police and me, and now my children would be motherless.

Where the hell was my life? Wasn't it supposed to be flashing in front of my eyes right about now? Someone in the left lane honked, as I'd unwittingly started to veer too close. I swerved back into my lane. Maybe my brain had decided I needed to pay attention to the traffic instead of flashbacks.

"Just keep going straight till we're out of town," Dayton instructed.

We stopped at a red light. A man in a pickup truck pulled into the left-turn lane beside me. I watched him and tried to make little jerky motions with my chin that might attract his eye but not be so blatant as to inspire Dayton to shoot me on the spot. Dayton had leaned forward between the front seats, now resting the barrel of his gun in the crook of his arm but still pointing it at my head. He was so close to my face now I could smell his sweat and the lingering cigarette smoke on his clothing.

As the light turned green, Dayton chuckled. "What's the matter, Mike? Cat got your tongue?"

Oh, fine! I was going to get taken out of this world in the midst of honking cars and clichés! This really sucked!

Then again, as long as I was still behind the wheel and driving, I was unlikely to get shot. I glanced at his face in the rearview mirror. His scalp was still smoothly shaved, but his gray, mocking eyes now portrayed an unmistakable resemblance to his father. "Just tell me one thing," I said, finally finding my voice. "Why me? I don't even like the Saunderses. They don't like me, either, for that matter."

"Just your dumb luck, huh, Miss Molly? See, when my mom overheard about the cartoon and everything, it was just too perfect to pass up. I made it look like a radical feminist group because all of you libbers annoy the hell out of me. Look at what you've done to my mom. Shit. Trouble was, a group of crazy libbers wouldn't know that Mike

Masters wasn't Daddy Dearest's real name. So I looked up Masters in the directory. There you were, Jim and Molly Masters. How was I s'posed to know you'd turn out to be such a damned pain in the ass?''

Now *there* was a question for the ages.

We stopped at another red light. This time we were too far back to pull alongside anyone in the turn lanes. I wanted to get him talking. Maybe then he'd lose concentration long enough for me to signal a passing motorist or pedestrian.

"Why did you kill him? Was it for your mom's sake?"

"Yeah. Hers and mine. Last year, my mom contacted Preston at work and said she needed a job. The least he could do for her, right? But he just got her that damned waitressing job at the club. It was eating her up inside, waiting on you pigs. So finally I went to see him myself. At his office. Told the shit-head we needed a hundred thousand and we'd move away and be out of his life forever. He said forget it. That's when I decided to kill him."

Our lane started up again, and I deliberately lagged back, hoping to build enough of a gap between cars to attract attention to myself.

"Dear ol' Dad loves his money too much to ever let go of a hundred grand," Dayton continued. "But I knew I could get at least something out of him. Told him I was going to have a friendly little chat with his wife and with all of his socialite buddies if he didn't come up with at least ten thousand reasons to keep quiet." He paused and gestured with his gun. "Hey, step on it. If you want to stay alive till we're out of town, you keep up with the traffic and don't try nothin'."

"Sorry," I murmured. "I hate to tailgate."

"Yeah? Well, I hate slowpokes, and I got the gun."

I cleared my throat as we caught up to the Buick ahead of us. Time to try the standby ego-massage. Maybe he'd get to like me enough so he wouldn't want to kill me. That was highly unlikely, but there was little to lose at this point.

"I have to admit, your idea of setting up his drinking

buddies through threats from an antiporn group was brilliant.''

He grinned. "Yeah. I liked that, too. 'Specially how well it worked out, with you screaming at him 'bout entering your cartoon. See, I'd been keeping an eye on him. When he went to your house, I made my move and delivered your box. Then I called him on his car phone. Told him I needed the money now and I'd meet him at his home. He tried to tell me he didn't care if I tell the world he's my father, he just wanted me to have some money 'cause he was starting a new life for himself and wanted to set the past straight. Like I was stupid enough to believe that bullshit.''

We were nearing the outskirts of town. He pointed at the intersection up ahead. "Turn left onto one-forty-six. We're gonna head to the Northway. Maybe, if you're nice to me, I'll let you live clear till we get to the Adirondacks.''

So far, we were retracing the route I'd used to get to his mom's house. The hospital was around here someplace, but I wasn't sure where. If only I were more familiar with this part of town, I'd drive like a bat out of hell to the hospital, then try and make a run for it to the emergency room. He'd probably shoot me, but at least I'd get quick medical attention.

I silently cursed at myself as we reached Route 146. I had already blown my chance to get out of the car. The houses were set way back from the roads and there were few traffic lights. The speed limit was forty-five all the way to Carlton, though I doubted he'd be foolish enough to have us go there. He'd probably have me turn off for the Northway in a couple of miles.

"Since I'm going to die soon, can you just answer a couple of questions for me? Why all the stained boxes? And how did the one stained box wind up in the Saunderses' closet?''

"Just didn't want to have to deal with that much shit. Not my thing, you know? And I stashed it in the closet to make it look like it had been there a while, so no one would suspect the messenger.''

Why couldn't there be a single patrol car or fire truck out on the road? Then I could honk and swerve all over the road and get help. "Did you mean to kill me that time you shot at me and Tiffany?"

"That was just a warning. I'd tried to keep outta sight for a while till this all blew over, just drove by the house a few times to see what was happening. Then I spot you and the pig's daughter getting onto the school bus. I gotta tell you. Man, you're like, nuttier than my mom.''

"So what are you going to do now, Dayton? The police know all about this. The sergeant I've been working with will be looking for me by now, wondering why I haven't returned from your mom's house.''

"And I suppose next you're going to tell me that if I let you go, you won't go to the police and I'll go scot free.''

"No, but if you let me go at least your mother won't get tied to this. If you kill me, they'll think she was in on it. You'll both go to jail for the rest of your lives.''

"She didn't have anything to do with it! She still doesn't even know where I got the money, or that I killed him!''

"I'm sure that's the truth but, Dayton, I already told the police that if anything happened to me, she did it and forced her son to help. Do you really think I'd be stupid enough to go out to a killer's house without even telling the police where I was going?''

If only the correct answer to that particular question had been no.

He flopped back into his seat, but one glance into the mirror assured me he was still aiming the gun straight at my head. "Here's another scenario. I blow your head off and dump your body. It looks like an act of random violence. While the police are still trying to ID your headless body, me and my mom are safe in Tahiti.''

Dear God. My stomach felt as if I'd been sucker-punched. "Please stop pointing that gun at me. If we hit a bump and you accidentally shoot me while I'm driving, we'll crash. Didn't you see *Pulp Fiction*?''

"Different kind of gun," he said with a shrug. "This one can only go off from the cocked position." He gestured with his free hand. "We're gonna turn left up ahead. We can't have you drive through Carlton and risk someone recognizing your car."

The road up ahead that Dayton indicated seemed to head out into the boonies. I'd never been on it before. I made the split-second decision that I couldn't afford to wait any longer. He fully intended to kill me. I had to try something, anything, to escape.

"Slow down," Dayton yelled, "that's our turn."

"Whoa, sorry," I said as we sped past it. "My mind was wandering. I'll turn around up ahead."

My heart was pounding. My only hope was to crash the car deliberately. He wasn't wearing his seat belt. He was in the backseat, though, which improved his chances of survival. I slowed down as if I intended to turn, but all the while scanned for trees to hit. Maybe I could swing the car around so the back would get the most damage. If only this Jeep had an airbag.

A police cruiser was up ahead in the opposite lane! I had to act fast before Dayton spotted it, too. There was a nice-sized tree alongside our lane.

I took a deep breath, slammed on the brakes, and jerked the wheel to the right.

TWENTY

I'm Going to Disney World!

I HOPED to orchestrate how my Jeep would hit the tree, but as soon as I swung the car off the road, we went into a screeching skid and I lost control. Dayton screamed, "Oh, shit!"

I covered my eyes and kept my weight on the brake as if that would save my life. It felt as if the car went sideways at a hundred miles an hour into the tree on the driver's side. The windows shattered. My body felt as if it was going to be jettisoned, but I was rudely jerked into place by my seat belt. My left arm struck something very hard and the pain shot through my entire body.

My head felt as though it had been used as a punching bag, but I stayed conscious. My one thought that I'd kept throughout the crash, was, "Get out of the car!" Even though I was dazed and barely capable of rational decision, that thought governed my actions.

My door was smashed. Without so much as a glance into the backseat, I released my seat belt, frog-kicked my way to the passenger side, unlocked that door, and dove out. I tumbled onto hard-packed earth and tried to scramble to my feet. Pain shot up my left side. I now knew for certain that my arm was broken. I managed to stagger toward the police car, which had just completed a U-turn and was just coming to a stop beyond my car and its tree.

A male officer was starting to get out of the passenger

door. I yelled, "He's got a gun." I ran toward the officer, supporting my left arm at the elbow. My arm throbbed. Pain stabbed at me with each step. The time it took me to get past the officer, protecting my backside, seemed to last forever.

The second officer, who'd been driving, got out. His gun was drawn. For a moment I thought I was hallucinating, but blinked and realized it really was Tommy Newton. "Get down!" he hollered at me.

In what may have been partially a faint, I dropped flat onto the ground next to the police car. Behind me, I heard Dayton cry, "Don't shoot! She's crazy! That woman tried to kidnap me!"

Tommy hollered, "Lie on the ground! Put your hands above your head!"

"I'm unarmed," Dayton cried. "That's her gun in the car, not mine! That bitch tried to shoot me!"

"Listen, punk," Tommy growled at him. "I happen to know this lady, so show some respect."

I couldn't hold the tears back any longer. I rolled onto my right side and raised myself up a little to look back through blurred vision. Tommy's partner slapped handcuffs onto Dayton, who was lying facedown on the ground. With his partner keeping a gun drawn on the prone and handcuffed Dayton, Tommy returned and helped me up, asking if I was all right.

I swiped away my tears with my right sleeve and said, "I think my arm's broken."

He opened the back door of his cruiser and helped me in.

I sat down on the edge of the seat, rocking myself in pain as I cradled my arm. Tommy was watching me, his eyes full of concern.

"What were you doing way out here?" I asked him.

"Your husband called the Carlton Club when you didn't answer at home. When you weren't there, he tried Lauren's and learned you were looking for some waitress. So he called and passed the info along to me. Just took me a while to follow your tracks to Lindsay Mintoff."

"That's her son, Dayton, the messenger." I gestured with my chin. "He did it."

A second police car pulled to a noisy stop behind us. The officers joined Tommy's partner and soon helped Dayton to his feet and marched him past Tommy's cruiser toward theirs. Dayton caught my eye and spat at me, calling, "You and your damned country-club friends will be making foursomes in hell!"

THE KIDS had signed my cast before we even left the hospital. Nathan had used his careful, though crooked, lettering. Karen had written *I love you, Mommy* with a red pen and had drawn hearts around it.

Jim and I hadn't had a moment alone, though he had given me a big kiss and a long hug when we first saw each other in the emergency room. I'm sure he felt just as unsure as I did about how much information we should let the kids hear. All I had told them personally was that the man who'd shot Preston had tried to kidnap me, so I crashed the car and broke my arm, but that the important thing was he was in jail now and we were safe. I didn't know if that was too much information or not enough. Nor was this the stuff of any child-care handbook I knew of that I could consult.

Jim helped me into the Toyota. I hadn't asked where his wrecked Jeep was and he hadn't volunteered the information. As we waited at a stoplight partway home, I said, "So. On a scale of one to ten, how mad at me are you?"

He shrugged. "At this point, I'm just grateful you're all right."

My sense of relief was overwhelming. Finally I realized that this was truly over, and I hadn't destroyed my marriage after all. But having just survived one car accident, I was particularly careful not to distract the driver. I merely patted his thigh as best I could, while reaching across my body with my good arm. "Guess we don't need those tickets to Florida anymore."

Jim grinned. "This morning I changed the reservations. The four of us are flying to Orlando Saturday morning."

"Orlando?" Karen cried from the backseat. "Nathan, that's where Disney World is!"

The children cheered wildly and exchanged joyful hugs, only their seat belts preventing them from bouncing off the ceiling with excitement. I put a hand to my chest in mock anger and said to Jim, "And you didn't consult me first? The nerve!"

Jim spoke into his fist as if he were holding a microphone and said, "Molly Masters. You've just purposely totaled my car and scared your family half to death. What are you going to do now?" He held the fake microphone to my lips.

Though I felt as if my heart would burst with my love and gratitude, I kissed his hand, then played along and said, "I'm going to Disney World!"

First Time in Paperback

Murder at St. Adelaide's

A FRANCES FINN MYSTERY

Kansas City private detective Frances Finn
returns to her alma mater at the request
of dying Mother Celeste, who claims that a
young nun who died thirty years earlier was
actually murdered. The Mother Superior knows
who the killer is, but refuses to point the finger,
insisting that there is no danger. But when
Mother Celeste is found brutally murdered,
Frances knows that there is indeed a great deal
of danger at hand and that someone has a
secret they want kept…at any cost.

Gerelyn Hollingsworth

"A good debut." *–Armchair Detective*

Available in November 1997
at your favorite retail outlet.

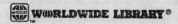

WORLDWIDE LIBRARY®